Wicked Creature
Kayleigh Rymer

Copyright © [2025] by [Kayleigh Rymer]

All rights reserved.

No portion of this book may be reproduced in any form without written permission from the publisher or author, except as permitted by U.S. copyright law.

Contents

Foreword	V
Dedication	VI
Map	VII
1. Ivy	1
2. Ivy	10
3. Ivy	16
4. Tegwyn	26
5. Ivy	37
6. Ivy	44
7. Tegwyn	53
8. Ivy	61
9. Tegwyn	70
10. Ivy	80
11. Ivy	87
12. Tegwyn	93
13. Tegwyn	106
14. Ivy	116
15. Tegwyn	130

16.	Tegwyn	137
17.	Ivy	148
18.	Ivy	158
19.	Tegwyn	171
20.	Tegwyn	183
21.	Tegwyn	193
22.	Ivy	199
23.	Tegwyn	211
24.	Tegwyn	221
25.	Ivy	228
26.	Ivy	238
27.	Tegwyn	245
28.	Tegwyn	258
29.	Ivy	265
30.	Tegwyn	272
31.	Tegwyn	280
32.	Ivy	288
33.	Tegwyn	300
34.	Tegwyn	309
35.	Ivy	317
36.	Tegwyn	323
Afterword		334
About the author		335

Foreword

Wicked Creature is a New Adult romantasy set in a fictitious world riddled with wicked faeries, twists, and turns.

The characters are young, prone to mistakes, and just learning to navigate falling in love and becoming adults for the very first time.

Trigger warnings:
One character experiences severe PTSD caused by traumatic memories from his past. There is swearing, scenes of a mature nature, and parental death as well.

Wicked Creature is written in British English. I tend to write in US English for my other pen names (since those stories are contemporary and/or set in the US), but I decided that British English would be my language of choice for this book. Since the story borrows from Welsh, Irish, and Scottish folklore, I thought it was the best option. However, if you find any genuine typos or spelling mistakes, I'd love to hear from you! You can email me at *kayleighrymerauthor@outlook.com*.

So, without further ado... I give you *Wicked Creature*.

For anyone trapped in the fog...
This book is for you.
I know you'll make it out, too.
Because I will be there on the other side,
waiting for you.

MAP OF LIONA

THE VEIL?

THE STRANDS

THE FAERIE

THE CAPITAL
LYON BORNE

1

Ivy

VULPINE EYES RUSH UP from the darkness, framed by hair of deep russet red, and I finally see his face—green gold with horns like twisted tree branches. When I reach out my hand to touch him, though, he slips away, and my cries echo through the void.

Always so near, yet so far...

One day, I will reach him.

One day, I will make him *mine*.

As he fades into the darkness, his voice resonates, a gentle balm on my soul, *"Forget me."*

I will never forget him, though.

He forever haunts my dreams.

I jerk upright, gasping for breath as I repeat the mantra in my head. *It was just a dream; it was just a dream.*

Yet as my mind adjusts, I spy a shadow in the corner of my room, and I stare at the apparition, transfixed.

It's him—the Fae from my dream. I recognise the horns, the glowing eyes.

His voice echoes to me still, *"Forget me..."*

And then just like that, he's gone.

Drawing a deep breath, I gather my bearings, reaching up to pat my clammy forehead. I could have sworn he was beside me, mere inches from my face. I felt the heat of his body and smelled the rich scent of his pine and woodsmoke.

I've had this recurring dream for several weeks, and I don't quite understand. Every time I close my eyes, he's there, *haunting* me. My heart won't stop pounding, even when I lie back in bed, trying to calm my erratic nerves. But all I can see is him.

They say the Fae are imperceptible to the human eye, yet they surround us every day, hiding in plain sight through various charms and glamours.

The only way to keep the Fae away is to position an iron horseshoe above your door or to adorn your house with rowanberries and pouches of salt.

But I don't want to keep this faerie away; I want him close so I can gaze into his golden eyes. They're simply mesmerising.

He's mesmerising.

I glance at the mural beside my bed. I painted it myself, and I think it really ties the whole room together. His likeness stares back at me from behind a birch tree, one claw exposed as he drags it down the white bark. His eyes shine as bright as they did in my dream, and when I reach up, stroking my fingers over the metallic gold that limns his cheeks, I smile. Most would consider him frightful, but to me, he's merely exotic.

If only he were real...

Tearing my gaze away from the painting, I glance at the other side of the room. My ocean mural remains unfinished, but one day, I will finish it. One day, I will get to see the real ocean and feel the spray of its fine mist on my cheeks.

A thump sounds on the stairs, and I turn my head towards the door. Bryce growls on the landing outside, raising the hair on my arms. That lovable mastiff is normally afraid of his own shadow, yet something has deeply unsettled him tonight.

I climb out of bed, untangling the sheets from my legs. It's probably just a mouse, but I should still check.

Grabbing the knife that I keep hidden beneath my pillow per Papa's request, I creep towards the door, holding the blade steady.

He fashioned the weapon in his forge several weeks prior, and I've kept it on my person ever since. But what need would I have for a knife? Nothing ever happens in Charstown. We're safe here.

Still, I've been somewhat restless these past few weeks, ever since the faerie turned up in my dreams.

I open the door a crack, investigating the landing outside. All appears well. Bryce sits in a sphinx position, curling his upper lip. A low growl vibrates in his chest. He's getting paranoid in his old age.

"What is it, boy?" I ask, kneeling down to pat his head.

The dog clambers up to his feet, a ridge of fur streaking along his spine as he snarls at the stairs. My own hair pricks on end, and then a lump lodges in my throat. With my heart in my mouth, I inch towards the stairs of our two-storey cottage. Darkness pools at the bottom of the steps, and at first, I can't see a thing.

But as my vision adjusts, I spy a silhouette of a woman in a white dress. I think she's Mama at first, but why would she be sitting alone at the bottom of the stairs at three a.m.?

I suck in a trembling breath. "M-mama? What are you doing down there?"

The woman doesn't move, and a shiver rattles down my spine at how unnaturally quiet she is.

I call out yet again. "Mama? Are you..."

A door opens on the landing, and then Mama steps out of the master bedroom, a yawn splitting her lips. "Ivy, what are you doing out of bed?"

The blood drains from my face, and I turn towards the stairs again, heart thumping in my throat.

The woman stares straight back at me this time, and I hold out a shaking hand, keeping my knife steady.

Whoever she is, she's not welcome here.

Mama's gaze settles on the strange woman, yet the blood doesn't drain from her face. In fact, she looks as if she knows the apparition. Sadness glistens inside her big hazel eyes.

"Mama?" I ask, keeping a tight grip on my knife. "Who is that?"

She doesn't reply. Instead, she presses her lips together and closes her eyes.

The thick stench of smoke reaches my nose, and I cough, trying not to lose my grip on the blade. Then the landing fills with a foul stench, and it takes me a moment to realise—that's the scent of burning flesh.

The woman's skin peels back from her once beautiful face, and I gaze into the orbital cavities of her blackened skull.

My arm trembles, but I don't move from my spot. A charred corpse stares straight back at me, and I blink. I must be dreaming.

Any moment now, I will wake from this nightmare.

She opens her lipless mouth, and her voice tolls like a death bell. *"The spell has broken. They're coming. Leave. Now."*

My heartbeat drums in my ears.

Leave? Where?

Mama grips my arm, squeezing tightly. "Ivy, pack your things. Only take what you need."

I still don't move, eyes transfixed on the stairs. The woman has vanished, yet the smell of her seared flesh remains. "Mama, who—?"

"Never mind her. Go, now. It is not safe here anymore."

She shoves me into my room, but I don't move for some time. I can't rid the image of the woman's skinless face from my mind. The way her flesh withered away until it was nothing but ash.

I peer through the gap of the door. Papa rushes down the stairs, yet before he slips away into the darkness, I glimpse his expression, and it rattles me to my core.

In my whole life, I have never once seen my father look so frightened. He has always been stalwart, fearless.

An immovable mountain.

He taught me how to hold a blade, and how to shoot an arrow. He taught me how to be as brave as he is. If he is afraid, there is something to be afraid of.

I snap into action, stowing what I can into a burlap sack. I only take what is important, as Mama instructed.

A lump blocks my airway when I glance around the room and spy my unfinished mural. Wherever we're going, I hope there is real seawater...

Unnecessary or not, I still pack several paints and brushes. I even grab my necklace, as I can't bear to leave it behind. I've had it since I was five.

Once I'm done, I step into my boots, glancing across the room at Bryce. He's barking at the window.

"What is it, Bryce?" I ask, tying the strings of my bodice. I tuck my necklace under my blouse, right beside my heart.

Bryce paws at the window, smearing the glass with his drool. His growl turns my insides cold, and I creep toward the window.

I rub my eyes to ensure I'm seeing right. A succession of cloaked figures marches up the dirt road to our cottage, a winding, curving snake encroaching on its prey.

And we're about to be swallowed whole.

I yelp when a raven lands on the ledge outside my window, pecking its black beak at the stained glass. Its silver eyes are trained on me.

I can't take my gaze off it. I have never seen a raven with silver eyes before.

Mama bursts into the room, and the bird takes flight, disappearing into a night as black as its wings.

"Come. To the stables."

She leads me away from my room and down to the kitchen. Papa has barricaded the back door, and I spy his crossbow in his hands.

I don't speak; I just watch as Mama tosses fruit into my sack. She wraps up a loaf of bread and a wheel of cheese, dropping those inside, too.

All the while, I keep my hand on my knife, the one tucked away inside my skirt.

Things will be okay. We will survive this.

She hands the sack back to me, then crouches to her knees to lift the trapdoor beneath the rug. "Inside, hurry!"

A cold wind wafts up from the cellar, clawing at my arms like clammy fingers, and I freeze. It's like I've lost the ability to move. Everything in me screams fight or flight. My body just isn't sure which to choose.

Something vibrates beneath my feet, and for a moment I think it's thunder. But then the rumbling draws closer, and the sound of hoofbeats crystallises.

I've never heard so many horses at once; I've never even seen a soldier before tonight.

Why have they come to the cottage?

Papa aims his crossbow at the door, never taking his eyes off the bolted wood. "Get to the stables. Take Belle and head north. I will hold them off."

His words pull me from my reverie, and I whirl around, staring at him aghast. "Wait... You're not coming with us?"

His blue eyes shimmer in the dim light. "No. You two go."

It's like someone pulled the rug from beneath my feet. I don't even have time to argue with him as Mama pushes me down the cellar stairs.

"No! I'm not going without Papa! I'll stay and fight—"

He jerks his gaze away from the door, pinning me in place. Only pain gazes back at me now, and hard, determined resolve. "No. I am more than capable of holding them back. You go."

"But—"

"Go!" he roars. The sound of hooves grows louder and louder with each passing heartbeat.

"Please, Ivy," Mama pleads. "Get down into the cellar."

I turn her way this time, yet she vanishes behind a shroud of tears. I have never felt so torn. Do I stay and fight with Papa? Or leave?

If only I had my sword, but I left it in the forge.

Papa had forged it recently—a gift for my upcoming birthday. He's been teaching me how to fight, and I was more than eager to learn.

Was he preparing me for this very moment?

Voices echo outside the door. The men have finally reached the cottage. I hear the piercing whinny of a horse, and I make my choice at last.

I don't even get to say goodbye. The last thing I see of my father before I disappear into the cellar is the back of his silver head, his body poised as he readies the crossbow.

Mama and I trip over jars and bags of grain as we stumble to the escape door at the end of the cellar. She grips my wrist, pulling me around to the stables at the back of the cottage once we're outside.

Their shouts surround us, and I'm pretty sure one of them has spotted us, but we don't stop.

We just keep going forward.

Once we reach the stables, Papa's chestnut bay, Flame, rears up on his hindquarters, crying out in alarm. Yet my own horse, a beautiful mare with a bright coat of shining silver, remains poised. Belle will be the one to carry us away to safety tonight.

We open Belle's stall, leading her out into the main aisle. We don't have time to tack her up, but I have no trouble riding bareback.

"Up you go," Mama instructs, keeping her voice calm. I don't know how she does it.

I climb onto the mare with ease, and once I'm seated on Belle's back, I reach my hand down. "Take my hand."

She steps away from my outstretched fingers.

I gaze down at her shadowy silhouette, wishing I could see her face, but it's too dark. "Mama...take my hand..."

She closes her eyes, shaking her head. "No, dear. An old bird like me will only slow you down."

Heat rises at the back of my neck, settling at the base of my skull. "Mama. Take. My. Hand. I won't leave you behind, too!"

She glances away from me, and I don't miss her tears. They glisten as they trail down her tawny cheek, capturing the light of the moon.

"I'm sorry it had to come to this. I just hope you understand one day. We love you, Ivy. We always have. But you must go on without us."

Anger boils in the pits of my stomach. "No! I won't leave without you. Just take my hand, and we can—"

She slaps Belle's flank, and the horse shoots off. The world flashes by, and once again, I never got to say goodbye...

I squeeze my eyes against the cruel wind, hoping and praying that this is another dream, and I'll wake in my bed at any moment.

Yet I don't wake. This is real, and I have no choice but to move forward.

Something heavy lumbers after us, and I nudge my heels into Belle's flank, urging her to move faster as I grip her mane.

Suddenly, a large black wolf jumps out from the trees, snapping its teeth at my calves. Belle increases her speed, and I have never seen her gallop so fast. She dodges trees with ease, and at one point, she appears to be flying.

Her coat burns as bright as the full moon, and I can barely believe it. I always knew she was special, but never *this* special.

She almost seems magical.

The wolf re-emerges on our left flank, and I scream. "Belle!"

The horse kicks the wolf with her hind legs, and the beast disappears with a yelp. I'm too afraid to look back.

It was a massive creature, and I'm pretty sure it had silver eyes...

I don't breathe, not until I no longer hear those giant footfalls, and it seems we're safe.

The wolf is gone.

Still, I won't relax. Not just yet.

We still have a long night ahead of us.

2

Ivy

PAPA TOLD ME TO ride north, so that's what I do, using the stars as a visual aid as he taught me.

At the first light of dawn, we stop by a brook for a much-needed rest. My muscles are stiff from riding through the night, so I take the opportunity to stretch my limbs.

The wolf never reappeared, so hopefully we've managed to outrun it.

I kneel by the brook and fill my waterskin. The horse laps up water beside me, and that's how we stay for some time—two lost souls on the run.

My face is reflected in the brook, rippling along the glittering surface. It's hard to believe I was still sleeping in my bed a mere eight hours ago.

Memories of last night rush to the front of my mind, and I inhale a shaky breath, the cool morning air piercing my lungs like knives.

Did Papa get the better of those soldiers? Did they manage to escape?

I squeeze my eyes shut, bringing my knees to my chin. They will be all right. Mama and Papa will have escaped...

I just don't understand. Why did those soldiers come to our cottage?

We are not criminals; we have never broken the law. So, why did I have to rush away like a thief in the night?

Despite my best efforts, a sob wracks my body, and no matter how hard I press my face against my skirt, the tears won't stop.

I'm alone, lost, and frightened, and the woods here are strange. The trees seem to grow differently, their clawed limbs stark black against a grey, merciless sky.

No. This is wrong.

I must go back; I must find my parents. I can't leave them behind. I *will* rescue them.

A memory of the ghostly woman returns, and I stop crying at once. *"The spell has broken...they're coming..."*

Who was she? And what spell? Maybe she was talking about the legendary spell that protects the town. I always thought it was just an old folktale.

According to legend, a witch once cast a spell around Charstown to protect its inhabitants from evil spirits, yet despite her altruistic efforts, they still burned her at the stake.

I flinch when something wet nudges my cheek, and I look up at Belle. My horse wants me to take a drink from the brook. Glistening droplets fall from her snout, and she's already had her fill.

I dip my hands into the brook, bringing the water to my lips. It's cool and fresh, and just what I need.

I take another sip and splash my face to wash away the grit from my eyes. It's best we move on, but another five minutes won't hurt.

We're alone out here. Only the birds keep us company, trilling in the branches above.

I smile at Belle, petting her cheek. "You were a good girl last night, getting us away so swiftly. Thank you."

I give her snout a kiss, and she nickers softly, closing her eyes.

I'm lucky to have her. She was a gift from my parents, and I couldn't imagine where I'd be without her. She saved my life.

My stomach growls. It's time for breakfast.

Grabbing an apple from my bag, I offer it to Belle, smiling when she bites into it eagerly. Then I dip my hand inside for another, stopping short when my fingers graze a smooth, hard surface.

Curiosity gets the better of me, and I tug out the object, surprised when I spy a rosewood box. A filigree pattern of gilded flowers decorates the outer edges, and it's one of the most beautiful boxes I have ever seen.

I don't even remember Mama sneaking it inside the bag, but she was always good at tricks.

Sleight of hand, she always called it.

I lift the ornate lid, gasping when I spy a dancing ballerina inside.

It's a music box.

Winding the lever, I place the box onto the grass, smiling when it plays a sweet melody. Such a lovely sound. It chases away the shadows of the forest, bringing a grin to my face.

I find a framed oil painting of a beautiful woman inside the box. She has raven hair, sapphire eyes, and full red lips, but her face doesn't ring a bell.

Who is she?

As I set the portrait aside, I notice a scroll of parchment at the bottom of the box. I unroll it quickly. My hands shake as I see my mother's scrawl, and now I read her words through glistening tears.

Dear Ivy,

Hopefully, by the time you read this, you are far from Charstown. Whatever you do, do not come back. Go beyond the lion's neck and keep riding north. That way, the king's men won't find you.

When you reach the mountains, find the Veil. There, you will find Aunt Elly.

Your father and I love you. We regret every moment of letting you go, but one day, we hope you'll understand.

Remember, you are our child and always will be. No couple could ask for a greater daughter.

P.S. Your father left you a gift.

A gift?

I gasp when I spy the pommel of a sword sticking out of the bag. Pulling it by the handle, I find myself holding a narrow blade with a pointed tip.

My sword...

But... *how?*

I swear I'd left it inside Papa's forge. Could it be another of Mama's tricks again?

I twist the blade in my hand, smiling through tears when I study my father's beautiful metalwork.

The knuckle guard is a gilded sea serpent that curves around the crossbar, and I think back to all our lessons.

Papa had been teaching me swordplay for the past few years, mostly in the art of self-defence, but I sure hope I never have to use it.

For now, I will hold on to that naïve thought.

There's a scabbard and belt inside the bag too, and I tie them around my waist, slipping the sword inside.

Well, no point in crying any longer. There's only one direction to go.

North.

I'm not sure if the Veil is a town or a city, and I've never even met my Aunt Elly before. I don't even know what she looks like, but I *will* find her.

And then, I'll find my parents.

I unroll my map onto a dry patch of grass, using rocks and twigs as paperweights. The kingdom of Liona spreads out before me, named for its resemblance to the mighty lion. The north makes up his head, and the south his foot and tail.

My eyes skim over the many towns and cities that I have only ever read about in books, but never had the privilege of visiting.

Charstown is situated to the east just below the lion's neck, and I still have a long way to go before I reach it.

Across the lion's head, I see a semicircle marking a vast stretch of mountains. The word 'Veil' is written there in dark ink. Again, I recognise my mother's handwriting.

I count my money: ten gold lions, five silver stallions, and several copper bits.

After gathering my things, I climb onto Belle's back and pat her mane. The path before us is unfamiliar, but we must go on.

There's no turning back now.

A new beginning awaits us.

"It's time to go, Belle."

A cold wind whispers through the trees, rustling the leaves of the forest, before brushing across my skin like icy fingers.

I'm being watched.

I turn to a nearby tree, where a glossy raven perches, its silver eye fixed on me. Dread sweeps through my veins. The raven at the cottage had silver eyes, too.

It arrived at the same time as the king's men. Could the two be connected? I doubt it. It's most likely just an ordinary raven... with eerie, human-like eyes.

Belle stamps her hoof, and a tremor ripples through the earth, rattling my bones. The trees shake, and the raven spreads its wings, disappearing into the grey sky.

One of its coal-black feathers drifts to the ground, and I shiver as a cold breeze wraps its talons around me. Ravens are omens of death, and unease twists in my gut.

But it's probably nothing to worry about. Maybe it's all just in my head.

And it's time to ride north.

3

Ivy

SEVERAL DAYS PASS, AND I find myself at the edge of a stony cliff, gawping at a giant, snow-capped mountain in the distance.

I've never seen anything so vast before. Maybe inside the illustrated pages of a book. But seeing one in real life is a whole different experience.

There are other mountains, too, and they're all just as imposing as the first, like sleeping behemoths waiting for someone to come along and wake them from their ancient slumber.

These rock formations have been here since the world began, and at the thought, the hair on my arms rises up and down.

What dreadful creatures will be waiting for me beyond those colossal structures? Stories of trolls and goblins rush to the fore, and I think of everything Mama taught me about the Fae.

At least I have my iron cross; I have my knife and sword, too, and sprigs of rowanberries and pouches of salt.

But will I really have any need for them? After all, I'm not sure that I really believe all those stories about the Fae.

I always wanted to believe. Anything to make the real world seem less dull in comparison.

Are they real?

I want to believe in pocket worlds or faerie circles made of toadstools, and I want to believe in the Fae court.

But seeing is a whole different experience, and I guess I'm about to find out if all those cautionary tales I read as a child were true, after all.

Because if they are true, once I enter that mountain range, the one shrouded in a ghostly mist, I'll be in Fae territory. And I have to wonder if I will ever come back out again.

But in the end, the only real monster I have to fear right now is the king himself, so go forth I must—even if I have to ride into the gaping maw of hell.

I urge Belle forward, and she gallops down the rocky slope and across the barren landscape.

The terrain turns rougher and craggier the closer we get to the mountains, but I keep my eyes peeled. At any moment, I suspect one of those sleeping giants might tear itself free from the earth and crush me under its fist. Yet they remain static, and I narrow my eyes against the biting wind until I reach the first peak.

Soon, I come to a stop and gaze into a misty valley. It's quiet. And dark.

Light ceases to exist beyond the mountains. Nothing but sprawling rock lies in waste ahead of me, but I have no choice.

Straight into the maw of hell.

From this point onward, I'll be leaving the kingdom of Liona and entering Fae country, if that's really what it is.

Here, the *Fae* are free to do as they please. They are free to enslave me and bend me to their will. This is *their* land, and I am merely trespassing.

But somewhere in that unholy nest of vipers lives my Aunt Elly, and I'll be damned if I don't find her in a matter of days.

By this time next week, I'll be having supper with my aunt, and I hope those faeries enjoy the chase.

If they want me, they'll have to catch me first.

A day goes by, and I still find no sign of the Veil.

But at least the sprawling rock has given way to evergreen forest. The pines stretch towards the sky, their topmost branches vanishing with the clouds, and I swallow a lump in my throat.

Everything seems so much bigger here.

I would do anything to see a simple hawthorn or a hazelnut—anything that sheds its leaves come winter.

These trees are frozen in time. Nothing moves, and I can barely see the sky.

The forest is draped in moss, giving the light a sickly green hue, and the ferns are as tall as Belle. I've had to hack several down with my sword, and I swear I woke some ancient evil from its slumber at one crucial point. Something malevolent awaits me in these woods, and whatever it is, it's far from friendly.

The faerie wilds are untameable, and it truly is disorientating. It could be days before I find my way out again.

I've checked my map dozens of times, and I've even used Papa's compass for guidance, but I feel like I'm running in circles.

I'm pretty sure I passed that tree with the gnarled branches a few miles back, but it's hard to tell. Everything looks so similar.

I need to top up my waterskin, but there's no sign of water. I climb down from Belle's saddle and touch the ground. No moisture. Only a carpet of dried pine needles.

I search the sky, but it's hard to see any geese through the thick canopy.

The sun should be setting soon, but again, it's difficult to tell. There's barely any light in this place.

It's best we get some sleep, at any rate, and continue our search in the morning. Belle is looking tired.

I tie her reins to a tree, kissing her snout goodnight. I stopped at a town a few days prior to pick up some supplies, and I even managed to find Belle a new saddle and bridle, too.

I also managed to stock up on rations, so we should be good for the next week or two.

I gather some rocks for a firepit, and after a few failed attempts with a rock and my knife, I finally get a spark going. Once the tinder catches fire, I wrap myself up in my cloak, holding my hands before the flames. The temperature has dropped drastically, and I'm afraid I'll freeze to death out here.

Hopefully, I will make it through the night.

I wake with a start.

Something dropped onto my head, and I look around the forest, heart beating in my throat.

That's when my eyes find the pinecone. Its scales have been chewed off, and I crane my neck to peer up at the branches.

I'm greeted by the sight of a bushy red tail, and a smile forms across my face. Finally, the first sign of life I've seen since I entered this dreary place.

A lack of humans must mean that wildlife can flourish here, and that's one good thing, I suppose.

However, my joy is short-lived when the squirrel drops another pinecone onto my head, and I fish it out of my hood, stretching to my feet.

It's time I had some breakfast of my own. I gaze into my bag, my hand freezing.

My food. It's all gone.

No apples, no bread, even my wheel of cheese has vanished. I know I went to sleep with a full bag of rations.

Panic rakes its dark talons down my spine, and I grip the hilt of my sword, wrapping my fingers around it tightly.

Who...or what...took my food?

I could hunt for food. But I haven't hunted in a long time.

Papa used to take me out in the woods all the time when I was younger, but I didn't have the heart to shoot a helpless animal. I'm decent enough with an arrow, and I know how to set a snare.

I shake my head. Maybe my mind is just playing tricks on me, addled by thirst and hunger.

However, when I check my bag again, I find that it's still empty. Not even a single crumb.

Someone must have stolen my food in the middle of the night, but surely, I would have woken to find the culprit. I had a restless sleep after all, tossing and turning on the cold, hard ground.

With shaking limbs, I climb up onto Belle's saddle, urging her forward. Maybe if I leave now, I can catch up with the thief.

A hush spreads through the forest, and I think I can hear people whispering about me. I take a deep breath, telling myself it's not real.

A shape moves in the corner of my eye, and I repeat the mantra: *It's not real, it's not real...*

Through the misty trees, I spy a glowing blue light, and it beckons to me in a voice so sweet. I try to pull Belle in that direction, but the horse refuses, carrying me away from the strange orb.

The light vanishes into the mist, and I finally understand.

A Will-o'-the-Wisp. Faeries that lure lost travellers to their deaths.

They're mostly found by fens and boglands, and if that's the case, then there must be water close by.

My waterskin is running dry.

Making up my mind, I tug Belle in the direction of the Will-o'-the-Wisp, yet she's adamant that we don't go anywhere near that floating orb.

"Belle, come along. There may be water that way."

But the horse is persistent, taking me further and further away from the water source.

Losing my patience, I pull on Belle's reins as gently as possible, leading her towards the water. "Don't be ridiculous, Belle. There is nothing—"

The horse rears back suddenly, and I slip off her saddle, falling to the ground with a yelp, but before I can gather my bearings, the eerie sound of a growl freezes me in place.

I turn towards a sharp set of teeth. They float in a face as black as midnight, and all I can do is stare.

It's a wolf, though far larger and far fouler than any I've ever seen. I fumble for my blade, finding my scabbard empty.

It's gone, and now I'm defenceless.

The wolf snaps its teeth, and I shuffle away on my hands and knees, never taking my gaze off its silver eyes.

Silver, just like the eyes of the raven that came to my window...

Belle shields me from the beast, light against dark.

The mare's coat beams as bright as the moon, while the lupine's black fur seems to absorb all light. They size each other up, and it's obvious Belle isn't going to let this monster anywhere near me. I wish I hadn't been so harsh with her earlier.

I will apologise to her later. After she saves me from this monstrosity.

The wolf's eyes are far too calculating, evaluating Belle's every possible movement, and that's when I realise... *Wolves hunt in packs.*

Yet this wolf hunts alone, coordinating its attacks with cunning and precision.

This wolf is *Fae.*

The blood drains from my face. There is no way Belle can defeat this creature.

The wolf feints to the right, trying to catch the horse off guard, but Belle is far too quick, kicking it with her leg.

It lands on its paws, then lunges for the horse's neck, and I scream her name, the sound rupturing my throat. "Belle!"

It happens so fast.

One moment, Belle is about to be slain, and the next, she burns with the light of a thousand suns. I shield my eyes, yet no matter how hard I try, her rays blind me.

The light intensifies, burning brighter by the second, and then as swiftly as it appeared, the light vanishes.

All is silent, aside from the pounding of my heart.

When I remove my hands from my eyes, I find myself alone. There is no sign of the wolf or Belle.

I rise up on trembling limbs, jerking left and right as I search fruitlessly for my horse.

All I find are her saddlebags.

I stumble towards the bags, gripping them tightly as I continue searching the forest. "Belle!"

Only my voice echoes back. She truly is gone.

No. I can't be alone in this place...

So, I search, search, search, wandering aimlessly through unknown terrain for my horse.

I won't give up. Not until I've reunited with Belle.

Where did she go? What happened to the wolf?

One moment, they were fighting, and the next, they were gone with a blast of light.

That strange whispering starts again, and now I know I'm *definitely* being watched this time.

They giggle like small children, darting behind trees in the corners of my eyes, but every time I turn to face one, pulling out my knife, they're gone.

But I know they'll return.

Time is never-ending as it stretches slowly, making it hard to tell east from west. The mossy trees close in, making it hard to breathe, yet I must go on.

Belle needs me...

Childish laughter echoes through the trees again, and I lose my nerve at last, throwing down my bags. I hold out my knife, whirling on the spot. "Show yourself!"

The giggling stops, leaving nothing but the taunting wind.

I tighten my grasp on the handle of my blade. If only I had my sword, but I lost it a few miles back.

"Cowards. Can't even face me!"

More silence, and I scoff, bending down to pick up my bags.

Something jumps out at me, knocking me off my feet, and I look up in time to see a tiny, childlike figure vanishing behind a tree.

They *are* taunting me, making me believe that I'm going crazy, but I'll have the last laugh.

I grip my knife tighter, hoping they see the threat. This knife is steel, and steel is an alloy of iron. I am ready this time.

Another blurred shape darts out from the trees, shoving me hard against the ground, and my knife fumbles from my fingers.

Horrid little things!

They peal with laughter, and I find my iron cross within the folds of my skirt.

Another solid push to the ground, and the cross slips from my fingers, disappearing beneath the undergrowth with my knife.

These faeries simply are too quick for me. They're small, so I can hardly make them out.

Crawling on my hands and knees, I gasp for air, counting down as I prepare for battle with an unseen enemy.

I only came here looking for my aunt. A woman I have yet to meet, but I truly mean these creatures no harm.

Surely, they must see that. Yet they don't care... They just want to make me suffer. Mother was right about the Fae. They truly are wicked.

Still, I refuse to give up. They will not make a fool out of me.

Climbing to my feet, I face the creatures head-on. But then I gasp when I spy a horse's silhouette up ahead. There's no mistaking it now.

"Belle!"

I rush forward, tears streaming from my eyes.

The horse turns her head my way, but I won't stop until I reach her side. "Thank goodness! I thought—"

The ground gives way beneath me, and I find myself tumbling into deep water.

I didn't even see that marsh, hidden by the mist.

And the thing I thought was Belle? Well, it turned out to be a monster with a mane of seaweed and sharp, needle-pointed teeth.

It wasn't a horse after all, but one of *them*. It tricked me, and now it will gladly drown me.

I try to swim away from the Fae horse with glowing red eyes and piercing fangs, but I may as well be swimming in tar. My limbs won't move.

This is the end. I really am going to die.

Something darts into the murky water, skewering the creature's eye, and I try to scream. But only bubbles escape.

Before I sink to the bottomless depths of the marsh, a hand grips the back of my cloak, yanking me up to the surface.

I gasp for breath, the cold air like knives in my lungs, but I welcome the sensation, even when my vision tunnels and I begin to lose consciousness.

The last thing I recall before I pass out are those glowing eyes of amber—eyes hidden beneath a cowl of forest green.

It's *him*...the male from my dream. Now I know I've *definitely* lost the plot.

Finally, I slip away, grateful for an end to this nightmare at last.

4

Tegwyn

As I live and breathe... A human girl.

I have to pinch myself to make sure I'm not dreaming. Nope. She's as real as the bow and quiver that hangs from my shoulder.

I drag her out of the marsh, lying her flat on the bank so I can check her pulse. It's faint but there.

My gaze finds the kelpie floating in the water, its blood-red eyes glazed over with death, and I send a silent prayer to the goddess Maghelena.

Forgive me.

What have I done? I killed one of my own just to save a human. I'm *definitely* going to hell for this.

I have no idea why I intervened. The moment I caught her trail through the woods, I became possessed; I had to find the source of that delightful, honeysuckle scent, and that's when I found her at the mercy of the kelpie.

Why is she here? The north is Fae territory. I'm surprised she managed to survive this long.

I locate her bags, finding one filled with rations, and another with a map and a music box. Then I sniff a couple of apples, hissing when I detect Fae magic.

Pixies—wicked little blights.

It looks like they glamoured her bags, making them appear as if they were empty. They just couldn't help themselves, could they?

What must have gone through the poor thing's mind when she thought her food was gone?

My eyes flick back to her unconscious form. The worry lines have vanished from her fair countenance, and she almost looks at peace.

But I know that face will be etched with horror the moment she re-opens those sweet sea-green eyes again. She made a grave mistake coming here.

Although she may not be a complete idiot; she came here bearing iron on her person. It's close by. I can tell by the burning itch of my skin, and the way my stomach threatens to eject its contents.

Iron is harmful to the Fae. It incapacitates us, and this girl is fully aware of that. The creatures of this forest won't take the slight lightly, and I suppose saving her from the kelpie was pointless in hindsight.

Either way, she's dead. There's nothing more I can do for her.

But I find myself unable to leave her side, and the longer I gaze at her sopping wet form on the grass, her chest gently rising with each breath, the more reluctant I become to do so.

I'm no idiot. I'm wholly aware of the effect she's having on me—and most other males, too, I bet, Fae or otherwise.

The girl is beautiful. Painfully so.

Anyone with eyes can see that, and I can't help but be drawn to her honeyed scent again as it makes me wonder...

Why am I so attracted to her?

Unfortunately, her beauty only makes her an even bigger target. What am I going to do with her?

I can't just leave her to the wolves.

If the cold doesn't get to her first, then the wicked denizens of this forest surely will.

I spy a glint of gold around her slender neck, and my resolve firms. If there's one thing faeries love more than a fair maid, it's jewellery. I'll take care of her…for a price.

The girl is coming home with me.

The pot bubbles and spits on the stove, sending clouds of vapour across the small, dark cave. It may be cramped and dark to some, but it has been my sanctuary for many years. I personally think the stalagmites give it a homely touch.

Or are they *stalactites*?

Maybe the girl will know the difference when she finally wakes.

She's still sleeping in the other cave, and my heart flaps in my chest at the thought, making me stir my spoon faster.

She's the first visitor I've ever had in this cave…

I straighten, then I swallow, using my cravat to wipe the steam that wets my face.

What do I do? Should I make tea? I'm sure I have an old, dusty set of porcelain lying around somewhere.

She groans, and I snap my head around, spying a shadow along the far wall.

She's awake.

Shit.

Suddenly, she gives a loud, shrill gasp, and then everything falls completely silent—well, all except the pounding of my heart.

Time may as well be frozen.

My skin breaks out in a cold sweat when I hear those soft footsteps, and my eyes roam the cave, noticing the dirt and grime. Cobwebs drape across the walls, and I curse.

Yet, they have nothing on me: the most frightening entity in this entire cave.

She's coming closer, so I grab my cloak from the back of a chair, using it to mask my face. Then I find my gloves, pulling them up to my elbows. I even retract my claws so as not to startle the poor thing.

Finally, she steps into the cave, and I feel those big eyes boring into my spine. I don't dare look over my shoulder; I'm afraid to see what kind of face she's making.

She does nothing else but stare, and the suspense is *killing* me. One of us must break the ice, or we could be at this forever.

She speaks, "Who...who are you?"

The sound of her sweet, dulcet voice catches me off guard, and I'm at a loss for words. My mouth dries, and I lose the ability to breathe.

What's happening to me?

Somehow, I muster enough strength to offer her my hospitality. "Please...take a seat."

She doesn't move an inch, so I angle my head, examining her from the corner of my eye.

Maybe she didn't hear me.

Drawing a breath, I say with a little more force, "I said, take a seat."

She flinches. So much for being amicable. It's just hard to speak gently when you have a rasp to your voice.

One second passes by. And then two by the time she whispers, "You...saved my life."

My heart skips a beat, and I drop the spoon, gazing at the wall before me. I did save her, and I'm still pondering why.

I murdered a fellow faerie just to save a human. What is the world coming to?

"Th-thank you," she mutters, and something warm and buttery fills my veins, turning my mouth into a strange shape.

I think I'm...*smiling*.

"You're welcome," I reply, cringing at the way my voice trembles.

Silence hovers over us like a heavy cloud, and in a bid to break the tension, I offer her a seat again. "Please, sit."

She does as I ask this time, sitting with her hands on her lap. I feel her probing gaze the whole time I stir the stew.

Her small intake of breath redirects my attention to the table. "Where...where are my bags?"

Shame trickles down my face, and then I close my eyes, rubbing the bridge of my nose.

This will be interesting...

Since I'm a faerie, and therefore cannot lie in fear of upsetting my goddess, I decide to give her the truth. "I've confiscated them."

A brief pause. "Why?"

How do I tell her that I have trust issues, and I've hidden her things deep away in my lair where she can't find them?

She had iron in those bags. I had no choice. Iron makes me sick, so I cannot permit her to have it in my cave.

I try to change the subject, grabbing the spoon. "Supper's almost ready. You must be hungry."

She thinks long and hard for a moment, and I can almost hear the cogs of her mind spinning. Then she rises, heading for the exit. "Thank you for your hospitality, kind sir, but I must be on my way. So, if you would please show me to my bags."

I watch her, dumbfounded. "Won't you at least stay for supper? It would be terribly rude if I didn't at least offer you a warm meal."

She pauses, eyeing the stew warily.

There's no point in beating around the bush. She knows what I am; there's no missing the way my eyes glow beneath the hood.

The girl is smart. She knows not to accept anything from the Fae, be that food, gifts, or favours. But I mean no harm, truly. I genuinely do just want to give her supper.

I lift the pot, and she steps closer, giving an investigative sniff. "Is that rosemary?"

An ironic choice, really, given the name, but yes, it is rosemary.

"What else?"

Before she can protest, her stomach growls, and I snort.

She gives me a withering look, then sighs, taking her place at the table again. "All right. One bowl, and then you can take me to my bags and show me the way out. *Please*," she adds, remembering her manners.

I pour a generous amount of stew into a bowl, placing it onto the table before her, and she studies its contents carefully.

I watch, amused, as she brings the spoon to her lips, seeming to be at war with herself. It's good of her to be cautious, but really, it's just mushroom stew.

Not glamoured or poisoned in any shape or form.

Finally, she slips the spoon into her mouth, eyes lighting up with surprise. "This is actually delicious."

I scoff. "Well, don't sound so surprised."

She doesn't hear my retort as she helps herself to another spoonful, and maybe I did spike the stew with some magic after all. The girl is obsessed.

She clears the bowl in minutes, and I stare, impressed. "My, you must have been hungry."

She nods, wiping the grease from her lips. "Can I have more?"

I watch as she devours another bowl, and the moment she's finished, she leans back in the squeaky chair, closing her eyes.

She's a far cry from the helpless girl who was drowning in the marsh just a few hours ago. I've lulled her into a false sense of security.

I inch closer, expecting her to recoil, yet she stays put. When I grab the spare chair, she doesn't flinch. She continues to hug her belly, eyes closed in deep thought.

I drum my fingers on the table. "I hope you don't mind my asking, but what are you doing all the way out here? You're a far cry from civilization."

Her eyes shoot wide open, and then she jumps to her feet, saying with more urgency, "Please, take me to my bags. I wish to leave."

I regard her curiously. She's trembling, avoiding my eyes. Is she afraid or something?

"People usually don't come this far north unless they're running from someone. *Who* are you running from?"

She sighs, "Please...if you would just take me to my bags, then I will be out of your hair."

I tap my chin. "Are you running from your family?"

Finally, she looks me straight in the eyes, and there I meet those twin flames of green. "I won't ask you again. Please, take me to my things."

I watch as her hand slips into her pocket, and I bet she's looking for her iron cross. Her face blanches when she finally realises it's gone, and then she throws an accusatory glare in my direction.

I decide to play the dumb card. If we're going to continue playing this game, then so be it.

Besides, it's been a while since I got to be the bad guy.

My eyes move to her clothes. Her boots have certainly seen better days, and her nightdress is torn and dirty.

She steps away from the table, extending an olive branch. "Again, I thank you for your hospitality, sir, but I must leave. I have somewhere important to be."

Again, I disregard her thanks, balancing my chin on my hand. "Let me guess. You're searching for the *Veil*."

She looks at me incredulously. "You...looked through my things?"

I lift my shoulders with a shrug. "I'm a curious creature..."

She becomes visibly flustered, and her cheeks turn an adorable shade of red. "You had no right!"

I give another shrug. "Had to know who I was bringing home to my cave. You could be up to anything out here."

She growls, and I've never heard anything so inhuman.

Maybe she's Fae, too.

"Oh, that's rich, coming from a..."

Her voice trails, and then her face drops five shades lighter as she realises the error of her ways. It's okay, though. I'm quite the forgiving creature.

Most of the time.

I rise, throwing down my hood. She stumbles, tripping on her own clumsy feet, and you would think she had seen a ghost with the way she stares at me. But she wouldn't be far off the mark, I guess. Especially as my ire summons the very shadows of the cave, making them crawl their wicked way towards her. It happens all the time when I'm particularly pissed or threatened.

"I'm a *what*, exactly?" I whisper, a low growl vibrating in my throat.

The human stammers, all that previous gusto gone.

My eyes flash. I come around the table, stalking her like a predator with shadows in tow. "Go on. Say it."

She doesn't take her eyes off me as I back her up against the wall. When I stop mere inches away, she squeaks, making my mouth stretch with a sneer.

"Well, go on. *Say it...*"

Finally, she shuts her eyes, bottom lip shaking as she mumbles, "Fae."

A snigger escapes my cruel lips. "That's right, and don't you forget it, *princess*."

She turns her face away as I scrutinise her for a few moments longer. When I've had my fun with her, I move back towards the chair, kicking my legs up on the table.

When the shadows withdraw, I pull out my bronze knife, spinning it around in my fingers. She remains by the wall, her heavy breaths filling the cave.

I roll my eyes. "You won't get far looking for the Veil. That town hasn't been seen in centuries."

It takes her a while to respond. When she finally does, I can't help but smirk. "And why should I take your word for it?"

I sigh. "Then don't. Unless you want to become kelpie food again, I wouldn't bother. You'll be dead before you ever find the Veil."

She laughs, but it doesn't quite reach her eyes. "Well, that's a risk I'm willing to take."

She peels away from the wall, moving for the exit, and she doesn't even ask for her bags, finally giving up on them, I suppose.

I chuckle, "I guess that's one less human in the world to worry about."

She ignores the harsh comment, continuing for the exit. I glance at the chain around her neck.

It's time to strike a deal.

"I'll make you a deal. Your necklace for a room. You'll get hot meals and a place to sleep. Even brand-new clothes."

I really hope she takes up my last offer. Her flimsy nightdress is looking worse for wear.

Shocked, she grabs her necklace, staring at me aghast. "So, that's what this was all about? You were just after my necklace?"

I hold up my hands. "You got me. Look, I don't care what you do. You're not my problem, but if you want sanctuary, then you pay. A pretty fair deal, if you ask me."

She backs towards the exit. "As if I would ever bargain with a creature like you..."

I arch a brow. "Smart of you, but you don't really have a choice. There is far worse out there than kelpies and pixies, *princess*. You will not survive on your own."

She pinches her eyes shut, taking everything I say on board. A tear drips down her cheek, but I pretend not to notice.

Finally, she takes a deep breath, looking me straight in the eyes. "Fine. I will give you my necklace... on *one* condition. You let me stay for as long as I need. At least until I find a way to search for the Veil."

A sneer stretches my lips again. "Of course... Would I lie to you?"

Dumb question, considering I can't lie to her. It's just something I've always heard the humans say.

They always sound so insincere.

She hesitates for a few moments, holding on to whatever dignity she may have left. It must be awful to realise you've been duped by a faerie.

Once she hands over the necklace, there's no going back. It's a binding contract. Of course, she's still free to leave, but the consequences will be her choice.

Certain death or a room in my mountain.

With a heavy sigh, she unhooks the necklace, tossing it across the table. I catch it in my hand, and the air ripples with magic once our bargain is complete.

My mouth salivates when I spy the diamond sigil. This should fetch a nice price on the black market. Then, when I have my riches, I can leave this godforsaken country and live out the rest of my days on a deserted island.

Pure heaven.

I pocket the necklace, donning my business hat again. "Our deal is done. You may do as you please." I wave her off.

She looks up. Candlelight dances in her eyes, and for a moment, I think she's going to kill me. But then she dashes out of the cave, making me chuckle.

She's just too easy to tease.

5

Ivy

My breath ricochets off the cold walls as I run down a long, winding tunnel. I have no idea where it leads, and I don't care.

I'm not safe here, and it won't be long until I'm duped yet again.

That faerie...he *tricked* me, and I can't believe I let him get the better of me. He's nothing but a crook.

Never accept a favour from the Fae, no matter how tempting the offer may seem, because absolutely *everything* comes with a price.

It just reminds me of how alone I am. There's no one left in this world who I care about, and I must be wiser if I hope to survive.

So, no more bargaining with the Fae.

A bright light shines up ahead, and I rush forth.

Finally. A way out.

Unfortunately, I almost topple over the edge of a cliff once I reach the light, and I rear back, chest heaving as I stare at the sharp precipice.

A sprawling valley lies beyond, stretching far and wide, an all-encompassing sea of mist and trees that hugs the grey sky. It's hopeless.

I am utterly trapped, caught in that wicked creature's snare of sticky lies.

A biting wind almost knocks me off course, and I fumble along the wall with my hands, searching for the mouth of the cave.

Once I'm tucked away inside, I drop to the ground, wrapping my arms around my legs. The only thing I can do now is gaze wistfully across the stark landscape, wondering if my parents are out there somewhere...searching for me.

I know we'll be reunited again, and I make a silent promise, hoping they'll hear me.

I will find you, Mama, Papa. Mark my words.

It must be hours before he finds me.

Once again, I find no sympathy in his golden, fox-like eyes. Only cold indifference.

Mama once told me that the heart of a Fae works a little differently from ours. They lack what we call a conscience or empathy.

This wicked creature honestly sees no fault in his actions. He thinks he's justified due to the lore of his people.

They never give freely. It's just not in their nature, and in turn, they hate to be in debt to anyone. Hence why they seldom accept favours.

That's why they're considered cruel by my kind. A faerie's favourite pastime is to trick poor, gullible humans into doing exactly as they please—as I've had the misfortune of finding out myself. But a part of me always believed there were some good faeries out there.

There are three classes of Fae: Seelie, Unseelie, and Rogue.

I don't know what category my new captor falls under, but I do hope it's the merciful kind. Since he likes to trick poor girls into giving up their necklaces, I highly doubt it.

"Thought I lost you for a moment, princess," he croons in that unearthly tenor, the one that shakes the marrow of my bones.

I refuse to look at him. Instead, I burn a hole into the dark ore of his mountain.

He glances at the cliff warily. "You... weren't thinking about jumping, were you? I know I'm unbearable, but I never would have dreamed I'd be *that* unbearable..."

His small talk won't work with me. If he thinks for a moment that he has any chance of clemency after what he did, then he can kiss my derriere.

More silence passes between us as I keep my eyes on the distant horizon. A strong gust of wind blows through the tunnel, so sharp that it almost blows out the flame of his oil lamp.

"Well, then...let's show you to your room."

That catches my attention, and finally, I meet his fox-like eyes. They glow in the dark, startling me at first, but I swallow my dread, speaking clearly, "My room?"

I can't see his face since it's bathed in shadow, but his eyes narrow with what I can only assume is exasperation. "Yes. As per our bargain. Did you forget?"

No. Of course I didn't.

In exchange for my necklace, he promised me a bed and warm food. But if I had known what his kindness would have cost me, I never would have agreed to return to his cave in the first place.

But I didn't have much of a choice in the matter. I was unconscious. He must have carried me up himself, and the thought makes my heart flutter.

Did he only save me just so he could trick me? I will never quite understand him. He's an odd creature, a true enigma, and I curl my fists, refusing to meet his gaze.

He sighs, heading down the tunnel. "Let's go."

It's getting harder and harder to resist his offer. Not that I expect much in the way of comfort, but better than sleeping outside in the woods. I haven't slept in a bed in days.

I rise shakily to my feet, following him down the tunnel. I feel the walls closing in as we descend further into his lair, and I'll probably never find my way out of this mountain again.

He walks at a languid pace, his oil lamp swinging freely. It causes shadows to dance across the walls, and it's getting darker and darker the farther we go.

Several times I lose him, but it's hard to want to be anywhere near him in this damp, cool place. I trip on a jutting rock, and he laughs, calling me a 'clumsy human.'

He stops abruptly, and when I bump into him, I get a strong whiff of pine and woodsmoke. I jump back immediately, trying to maintain a safe distance.

That was a little too close for comfort, and it would be so much easier to hate him if he didn't smell so pleasant.

No wonder these creatures can trick us so easily.

He regards me strangely, and again, I don't meet his eyes. He likes to stare at me a lot, I've noticed, and I find it unnerving.

"You're not very graceful, are you?"

I hold my tongue, refraining from what I really want to say. Quite frankly, I don't like him. I'm afraid of him, much to my chagrin, and that bold girl with the knife has long gone now—she drowned in that icy marsh with the kelpie.

He snorts, vanishing into a cave that I hadn't noticed before.

I gulp, stepping away. I can't go in there...

He pops his head out again. "Well?"

I fight the urge to run back up the tunnel. Maybe I should have jumped off the cliff after all, but it's too late for regrets now.

Once I step into that cold, black cave, I will never come back out again.

The faerie materialises before me, and I yelp, fumbling my way backwards. I didn't even see him coming; he's such a sneaky devil.

With quick reflexes, he snatches hold of my arm, stopping my fall, and despite how frightened I am, I find his gaze.

His fingers are like a vise on my wrist, and I can feel how strong they are. If he wanted, he could snap my arm like a twig.

I can't stop staring at his hand as he continues to hold me fast. He wears brown leather gloves with holes at the tips of his fingers.

My heart pounds. They're for his claws...

With a scoff, he lets go of my arm, stepping into the cave. "When you're done yelping and tripping, come inside."

He may have saved me from my fall, but he's still my enemy. I can't forget that.

Never let your guard down.

Finally, I follow him inside, stopping dead in my tracks. My skin grows cold all over when I spy a large animal in the middle of the cave.

For a moment, I think it's the black wolf—the one that chased me all the way to the north.

I still don't understand what happened to that creature, or Belle, for that matter. Both horse and lupine just seemed to vanish into thin air.

Then light washes over the cave, and I find myself gazing at a pile of furs. The black pelt of a wolf lies on top, and I also spy a bobcat, a bear, and a deer pelt, too.

"Well, sweet dreams."

The faerie takes his leave, and I stop him. "Wait."

He pauses at the mouth of the cave, giving me the profile of his face. "Yes?"

I suck in a breath. I have no idea what to say. I guess I'm still a little stunned; I thought he was leading me to a cell.

The Fae enslave humans and keep them as prisoners. At least, so I was taught.

"Is this where I will sleep?"

He gives an exasperated sigh, leaning against the wall to cross his arms. "Obviously."

I glance at the pelts. "On the furs?"

"Yes. Is there a problem?"

I shake my head. "N-no..."

"Well, then, go to sleep." He moves for the exit.

There's not even a fire pit in here or anything to keep me warm. The furs are all I have.

"But... what about the cold?"

"Not my problem."

Anger writhes inside me, hissing like a pit of threatened snakes, and finally, I lose my nerve. "My necklace was worth more than this!"

The faerie spins, and I flinch when I meet those flaming eyes. "If you want more, then you'll have to bargain for it. So, pay up or shut up."

I press my mouth into a line, eyeing him evilly. I really do hate him, and obviously the feeling is mutual.

With a roll of his eyes, he moves back towards the tunnel.

"Monster," I mutter under my breath.

He's in front of me before I can so much as blink, and I scream, falling back onto the furs. How on earth did he move so fast?

My heart thrums in my ears, and I wish I had something, *anything*, to protect myself. Something made from iron, preferably.

The creature doesn't speak. He just glares, baring his teeth and those terrible fangs. His claws are extended, and I scramble on the furs, trying to get away from him.

His pupils have narrowed to slits, and it's like gazing into the eyes of death. Shadows rise around him, stretching towards me like talons, and a dreadful lump sticks in my throat.

So, I wasn't imagining things before. He really did summon shadows. I'm no match for him after all.

"What did you say?"

His voice is cold liquid trickling down my spine, freezing my muscles in place. But I still hold my head high, meeting those murderous eyes. "Monster."

He takes a moment to respond. Then he whispers, making the hair rise at the back of my neck. "I'm not the monster here."

I don't reply. I just continue to stare at him, struggling to breathe. My laboured breaths fill the cave, and I've never felt so helpless.

With a final growl, he jerks away, taking his shadows and his pine and woodsmoke scent away with him.

He didn't even leave the lamp. Now I am left in total darkness.

I lie down on the furs, trying to get as warm as possible. It's too dark, and if only I could convince myself that monsters aren't real.

But one just left this cave...

Despite how scared I am, sleep still finds me. It's been an exhausting day—no, an exhausting week.

I dream about wicked faeries throughout the night.

6

Ivy

A BLACK WOLF JUMPS out from the shadows, snapping its sharp teeth at my face, and I jerk back, yelping in fright.

My thin, rasping breaths echo through the darkness, and I pinch my eyes shut.

It was a dream, just a dream...

As I wake fully, I gaze around, trying to make sense of my surroundings. I'm sitting inside a damp, cold cave, and for a moment I can't remember how I got here.

But once the memories come crashing back, I roll over onto my side and vomit onto the ground.

How could I have forgotten?

I'm trapped inside that wicked creature's domicile, and I will probably never see the light of day again.

That's when I realise...the cave is no longer pitch black. Faint light shines from somewhere, so I search for the source. It looks as if someone sneaked inside the cave while I was asleep and placed an oil lamp down beside my bed.

I don't understand.

I could have sworn I saw him leaving with the very same lamp the previous evening. Did he have a change of heart?

No, that can't be right. The Fae don't do random acts of kindness. Well, not unless there is something in it for them.

So, what did he have to gain by giving me the lamp? Nothing, really. It doesn't add up.

Wiping the tear stains from my cheeks, I rise from the furs, limbs stiff as I give an awkward stretch.

That's when I spy the dress hanging from a stalagmite, and I move across the cave, running my fingers over the smooth fabric. The skirt and bodice are made from the finest sky-blue silk, interwoven with silver thread to form a brocaded, floral pattern. I trace my finger over a rose, unable to contain my surprise.

The dress is beautiful and far too grand for a simple country girl like me. How on earth did he manage to procure such a gown? There's a pair of leather boots, too, and a royal blue cloak of damask velvet.

How did he know blue was my favourite colour?

No…I can't accept these. I did pay for them with my necklace, but I have a feeling they weren't rightfully his to give away in the first place.

But I do need a new set of clothes. My nightdress is torn and covered in dirt, and I did have a similar cloak back home.

I finally make up my mind, slipping on the dress. The bodice hugs my waist, and it feels like wearing a second skin. When I spin, the light catches the silver thread, and for a moment I fancy myself a queen.

I try on the boots, lacing them up at the front, then tiptoe down the tunnel, careful to avoid the stalagmites that protrude from the ground.

There are stalactites hanging from the ceiling, and I feel as though I'm walking through the mouth of a mighty dragon.

Thank goodness for the lamp, for I wouldn't have been able to find my way through the dark.

A warm glow shines ahead, and I step into the main chamber, the one where we first met.

He's nowhere in sight. Should I be worried? For all I know, he could be lurking in the shadows, watching me.

Shaking away the thought, I decide to search the rest of his home.

We're inside a mountain, one containing a labyrinth of tunnels. It's going to take a miracle to find my way out.

I stumble upon a tunnel with a waterfall, and as I step closer to the cascade, narrowing my eyes against the spray, I glimpse a verdant valley of green and purple beyond.

The other side of the mountain.

It's breathtaking, and nothing at all like the sprawling forests to the south.

A silver stream glistens in the sunlight, snaking across hills of vibrant heather. It's a true work of art, one I wouldn't mind capturing on canvas one day.

Cupping my hands together, I collect the water from beneath the cascade, then take a sip. The water is fresh and soothing, and I help myself to more, suddenly aware of the urge to relieve myself.

Let's just hope the faerie has a privy inside his mountain somewhere...

I hurry down the tunnel, spying a shaft of sunlight streaking across the stone ahead, but my hopes are soon dashed the moment I find myself in yet another cave.

It's a storage room of some kind, and it appears he's a collector.

Beams of light pierce through cracks in the ore above, and as I move in the dress, the fabric whispering with each step, I stir up a cloud of dust.

I have never seen so many books—towers upon towers reaching the ceiling. There are antiques, such as a grandfather clock and an old candelabra, along with useless bric-a-brac he couldn't possibly have any use for.

I cover my mouth, holding back a snort.

He's a *hoarder*.

My eyes find a globe, and I spin it on its axis, taking note of the continents of the world. Then I approach a table strewn with metal cogs and lengths of wire, picking up a kaleidoscope.

When I've had my fun with the contraption, I gaze around, pursing my lips. He should really consider hiring a maid. This cave is filthy and dangerous.

There's a bureau in the corner. That must be his office. Unlike the rest of the cave, it's free of clutter. There are rolls of parchment stacked inside a nook, alongside a jar of ink and several feather quills.

With a glance over my shoulder, I pick up a scroll, skimming his handwriting. His scrawl is slanted and neat, though marred by several blotches of ink.

A flash of light flickers at the edge of my vision, and I turn quickly, searching for the source. What was it?

That's when I feel a tug at my hair, and I yelp, dropping the parchment back onto the desk.

My breaths echo as I search for the culprit, certain it's one of his little friends... just like the ones that tricked me in the woods.

But when I reach behind my head, I discover my hair has been tied into a long braid.

Before I can question the strangeness further, my eyes fall on the golden spine of a book tucked into one of the stacks.

I don't believe it. I had the exact same book.

If I could just pull it out... but I don't want to be crushed to death by a stack of books. Still, that fear doesn't stop me from gripping the spine between my thumb and index finger, trying to slip it free.

If I could just...

"What are you doing?"

With a sharp squeal, I knock my shoulder into the stack of books, and the whole tower topples down.

Covering my head, I brace for the inevitable blow, but he clicks his fingers, and the books fly neatly back into place.

I stare in utter disbelief. It's not something you see every day, and it must be nice to just click your fingers and make everything right as rain again.

Now all is silent. Save for his angry breathing.

Finally, I summon the courage to look his way, flinching when I meet those glowing eyes in the shadows.

He looks like a thing of nightmares, especially as he summons tendrils of inky darkness like some deep-sea squid.

My heart thumps, and I swallow hard, feeling the sweat dripping down my temple.

When he steps into a shaft of light, the shadows dissipate, and I meet the glossy black eye of a dead stag. He balances its weight on his shoulders, and his sheer strength astounds me.

"I... I was just looking for a way outside," I mutter.

He speaks through clenched teeth. "Well, you're not going to find it here."

I'm not sure how to respond. A clock ticks somewhere in the cave, and I'm already starting to regret my choice.

I really had no business being in here, nosing at his personal effects.

But I was curious.

"Get out."

I snatch up the lamp where I left it on his desk, scurrying out of the cave like a frightened mouse. Blood drips down his long, faded leather coat, and I quicken my pace before I end up like that poor deer.

He follows me down the tunnel, and I move faster, trying to put some distance between us. But he soon catches up.

I must be slowing him down. These tunnels are awfully narrow.

"Would you hurry along? This beast's blood is dripping into places it shouldn't."

I pause, momentarily distracted by his choice of words. "Wh-what...?"

"Out of the way!"

At his flippant bark, I press my back to the wall, letting him pass. The deer's head bobs on his shoulder when he walks by, and it looks like it's nodding *yes*.

I keep my distance, having the idea to go back to my room where I can avoid him. Because I plan to avoid him a lot.

Ever the curious creature, though, I decide to follow him instead. I want to know where he's going.

He stops several feet down the tunnel, angling his head, and that's when I meet that ornery eye of glowing yellow. "Are you my shadow?"

My brows knit at the strange question. "No..."

"Then stop following me!"

His voice rebounds off the walls, punctuating his point, and I finally get it: he doesn't want me anywhere near him, either.

That's fine. We can just avoid each other. That should make life easier for both of us.

But alas, I'm too inquisitive for my own good, and like the fool I am, I reach out, "Wait."

He turns, fixing those burning eyes on me again. My mouth dries, and where do I begin? I have no idea how to speak to him, but if we're going to live together, we can at least be civil to each other.

"I'm... sorry for what I said last night."

Unless my eyes deceive me, his face softens slightly.

I brush the thought aside, peering shyly at my feet. "And... thank you for bringing the lamp back to the cave. You... didn't have to do that. Especially after what I called you."

I hold up said lamp for his inspection.

He continues to stare at me, his expression unreadable, and my cheeks burn under his scrutinising gaze.

His jaw ticks, and it almost looks as if he's trying to smile. But then he scoffs and marches back down the tunnel again.

I try to keep up with his pace this time. "Would you be able to point me to the way out? I...need to go outside."

"Nature calling?" he muses, and my cheeks blush bright red.

"N-no!"

Now, a smile *definitely* appears on his lips, and it displays his fangs.

I shake my head, finding it hard to believe that I'm discussing my bathroom habits with a faerie.

Finally, we reach a fork in the tunnel. He points left. "That way should lead you to the foot of the mountain."

I peer down the tunnel. It must be miles long, but needs must. "Are you going down the right cave?"

He shifts, distributing the deer's weight across his shoulders. "Yes."

I should probably stop and head on my way, but I can't help myself; it's not every day you get to speak with a member of the Fae.

Besides, he doesn't seem to be in a talkative mood today. Last night, he spoke so freely with that silver tongue, but he was hoping to make a trade, I suppose.

Now that he's got what he wants from me, he's lost all interest. I wonder if he would even care if I returned once I finished outside.

"What's down that way?"

"The pantry."

"Oh. How interesting..."

He regards me irritably, and I have to agree. It's not the most riveting conversation I've ever had, either.

Finally, he turns towards the right tunnel. I hold out my hand again. "Hold on."

He spins, anger flaring in his amber eyes. "What is it now?"

I worry my lip, twiddling my thumbs. "What... what's your name?"

His eyes widen, and then finally, he loses the ability to speak. He swallows, brushing his gloved fingers over his cotton cravat as he mutters under his breath.

I take a daring step closer. "I'm sorry. I didn't quite catch that. Would you—"

"It's Tegwyn."

I move back, repeating his name. "Tegwyn. Such a beautiful name."

He rolls his eyes. "You humans really are good at lying."

My mouth parts in shock. "I wasn't lying."

With an exasperated sigh, he moves for the tunnel. Yet before he departs, I say, "I'm Ivy. Just in case you wanted to know my name, too."

I know he never asked, but I thought it would be polite. Besides, he only has to know the short version.

As if I would ever give him my full name.

Tegwyn stops, studying me carefully. Again, I can't read his face since it's shrouded in shadow, but his eyes do gleam.

He slips his hand into his coat pocket, passing me a bronze knife. "Here. Heather grows in abundance this time of year. When you return, you will find a stack of fresh linen in your room. Stuff it with heather and make yourself a bed."

I'm not sure what to say. I was not expecting his thoughtfulness.

"Thank you," I reply, but he's already gone.

That's all right. Because the first genuine smile I've had in over a week spreads across my face, and maybe life with the horned faerie won't be so bad after all.

7

Tegwyn

I WAIT WITH BATED breath while the goblin investigates the necklace. One of his beetle-black eyes is currently amplified by his monocle, giving his already haphazard face an even more alarming appearance.

His clawed finger caresses the diamond pendant, making my eye twitch. He's taking his sweet ass time, and it's more than I can bloody take.

When he displays his teeth, going as far as to *lick* the necklace with his tongue to confirm its quality, I palm my face. So uncouth, but that's the way of the goblin. They're as vicious as they are greedy, and this one is no exception.

I suppose I'm not much different. I, too, take delight in all things that shine and sparkle.

The goblin's grating breaths are like a hacksaw to my brain, and he's putting me on edge.

Finally, he finishes his careful ministrations, fixing me with his cold stare. "Five gold pieces."

It's like someone punched me in the gut.

I shake my head. "No. That necklace must be worth at least five *hundred* pieces. Look at the sigil."

The goblin sneers. "*Five pieces.*"

I slam my palms down hard, raking my claws through the faded wood of his worktop to get my point across, yet the goblin displays little fear.

He merely stares, his beetle-black eyes completely unimpressed, and it doesn't look like my pitiful attempts at coercion are going to work in my favour. He's as old as time itself; I bet he was a wee lad during the Goblin Wars a thousand years ago.

I give him back his personal space, inhaling deeply. Then I meet his amplified eye, noticing how it shines blood red in a certain light. "I don't think you quite understand. That is a *Seaworth* sigil. One of the oldest kingdoms in the country."

He shows me his jagged teeth. "Do I look like the sort who cares about some forgotten kingdom, boy? *Five* pieces. That's my final offer."

My jaw ticks, and then I resist the urge to punch him in that crooked cucumber of a nose. I plead my case further. "They lived on the back of a giant sea monster. Does that amount to anything?"

I must appear desperate, but I don't care; I need the money.

"Two gold pieces," he growls.

I dig my claws in that little bit more, gouging the rotten wood of his worktop. Bloody old codger. He's just asking for a black eye, yet his mind is set. Two gold pieces.

Maybe I should have kept my mouth shut, but it looks as if the swindler got *swindled* in the end.

Poetic justice, I guess.

The only reason that necklace was in my possession in the first place was because I tricked some gullible girl into thinking she owed me. I'm getting exactly what I deserve.

But I still stand by my belief. That sigil is worth at least five hundred gold pieces. More than enough to buy my safe passage across the Haunted Sea.

Ivy's face rises up before me, and I blink her away. It's as if she's burned into my retinas, because every time I close my eyes, there she is, smiling at me.

I recall our conversation in the tunnel, and I just don't understand why she'd been so civil with me.

I have been nothing but *uncivil*, yet she offered me a sweet, dimpled smile all the same.

I know what she's doing.

She won't charm me so easily. I'm as stubborn as solid brick.

I snatch the necklace back from the goblin's withered hand, showing him my back. "You can shove your two gold pieces up your *bunghole*."

He scoffs. "Suit yourself. And a word of advice—don't go walking around these parts carrying that human filth like some good-for-nothing scallywag. Unless you want to get lynched. Also, take a bath. You *stink* of human."

The goblin slides the shutter over his window, and once he's out of sight, I sniff my coat. Ivy's honeysuckle scent clings to the leather. How is that possible? We've barely spent any time together.

I glance over my shoulder. The goblin's shop sits snugly inside a muddy hillock, one hidden by thick moss and craggy rock.

He's the closest pawnbroker this side of the mountain. There are others, of course, but I'm too tired to search for them now; I just want to head home and kick my legs up on the table.

Besides, Ivy will be missing me. Mustn't keep her waiting.

I scowl at the wreckage of the cave, finding a quiet spot in the shadows where no one can see me.

The moment I returned home, I ransacked the entire mountain from top to bottom, but in the end, my efforts yielded no results.

No scrap of gold whatsoever.

I still don't have enough. I pick up a vase, smashing it against the wall. Maybe I could sell a few of my stolen goods. Or perhaps I could go down south and pilfer more towns.

But then I'd have to leave Ivy alone in the mountain. Not that she's any concern of mine, but I'd be breaking the terms of our contract if I left her here to defend herself, and I refuse to be in debt to a human.

No matter how pretty she may be...

I promised her sanctuary and protection, and to go back on my word would break the ancient lore of my people.

Besides, human treasure is worthless to the Fae. They look down on anything crafted by the hands of men. I may have to search for alternative methods of travel. One way or another, I will be getting on a boat by winter's end.

And I know just the Fae who can help me get there. Bannog the Bold.

He lives in a village just west of the mountain. He's a clothier by trade—he weaves cloaks and glamours of the finest quality, and the best part—they are completely permanent.

A faerie never has to worry about budgeting their magic with one of Bannog's designs. But his glamours aren't cheap, and I may as well just dig the knife in now.

A piece of broken porcelain lies on the ground beside me, and I pick it up with my gloved fingers, losing myself in its floral design.

It looks and smells just like honeysuckle. Her scent really does linger.

I still don't understand what circumstances brought her here. Humans don't dare venture this far north unless they have a death wish.

Maybe she is running from someone. That fair-haired maiden is keeping something from me, and I'm going to find out. I always do.

My eyes skim over the wreckage, landing on a discarded vase. A spray of flowers spills out like guts, and I roll my eyes.

She's certainly making herself at home. She even dressed the table in a white lace cloth, and she's cleaned, too.

The dust and cobwebs are now a thing of the past.

A sharp pinch comes to my hand, and I gaze down at the porcelain shard. I gripped it a little too tightly, and now I have no choice but to use Ivy's pretty tablecloth to staunch the blood.

The shard even cut into the leather of my glove. How long have I been stewing?

Look what you did, idiot.

"Go away, Rosemary. I'm in no mood for your depressive shit."

Couldn't even watch what you were doing. Such a beautiful tablecloth, too. Not like it was yours to destroy, anyway. Just another thing you stole, thief!

A low growl rumbles in my chest. "I said, *go...*"

She laughs. *And you thought the goddess would grant you a favour for once. Turns out that the necklace was as worthless as you are in the end. You'll never leave this place. You will never be free, never find happiness...*

I cover my ears, but my attempts to block out her voice are merely in vain. Her cruelty drones on, slipping through the cracks of my mind.

A haunted cry echoes down the tunnel, and I remove my hands from my ears. What the hell was that?

When the cry doesn't return, I cast my gaze around, clicking my tongue in frustration. What a mess. I really ought to start cleaning.

A blood-curdling scream splits right down the centre of the mountain, and I leap to my feet, stretching my claws.

It looks as if another banshee sneaked inside the mountain, and this time, I'll fucking kill her.

I search the tunnels, scraping my claws along the walls to get them nice and sharp. When I find the bitch, I'm going to rip her jugular out.

The banshee's cry is coming from Ivy's room, and it's like the goddess herself strikes me with a bolt of white-hot lightning.

A banshee's scream can make a human haemorrhage.

Ivy could die in a matter of seconds.

With a snarl befitting a demon from the dankest pits of hell, I hurry to her room, storming inside. My eyes dart around the cave, searching for the banshee.

I don't see her, but I do spy a writhing shape beneath the furs and blankets of Ivy's bed. When I yank them away, I find the human tangled up in her own limbs, and I don't move. I don't even breathe.

I just...*stare*.

What the hell is *wrong* with her?

She doesn't appear to be suffering from a haemorrhage, and now that the adrenaline has vanished from my veins, I finally see...

Ivy was the one screaming.

She's deep in the throes of a nightmare, twisting and turning on her plush bed of wild heather. That banshee's cry still ruptures from her throat, and something tugs inside my chest, sinking to the depths of my soul like an anchor descending towards the seabed.

She looks so helpless, so frightened, and I'm completely at a loss.

So, I just continue to stare. A lot of good I am.

"No, no! *Please!*"

I come back to my senses, gripping her shoulders. "Wake up!"

Her lids fly open, and then our eyes lock. Her sclera shows, and I can't look away.

That sinking sensation returns to my gut until I'm drowning in a bottomless sea. What is happening? Why do I feel like this?

Her pulse thumps through her whole body, and my anchor descends, lower and lower, until that sea becomes the evergreen of her precious eyes.

They pin me in place, and any moment, I expect her to scream at the sight of me. I'm just another nightmare in the end—a detestable thing to be feared.

But then her eyes soften, and her shoulders sag as she recognises me. "T-Tegwyn."

I swallow a lump in my throat. "Yes, it's me... S-surprise."

Well, this just got awkward, but what else was I supposed to say? I'm not the most sociable creature.

She shuts her eyes, blowing a sigh from her lips. "Thank goodness. They were *here*..."

My heart rate spikes. She's about to spill her secret. "*Who* was here?"

A sheen glazes her eyes, and it's like I'm no longer present. "Soldiers. They came back for me."

I cock a brow. "Soldiers?"

She starts to tremble, but I force her to look at me again, letting my eyes flash. They reflect off her big, guileless pair, and I'm scarier than any banshee.

"What soldiers? *Tell me...*" My voice lacks all empathy, but I need to know who she's running from.

Ivy whimpers when I grip her a little too tightly, and I loosen my hold. I forgot to retract my claws before I grabbed her, and I've left nasty red welts on her porcelain skin.

That's what I do: I destroy everything I touch.

When I let her go, she grabs her furs and blankets, holding them close. Now her heavy gasps fill the cave. I'm not going to get my answers.

Not seeing any point in sticking around, I take my leave, heading for the exit. She grips my wrist, holding on like I'm her last lifeline. "Don't go."

My heart hiccups, and it takes me a moment to adjust to the sudden contact. I go to make a smart remark, but when I meet her shining, dewy eyes, the words die in my throat.

She genuinely wants me to stay and protect her from all the scary monsters out there.

It's too bad that I'm just another monster in the end.

With a heavy breath, I sit down beside her, sinking deep into the mattress. It seems she got enough heather, and at least she's sleeping comfortably.

I was just in a bad mood that first night.

She doesn't let go of my wrist, even long after she drifts off. When I start to get pins and needles, I still don't take my arm away. It seems to placate her.

I don't understand. Does my arm with its sharp claws really bring her comfort?

I watch her sleep. She really is a sight for weary eyes. The oil lamp casts her in a soft glow, giving her face a warm, velvety texture, and I'm tempted to brush my finger down her cheek.

But I would only cut her with my claw.

Well, it looks like I'm staying with her for the night. May as well get comfortable.

8

Ivy

I SNEAK DOWN THE tunnel the next morning, head pounding like a drum. Hopefully, Tegwyn left to hunt; I don't think I can face him today, not after what happened last night.

To my relief, he's nowhere in sight when I step into the kitchen, just like he was nowhere to be found when I woke, my bedside empty and devoid of his presence. I can't believe I begged him to stay.

I just couldn't bear to be alone. Not after the nightmares...

The dream had felt so real—I was absolutely convinced that the soldiers had found me.

I must have looked completely hysterical. Worst of all, I exposed a vulnerable side of myself.

I'm not sure if I can wholly trust that Fae. As a matter of fact, I wouldn't be surprised if he has a trick waiting up his sleeve for me. Any way to exploit me.

I'm greeted with a wall of darkness when I enter the cave. Holding my lamp out before me, I shuffle into the cold chamber, letting the soft light wash away the shadows.

It looks as if a certain *someone* left the kitchen in complete disarray, pots and pans scattered across the floor. Something cracks beneath my boot.

What on earth did that mischievous faerie get up to last night?

Something shifts in the corner of my eye, and I jump, dropping the lamp. It clatters to the ground, yet I can't tear my gaze away from the haunted figure sitting at the table.

Has he been in the kitchen this whole time? Or has he just arrived? I can never tell with him.

I've seen him in action—he's fast. One place one moment, and another the next.

The lamp continues to roll, making the shadows dance across the cave. Tegwyn doesn't move an inch. He merely stares with that vacant expression, eyes glowing like firelight.

Something isn't right. Still, despite my trepidation, I brave a step. "Tegwyn?"

No reply. He doesn't seem to hear me or even acknowledge my presence.

My hair spikes along my arms, yet I try his name for a second time, "Tegwyn? Are you all right?"

Slowly but surely, the faerie comes back to life, blinking his eyes. Then with a deep inhale, he peers off, voice hoarse, "I'm fine."

I wince. His throat sounds sore. Maybe I should offer him a drink of water.

Bending forward, I pick up the lamp and place it down on the table. "Have you been sitting alone in the dark all night?"

He looks right through me when he whispers, "Wouldn't be the first time."

I open my mouth to speak, but no words escape. Truth be told, I'm at a loss. He really is a strange creature.

Though strange he may be, he seems... *lost*. As if he can't quite remember where he left his shoes.

Grabbing the pot, I collect some water from a barrel, wondering what flavour of tea he likes as I place it over the hearth. In the end, I grab some lavender, sprinkling it into the water. From the corner of my eye, I watch him as he studies me carefully. So far, he hasn't mentioned the nightmare, and I hope it stays that way.

But then I freeze like a rabbit when he utters, "So... I've been wondering..."

A lump sticks in my throat.

He leans forward on his chair, yellow eyes burning in the lamplight. "What happened to you before you arrived here?"

I bow my head, swirling the pot with a wooden spoon as the lavender infuses with the water. Sweat beads on my forehead, but I resist the urge to wipe it away.

"Answer me. Truthfully."

There's no point in lying. But I don't have to tell him the whole truth, either. After all, I owe him nothing.

He got what he wanted from me. And I won't give him any more of myself.

"No. It's my business and mine only."

He rises, and before I can blink, he's by my side, making me drop the spoon in fright.

I place my hand on my heart, trying to calm my rapid breaths. This is ridiculous; if I hope to live with the faerie peacefully, then I must get used to his lightning reflexes.

Tegwyn merely smirks when he sees the effect he has on me, his eyes burning my skin like a brand. "You know I'll find out eventually."

"No, you won't," I reply, stirring his tea for him.

I hope he likes it bitter, like his soul.

He leans in closer, flaring his nostrils, and I turn to him, aghast.

Wait. Is he *sniffing* me?

Tegwyn chuckles when he meets my horrified expression, giving me back my personal space. "You're cocky all of a sudden. What happened to the snivelling baby I had to tuck to sleep last night?"

I whirl around, finding his scheming eyes. "I did *not* snivel!"

And there he is again, the *wicked* creature...

I can almost hear the cogs of his evil mind spinning as he keeps that calculating gaze on me. "Something happened to you out there. And I'm going to find out what."

With one last scrutinising glare in my direction, he slips away into the shadows, leaving me speechless.

I glower at the spot where he vanished. He can try all he likes, but I will never spill my secrets. They will die with me.

Forget lavender tea. He can die of thirst for all I care.

I start cleaning up his mess, picking up what looks like a calendar. There are notes attached, things he reminds himself of time and time again.

It looks as if he plans his heists. Every town and village he plunders.

My heart thumps when I spy the name *Charstown* in his notes, and then a hazy memory returns.

Well, I think it's a memory, but it's blurred at best. A scuffle in the cottage, vulpine eyes gazing back at me from beneath a dark hood.

And blood. *Fae* blood, leaking between the tiles of our kitchen...

I drop the calendar, gasping for air. Something pounds behind my eyes, and I lean back on the table, gripping my head.

Maybe we have met before... In another life, perhaps.

Back when I was still carefree.

Back when I still dared to dream.

To distract myself, I read the current date on the calendar. October tenth, two days before my birthday.

I'm going to be eighteen.

That's when the tears fall from my eyes. My parents were going to take me to see the ocean, but now, they never will.

Well, not if I can fix it.

Yanking my cloak from a hook, which is just a pair of mounted deer antlers on the wall, I storm up the tunnel, heading to my cave.

I *will* see the ocean.

And no soldiers or scheming, manipulative faeries will get in my way.

It's time I resumed my journey. My Aunt Elly will be waiting for me in the Veil, after all.

I slip several times as I go down the slope, meandering between the tall trunks of pines.

The contents of my rucksack jostle behind me, bouncing in perfect rhythm to the beats of my heart.

It's not like he'll miss me. I was just a means to an end—a way to get his grubby hands on some jewellery. He can have the necklace. In the end, it's just a thing.

It could never replace my parents.

Adrenaline flares through my veins, filling me with a confidence I haven't felt in weeks.

I can do this.

Unfortunately, fate has other ideas in store. I spy a mass of thick black smoke weaving between the trees at the foot of the mountain. It lurks in the dark, misty forest below, searching endlessly for prey, and cold waves of dread ripple down my spine.

At least…I think it's smoke. Its body is incorporeal, yet it moves like a tangible thing.

I backpedal, hoping it hasn't sensed me yet.

It *is* alive, as I previously feared. And hungry...

It pauses the moment I stumble on a rock, swivelling its head slowly in my direction. The creature's face is nothing more than a vortex of spinning shadow, yet its teeth are bone-white and jagged like knives.

It floats closer, stopping at the foot of the mountain where I stand, six feet away.

I can't look away from its swirling shadows. It's like gazing into an abyss, a place where there is no beginning or end. Only darkness.

Finally, it changes form, morphing into a black wolf with quicksilver eyes. It howls, and I yelp, stumbling down the slope towards its gaping mouth.

Luckily, I grab onto a sapling tree, getting my fingers sticky with sap, but I hold on for dear life.

The creature is taunting me, knowing exactly what keeps me up at night.

It saw inside my head.

This thing is nightmare personified.

Something moves in my peripheral vision, and before I can turn, a gloved hand clasps my mouth, dragging me back.

I'm shoved hard against a tree, and before I can protest, a warm finger presses to my lips, shushing me. Tegwyn's face hovers into view, and I meet his vulpine eyes.

"Don't make a sound," he whispers.

Behind us, the smoky creature shrieks in anger, and I shudder, closing my eyes.

This is it. I'm about to die...

Whatever that thing is, it's going to kill me.

Tegwyn doesn't remove his finger from my lips, yet all I can think about is the wolf and my possible demise.

"Ivy," he rasps.

I shake my head, just wanting it to be over.

"Ivy, don't let your fear consume you. Think... think about something else...something that makes you...*happy*..." He spits out the last word as if it's venom on his tongue.

Finally, I open my eyes, meeting his shining yellow pair.

All the breath leaves my lungs. He has shimmering flecks of gold inside the yellow, and I stare at them, captivated.

A ring glows around his pupils, resembling an angel's halo, and I can't look away. Never before have I seen so many shades of gold...

There are shades I can't even describe. If only I could paint his eyes...

His pupils dilate, and a hush spreads through the forest.

What...what was I afraid of again?

"It's gone," he observes.

What has gone?

"It seemed you repelled it. As soon as it sensed your happiness, it fled. Bugbears feed on pure fear, after all."

I shake my head, disoriented. What on earth is he talking about?

A sardonic grin sneaks across his face, upper canines making their appearance yet again.

The metallic gold of his eyes still catches the light of the sun, and...when did the weather change?

Before, it was grey and murky.

"What were you thinking about?"

I try to think back. Of course. That creature—bugbear. It morphed into a black wolf, and I froze in terror. I thought it was going to eat me.

But then he came to my rescue.

It was only when I looked into his eyes that I stopped feeling afraid. All I could think about was painting his golden eyes onto a canvas.

My cheeks flush, and then I look away, embarrassed.

Tegwyn's smirk stretches. "You were staring at me awfully hard just now."

I inhale a breath. "No, I wasn't."

He narrows his gaze. "Hmm, I may not be able to tell a lie myself, but I can still sense a lie on your sweet lips, *Ivy*..."

Oh, how I wish the ground would swallow me whole. Maybe that bugbear would be inclined to come back and finish the job.

His finger is still pressed to my lips, tucked neatly in the hollow beneath my nose, yet his claw remains inside his glove.

Finally, he removes his finger, taking his warmth and piney scent with him.

I shiver in their absence.

He steps back, amber eyes appraising me as he looks me up and down. The golden rings encircling his pupils burn even brighter than the sun now.

I can still feel a ghost of him on my lips, and I reach up, massaging where he pressed his finger.

A speck of blood beads on my fingertip.

Tegwyn's eyes track the movements of my finger, and if I'm not mistaken, he appears ashamed.

"Sorry. Sometimes my claws have a mind of their own."

I keep rubbing at the graze on my lip, swallowing hard. He truly is capable of so much horror. Yet, there is still some beauty to be found inside him, albeit hard to find.

I spy it whenever I gaze into his gilded eyes. He's the worst kind of puzzle.

The faerie shows me his back, marching up the mountain. "Well, let's go before the bugbear returns."

I shut my eyes. I guess I really was a fool, thinking I could go at it alone. I'm lucky he arrived on time. If he hadn't, I'd be dead.

That's *twice* he has saved my life.

Whether I like it or not, he's the best option I have right now. The Veil will have to wait. I need to survive first.

Finally, I follow him up the mountain, turning my back on the forest.

9

Tegwyn

I've just finished my latest perimeter check of the mountain. Since the unfortunate bugbear incident, I've become rather obsessed with setting up various wards to keep it away from my home.

Now that I have a human in my midst, all kinds of faerie ilk will be surrounding my mountain in hopes of devouring her.

And they won't just devour her; they will consume her soul, slowly sucking the essence from her lungs until she's nothing but a husk.

Over my dead body. If any bugbears want Ivy, then they'll have to get through me.

I never thought I would see the day I'd be protecting a human, of all insufferable creatures, but payment is payment.

Ivy paid a handsome reward for safe sanctuary at my mountain, so I'm just giving the girl her money's worth. If it wasn't for our bargain, I probably wouldn't even care what happened to her.

Maybe...

It's hard to tell these days, but she does intrigue me. The human is obviously hiding something from me, something that she clearly doesn't want me to know about. If she thinks the bugbear will distract me, then she is gravely mistaken.

I will find out.

Her face flashes up before me, and I pause mid-step. She's on my mind constantly. I guess I'm just not used to having company in the mountain.

Up close, her sea-green eyes have streaks of blue, and they remind me of starbursts. Her eyelashes are the length that many human females desire, curling softly at the tips to rest against freckled cheeks, and her lips...*fuck*... They are as soft as the petals of a budding rose...

My heart thuds, just thinking about their shape and texture, and it's no surprise I pricked her with my claw.

When I get excited, my claws come out, and I try to recall what I was thinking about.

Oh, of course. I was thinking about sucking on her rosebud lips until they were swollen with my teeth, and the blood fires hot through my veins, making my claws act of their own volition—claws designed for rending flesh, but they're good for tearing off corsets, too.

I need to get a hold of myself. An ice-cold shower under the waterfall should do the trick.

A silvery light dazzles up ahead, and I shield my eyes, peering through the trees. It's coming from a clearing, and I pick up the pace, eager to find the source of that ethereal light. I know that kind of magic, and it can't be...

Finally, I arrive at the clearing, and the breath leaks from my lungs the instant I see it.

The creature chews at fresh shoots of grass, shaking her long, silvery mane. When the sun catches the individual strands, strands that shimmer with pure, untainted magic, I drop my quiver of arrows and get down on one knee.

The unicorn contemplates me with her jewel-black eyes, sighing softly with a shake of her head. Her mane stuns me yet again, and even with Fae eyes, it's hard to make out her silhouette.

I've forgotten how to breathe.

Even amongst the Fae, there are creatures so rare, so enchanted, that they're considered legendary.

The magical mare doesn't move, frozen in time as she appraises me with that glittering eye of deep onyx, as if she approves of my bow.

The beginnings of a horn peek from her forelock. That's where she stores her magic.

The equine stomps her hoof, and heat spreads through the clearing, chasing away the winter chill. I close my eyes, sighing in deep reverence.

It's like being kissed by pure sunlight.

The unicorn vanishes into the woods with a flick of her tail, and I stay put until she's out of sight, keeping my head bowed and knee planted on the ground.

She leaves a breath of spring air in her wake, and when I look up, I spy a glittering joy of snowdrops trailing behind her.

My heart pounds as I still don't move from my crouched position. I feel so blessed to have seen a unicorn in the flesh.

They haven't been seen in over a century. It was long believed that humanity had hunted them all into extinction, but it looks as if some may have survived.

I couldn't help but notice the silver gash on her right flank. Whoever tried to hurt that sweet, guiltless creature deserves to rot.

That gash was definitely the work of a Dark Fae, and I curl my fists, releasing a light growl. I swear, if I ever get my hands on that faerie, I will *kill* them.

Rising to my feet, I sling my quiver back over my shoulder, stepping towards the snowdrops. I pluck one up from the ground, twirling it in my fingers.

Morning dew drips from its silky white petals, and inside each dewdrop radiates pure magic. Using my own magic to preserve the droplets, I pocket the flower away, then begin my trek back to the mountain.

Time for some experimenting.

I lock myself away in my study later that evening, gazing deeply into the lens of a light microscope. I do some bookkeeping on the side, deciding to kill two birds with one stone.

The unicorn's magic looks even more spectacular up close, and I'm just grateful that I had the foresight to wear a pair of protective goggles. A single drop alone could blind the eye.

I reach across, adding another coin to the pile on my right.

One hundred and fifty gold lions, and I grind my teeth. Still not enough for safe passage across the Haunted Sea.

I'm Fae, so any captain worth their salt won't take too kindly to my presence aboard their ship.

I'll need to pay handsomely.

Many seafaring humans consider faeries bad luck on board. Many have had run-ins with merfolk at sea, so I doubt I'll be any more well-received. A typical glamour won't last long, so I need a backup plan. I could steal a boat, but I have no idea how to sail.

Bannog is my best chance, but it's just a shame he's out of my budget. I bet he only likes to be paid in Fae gold, too.

He may not even want money as a form of payment; he may prefer to strike a bargain with me instead. I hope he doesn't ask for anything too precious.

Fae currency is quite different. Silver crescents are shaped like half-moons, whereas stallions are round. Golden suns resemble a five-pointed star, whereas lions are oval. Our copper is the same, shaped like a hexagon.

Yet, there's one thing both currencies have in common—the face of His Majesty, King Corvis.

The Fae have been known to enchant their suns and crescents to resemble lions and stallions, and it fools many humans.

Most of the time.

We have no choice. Rogue numbers are dwindling, while the Seelie and Unseelie prosper in their castles and sprawling estates back in the faerielands.

I have no castle or estate. Nor do I have a single courtier or vassal to my name. Hell, I don't even bear a title.

So, I do what I can to survive, living life on a precarious edge.

Damn it. Where was I again?

Right, one hundred and fifty…

As I place another gold sun onto a pile, I peer into the microscope, adding more notes to my diagram.

One dewdrop hosts a slew of magic, and it's like peering into a miniature universe, one with a myriad of swirling galaxies and various star systems.

They blind and dazzle, so I adjust the visor on my goggles as I twist the dial on the microscope to get a closer inspection.

Breathtaking. It truly is like finding an undiscovered world, and I'm no different from a pioneer in that regard.

If only I could manipulate that unicorn's magic somehow into fashioning myself a disguise, but a single dewdrop wouldn't last. I would need more…

Bannog's disguises harbour unlimited magic. No one knows how he does it, but folk say he weaves the magic into the garments with his very own hands.

Some believe he was blessed by the goddess herself to be able to perform such a delicate task. Unfortunately, if I want to get my hands on one of his rare glamours, then I'll have to get in line. His waiting lists can be years long.

For most Fae, that's nothing. We're immortal and live a ridiculously long time. But I don't have the luxury of time.

One of these days, I am going to get caught. Fae who are captured and imprisoned by humans don't last long.

However, there may be someone who can help me jump the queue. Stannog, perhaps—Bannog's sour-faced cousin. He owns a tavern just west of the mountain.

I haven't given up on the necklace, though. Not yet. When I finally get a disguise, I can sell it on the human black market and get that five hundred.

Then, once I've accrued enough money, I can set sail and live out the rest of my immortal life on a deserted island where no one can bother me ever again.

Maybe I will make myself *king* of that island.

One can dream.

With a steady hand, I add another coin to the pile. My magic keeps them intact, for now, but there will come a day when I won't even have a single drop left in my veins. I may even become *mortal*...

Perish the thought.

Footsteps echo down the tunnel, and I heave a sigh of frustration. Just when I found a moment's peace.

My claws retract as her honeysuckle scent finds its way to my nose. Sometimes I *abhor* these heightened senses. It makes ignoring her all the harder.

She steps into the cave. I really should have made more of an effort at hiding this place. These are *my* private quarters.

Her sweet scent drifts my way, and I shut my eyes, ignoring the roaring rush in my head.

Does she have any idea what she does to me? Probably not. She's as gullible as she looks.

I rein my beast in, willing my claws back inside my gloves.

"Oh... I thought I would find you here," she remarks casually, and I roll my eyes.

I speak through gritted teeth, "Yes, so you have. Now feel free to leave again. I'm quite busy. Your foolish talk can wait."

She falters at my dismissal, and I regard her from the corner of my eye. Her form wilts.

Maybe I was a little too brusque.

What can I say? Wickedness runs through my veins. I just wish she would hurry up and take the hint. I need to focus.

Ivy steps further into the cave, bringing her tantalising scent with her. "There's no need to be so rude. I only came to say hello. You've been gone all day. Did you find any more bugbears?"

There's no missing the shudder as she recalls the memory of the bugbear, and I finally give her the attention she so obviously craves.

"No. It appears the creature was alone, but fret not. I've set up various wards to keep it away from the mountain."

While using up all my magic in the process, princess...

It is quite strange. I'm sacrificing what little magic I have just to keep her safe. Maybe I did get the short end of the stick in our bargain after all.

She's going to drain my reserves at this rate.

"Thank goodness. At least I don't have to worry about any nasty bugbears from now on. I've barely recovered from that last one."

She giggles nervously, and I study her again.

I think she's trying to make small talk. She can't be *that* desperate for companionship, can she?

Now silence lingers in her stead, and I suppose her singsong voice does make an agreeable change to the dreariness.

Ivy is slowly bleeding life back into the mountain, and I'm not sure how to handle it.

I regard her once more in my peripheral vision. It appears she has nothing left to discuss. Still, I indulge her a little longer. "Is there something else you need?"

"Yes," she replies. "Since it's safe to go back outside, I was wondering if it would be okay if I collected firewood. The hearth died an hour ago, and I've grown rather cold."

I snort. "Well, wear a coat."

She watches me incredulously. "Well, I'm sorry for thinking that you would care."

"I don't."

The human stares at me, dumbfounded, and I guess it's too late to take back what I said.

Finally, she breathes a melancholy sigh, then vanishes from the cave.

Thank the goddess. Maybe now I can get some work done.

I turn back to my bookkeeping, placing another gold piece onto an enchanted pile.

Steady, focus...

The coins wobble, and I hold my breath.

To my relief, the pile remains intact, and I wipe the sweat from my brow. I've got this.

My magic might not fail me just yet.

"It's my birthday tomorrow."

I lose focus, and now I watch, helplessly, as the pile topples across the desk, right along with my magic and pride.

She made me lose my concentration, and all I can see now is bright vermilion.

Ivy visibly pales when I turn, giving her my undivided attention.

"I... erm..."

I have no idea what she sees in my eyes, but it's enough to render her utterly speechless.

My lip curls, exposing my fangs. "Leave..."

She bumps into the wall, fumbling her way out until she vanishes with the wind. Once she's gone, I throw my arms up, yelling at the top of my lungs. *"Fuck!"*

I kick my bureau like an insolent child, making more coins scatter in the process. Great. Now I'm going to have to start from the beginning.

Stupid girl. *"It's my birthday,"* I mock in a high-pitched voice.

What did she expect me to do, dance in celebration of the day she first drew breath? She really needs to grow up.

Still, it must be nice to know the day you were born. I only know the season.

This will be my twentieth winter.

I clear away the coins, opening a drawer to collect the ones that fell inside. My hand grazes a wooden carving, and I pull it out, turning it around in my hand.

It's a carving of an old farmer and his young daughter, and I wish I hadn't set sights on this wretched thing. For one, it doesn't even look like them. But as time wears on, I find that I'm forgetting their faces, and maybe one day I will forget what they looked like entirely.

They always celebrated my birthday, no matter how much misery I brought into their lives.

Maybe I took it too far tonight. The look of horror on her face will forever haunt me.

Just maybe I can do something to make it right again.

I just don't know where to begin.

10

Ivy

I'VE NEVER SPENT A birthday alone before, so when I wake on the day in question to find myself inside a dark, cold cave without a single friend in the world, it isn't easy.

Maybe if I close my eyes, I will wake in my old bed, and this whole nightmare will finally end. Maybe I will wake with Bryce panting by my side, and Mama bringing me breakfast in bed.

She always made me breakfast in bed for special occasions—breakfasts with poached eggs, fresh blueberries, and buttered toast.

Last year, she and Papa bought me an easel and a brand-new set of paints.

It's utterly hopeless. In the end, I lose the battle with my warring emotions, and the tears fall at last. Yet through the despair, I hear a distant voice. *Get up. Not all is lost...*

It sounds a little like my mother's voice.

Sitting up, I wipe away the tears and rise to my feet. I've had my little cry. Now it's time to be strong; I must be strong if I hope to survive the North and its vicious vipers.

The Fae truly are cruel, just like I was taught. They are selfish, manipulative, and only care for themselves.

Telling Tegwyn had been a grave mistake. I'd miscalculated, reading the situation entirely wrong.

The look of pure loathing in his eyes was proof enough. He hates me, and he wants nothing to do with me.

He only tolerates me because of the binding of our magical contract.

I sensed the ripple in the air the day I traded my necklace for a bed in his cave, and it was enough to shake the very foundations of the earth.

It's an old, ancient magic that is by no means to be broken or tampered with. But nothing in the contract specifically states that he must be nice or even friends with me. That's fine, though, because I don't care much for him, either.

I go through the motions, slipping on my dress. Then I step into my boots, brushing the lint from my skirt.

My fingers disappear beneath my pillow, searching for the weapon. When my fingers graze cool metal, I pull it out, gazing down at the shining bronze.

Tegwyn had given me this knife on my second day here. He told me to go and clip some heather on the slope so I could use it to stuff my bed.

He didn't have to do that. It wasn't in the contract. As far as he was concerned, he'd already done his due diligence, giving me a bed made up of furs, no matter how uncomfortable they may have been.

He also protected me from the bugbear. The faerie could have just sacrificed me to that vicious beast, getting me out of his hair once and for all. He already had my necklace by that point.

Yet, he protected me... Maybe he *does* care deep down, but he just has an odd way of showing it.

Finally, I pocket the knife, moving down to the kitchen to find it empty as usual.

After a warm breakfast of porridge, I grab my cloak from the mounted antlers, heading further down the mountain.

A morning hike along the northern slope should help clear away the cobwebs. As long as I stay within the safety margins of Tegwyn's wards, I should be safe from bugbears or worse.

A golden sun glimmers in a clear, sapphire sky once I emerge onto the grassy slope at the mouth of the tunnel, inhaling deeply. It may be sunny, but the weather is crisp cold, and fogs the breath.

I veer right, heading for the northern slope where the heather grows in abundance. It's a beautiful sight to behold, and one of my favourite places to unwind.

A peaceful, craggy footpath leads the way, rocky outcrops towering above me on either side as I watch wild goats scaling the cliffs and creeping across narrow ledges to reach tufts of thick grass.

When I finally arrive at my destination, a sigh leaves my lips, and for the first time today, I smile.

The slope is blanketed in purple heather and yellow gorse, and the bright colours lift my spirits, right along with their sweet scents.

If I had my easel, I would paint every single one.

A brook twists down the hill, a bright, glistening ribbon of crystal-clear water. I plan to take a dip today, cleansing my mind, body, and soul.

Following the brook, I trek further down the path, wending between bushes of gorse until I stop at a bank of smooth rock.

Untying my boots, I submerge my toes in the water, shivering when it sends ice-cold knives up my leg.

Despite the frigid temperature, I plunge my foot deeper, freezing my bones. This is where I come to bathe, but every time I strip off my clothes, I feel as if something watches me.

I've heard harrowing tales of Fae snatching away maidens who've wandered too far. Perhaps I should tie my dress back up.

But I've already loosened my corset.

I slip out of the dress, dragging it down until it bunches at my waist. When it drops to my feet, I step out carefully, bundling it up and placing it onto the smooth rock.

I start taking my undergarments off, too, despite my apprehension. I pop the buttons off my bralette and tug off my silken panties until I'm completely naked.

Finally, I step into the freezing brook, holding my breath as I drop to my knees. My hair hangs like a golden veil around my shoulders as I shut my eyes, tilting my face towards the sky.

Sunshine kisses my cheeks, and I dip my head back, letting the cold water soothe my scalp.

Water drips in rivulets between my breasts, gooseflesh encircling each peak, and it's so cold. My lower lip trembles, yet I sink deeper until no part of me remains above the surface.

The water is murky, but I keep my head under. I used to hold my breath in the lake all the time back at home, and the longest I've gone is two minutes.

I try to repeat my record, but when the pressure builds up in my lungs, I breach the surface, gasping for air.

So cold…

My teeth are chattering.

Yet I remain in the brook, gazing down at the fine hair of my arms. It pricks on end, resembling needles.

A stick snaps behind me, and I cover my breasts, jerking my head towards a grove of trees. A shadow moves behind the trunk of a pine, and my heart thumps. I am not alone. Someone or *something* watches me.

I search the bed of the brook for a sharp rock, keeping a hand across my chest as I feel my way across loamy soil; I left my knife in the folds of my dress, so I'll have to improvise.

When I find a rock sharp enough, I raise it high above my head, ready to hurl it at the peeping Tom.

The shadow moves again, and I grit my teeth, tossing the rock.

I don't care if the Grim Reaper himself awaits me behind those pine trees. No one, and I mean *no one*, watches me bathe.

The rock makes contact, and then someone shouts, "*Fuck!*"

My heart hammers when I recognise the voice, and then I scream his name, wrapping my arms around my breasts, *"Tegwyn!* You pervert!"

I grab another rock, and I hope this one knocks him out. He deserves it.

"You were watching me? I can't believe you!"

The Fae steps out from behind the tree, covering his eyes. "I wasn't watching you. Don't flatter yourself!"

I growl, readying the rock to launch it at his horned head. "Now you're insulting me? You really are despicable!"

He removes his hand from his eyes, pinning me with that cold, vicious stare, and not once does his gaze wander.

Still, I sink beneath the water, using my hair as a veil.

"I was here *far* before you arrived, princess. Besides, modesty is a foreign concept for the Fae. So...don't think I haven't seen it all before. You're nothing special."

I roll my eyes. "Well, that's reassuring."

Silence stretches for an age as I remain in the water. Somehow, I can't stop the ache that forms in my chest.

Nothing special...Is that what he thinks?

I've never been with a man. I'm inexperienced, while he, on the other hand, has most likely bedded hundreds of females. I bet they were all Fae, like him, and ten times more beautiful than I could ever dream of.

Who am I kidding? Of *course* he wasn't watching me. Compared to the Fae, I'm nothing. Hardly worth a second glance.

His eyes remain respectfully on my face, and I guess he truly did mean what he said; he isn't interested whatsoever.

Still, I have to get out of this water sometime; I can no longer feel my toes.

"Well, now that we've established that you weren't, *indeed*, watching me, could you turn around? I need to get dressed."

He hikes up a brow, regarding me strangely. Are faeries truly that blasé about nudity? Or was he just saying that to mess with me?

Tegwyn sighs, turning back towards the trees. "Do what you must."

He disappears, but I wait a few more moments before I climb out, dripping water onto the rocks.

As I slip into my clothes, I look to where I saw him last, wondering what he was doing in that grove in the first place. My hair hangs wet about my shoulders as I meander down the slope, coming to a stop behind a tree.

He sits by the brook, the water running as smooth as silk over the glistening rock. He looks so serene beneath the shining sun. His horns glisten as brightly as bronze, and I wonder if they're just as sturdy.

He snorts, "Now who's the peeping Tom?"

Tegwyn swivels on his rock, an accusatory look in his gleaming eyes. I bow my head, shame heating my cheeks. "I wasn't looking…"

Again, he arches a brow, seeing right through my lie. Then he chuckles, returning to his task. He's sharpening something with a bronze knife, and I step closer, curiosity getting the better of me.

"What are you doing?"

"Nothing that concerns your mortal eyes. Now go on, off you go to sing to a meadowlark, or whatever it is that you do in your spare time. I need to focus."

He's dismissing me, and again, I feel that sharp sting of rejection. I guess I should leave, then.

As I walk up the slope, I feel his burning gaze on my spine, but I don't bother turning back. If he wants to be alone, then fine, I'll go.

Who needs him, anyway?

11

Ivy

I don't return to the mountain until dusk. Apart from the embarrassing encounter with Tegwyn in the woods, I had a surprisingly pleasant day.

However, I couldn't stop thinking about my parents the whole time I was out on the slope, making a wreath of flowers for my hair.

Anything to take my mind off the day.

Anything to stop me from spiralling down the path of despair. Wherever my mother and father are, I hope they're happy. I hope they're not hurt.

I pause at the threshold of the kitchen, taken aback by the sight of Tegwyn with his dirty boots on the table.

Sometimes, I forget how alarming he is. His bright golden eyes gleam in the dark of the cave, reminding me of the eyes of an apex predator.

Once upon a time, those brilliant eyes used to captivate me, visiting me every night. But then I soon realised that the dream had been an illusion all along.

I grimace as he noisily chews on a quail leg. He really is a sight for weary eyes. Maybe I should paint him in his finest moment.

Yet, as messy as he is, I keep stealing glances at his horns. They are majestic, and I guess there is still some beauty to be found in this cruel world.

"What?" he grouses, glaring at me sideways.

I shake my head, coming back to my senses. "Nothing. I was just thinking."

He scoffs, taking another bite from his quail leg. "Well, think somewhere else."

Once he's finished, he tosses the bird's remains in the empty hearth, then picks at his teeth with a claw.

So uncouth.

I forget he is *Rogue* at times—Rogue Fae aren't known for being as cultured as their Seelie and Unseelie counterparts.

Finally, he offers me his undivided attention, falling as still as a statue.

I raise a brow. "Are you all right?"

He takes a moment, swallowing several times. Then he wipes his greasy mouth, and I'm pretty sure I spy a red blush beneath the golden-green hue of his skin.

A smile spreads across my face. "Are you blushing?"

He mutters something unintelligible, and I step closer. "Pardon?"

The faerie sighs, rolling his eyes towards the stalactites, "I said, nice flowers."

Alarmed, I reach up, brushing my fingers over my flower wreath, and now my own complexion takes on a reddish shade. "Thank you."

A painful silence stretches in the vast space between us, and just when I thought that things couldn't get any more awkward.

What else are we to discuss? We don't have anything in common.

I go to take off my cloak, but then he stops me, getting to his feet. "No. Keep it on. You're going to need it."

I wrap it back around my shoulders. "What for?"

A mischievous glint gleams in his eyes. "It's a surprise. Follow me."

He shoots towards the exit, and I startle, moving after him. Now our only source of light is his glowing eyes as we meander through the dark.

I try to keep close. He may be a little scary and messy at times, but I would rather not lose him to the shadows. Besides, I still find his scent pleasant, like pine and wood smoke.

"Have you had anything to eat?" he asks casually.

All I spy are his shining eyes, and once again, those vertical pupils regard me with indifference. It's quite rare to see the whites of his eyes. Only when he is particularly mad, they show.

"I had a few berries earlier," I reply.

Tegwyn sighs. "Suppose they'll do."

We continue down the tunnel, and I'm not sure how much time passes by the time we reach the slope. Under the cool blanket of night, we descend, and I shiver the whole way down, tightening my cloak around my body. "Where are we going?"

"Out."

Fog escapes my mouth. "A little more clarification would be nice."

He smirks that evil smirk, tapping the end of his upturned nose. Then he's on the march again, showing off his impressive stealth.

I'm not as surefooted as he is, and I find myself stumbling several times, using trees as an aid. All the while, I search the shadows, worrying my bottom lip about bugbears. Once or twice, I spy a dark shape in the corner of my eye, but it turns out to be a harmless bush.

Just a few more yards, and I'll be at the foot of the mountain.

Tegwyn is already waiting for me by the time I get there, leaning against a tree. He checks his claws rather impatiently. "I was wondering when you'd finally show."

I toss him a withering look, doubling over as I gasp for breath. "Well, I'm here now. No need to worry about me."

"I wasn't worried."

He vanishes into the inky darkness again, and I just about manage to keep up. When he chuckles, I glare at the back of his head. He really is heartless.

"Don't worry, human. We're almost there. No need to piss your knickers."

I ignore his rude comment, gazing around the forest. All I see are moonlit trees.

"Where—?"

He pauses, holding up a finger. "Just *listen...*"

So, I listen.

A lone vixen barks in the night, and then an owl hoots upon his perch in a shadowed tree. But there's not much else to be heard.

"I don't hear anything."

"Of course you don't. You're mortal, but just stop and truly *listen...*"

I roll my eyes. "Listen for what?"

"A shift in the wind..."

Okay. Now he is talking like a crazy person.

Still, I listen for the shift. Nothing happens.

I'm about to reprimand him when wind whips through the trees. It almost sounds like whispering—the ghosts of children who've long departed this world—and I grab onto Tegwyn's cloak.

A smile sneaks across his impish face, yellow eyes burning like embers. What does he find so amusing? "What?"

He sniggers. "I just wanted to see the expression on your face. Seldom mortals have ventured this land, and those who have... well, they barely make it out alive."

My brows knit together. "Land?"

"Look around."

I do as he says, gasping when I crane my neck to gaze at a towering behemoth of trees.

The forest has changed—giant redwoods have taken the place of pines, their twisting roots stretching across the moss-strewn ground like the limbs of a mighty Kraken.

"Come along, and do mind the tree roots."

I gaze at him, horrified. "Where *are* we?"

The smug faerie tosses me a conspiratorial glance. "Just follow me, *human*."

He steps over the roots with ease, while I trail behind him like the bumbling human I am. I lose him several times, but before the panic has a chance to sink its nasty fangs in, I spy his horned silhouette.

There's no missing his voice, either. "While we're young, Ivy."

I look across at him. He leans against a particularly large root several feet away, tapping at a broken pocket watch. "Do try to keep up. You don't want to spend too long out here."

I finally catch up, bending forward to plant my hands on my knees. "And where *is* here, exactly?"

Tegwyn points a gloved finger at a glowing square of light in the distance. It's a window.

"Who lives there?"

"You'll find out. Watch yourself. It's a rough establishment. Avoid eye contact with the other patrons, and you *may* just leave with your limbs intact."

I give a nervous smile. "How reassuring."

We hover along the edge of a clearing, gazing at a colossal house made from ancient stone. Its thatched roof is covered in moss, and it appears to be sunken on one side. I eye the giant door, the one choked in thorns and poison ivy.

My lip shakes. "Erm... Tegwyn?"

"Yes?" He turns my way, yellow eyes burning.

"What... what kind of people live here?"

He laughs, throwing up his hood, and now his eyes glow beneath the thick cowl. "It's best you throw yours up, too."

I take him up on his advice, following him towards the stone building. When we approach the door, we crane our necks.

A gulp bobs down my throat. Now that is one big door...

There are smaller doors fixed inside the larger, and the tiniest has to be as big as my thumbnail.

Tegwyn pushes the door that matches our height and slips inside, letting the sound of raucous voices pool into the night.

With a deep breath, I prepare myself, then follow him inside.

All sound diminishes the second we step into the building, and all I can see is a sea of shadowy faces with glowing eyes.

One or two shadows bear a set of sharp teeth, and then I'm met with a myriad of fanged smiles.

I make a beeline for the door, but then I crash face-first into a wall that wasn't there previously. My skin turns as white as frost as horror finally sinks in.

I am trapped with no way out.

Tegwyn coughs for my attention, and slowly, I face the room. So many angry faeries, watching me from every darkened corner of the room. There is no way I am going to make it out of here alive tonight.

Now I am nothing more than a corpse faced with a murder of crows.

12

Tegwyn

The pub patrons do not look pleased as I cast my gaze around, spying several faeries—a hook-nosed goblin and a withered hag covered in warts.

A giant, his bulbous head nearly reaching the rafters, grits his underbite with a vicious snarl, while a pair of seedy-looking trolls show me their middle fingers.

Rather rude, if you ask me. Yet, the worst scowl comes from the ogre behind the bar.

They may be rough around the edges, but the folk here are decent enough—when they're not tearing each other limb from limb, that is.

They're *Rogue Fae*, and like me, they live life on a knife's edge.

They also despise humans, mostly because humans have been persecuting them for the last hundred years.

However, they won't touch *my* little pet. Not while she's with me.

Besides, she needed to get out of the mountain; it can't be good for her to be cooped up inside a cave all day.

I lean in, whispering, "Stay close to me."

"Oh, I plan to," she mutters, hiding behind me like I'm the only thing in this world that could save her from these monsters.

We meander through the bar, and the whole time she keeps her head bowed, shoulders hunched, until we stop at a sticky table.

I place her in a seat, and she stares absentmindedly at a toadstool sprouting from a crack inside the rotten wood.

As I said, it's a rough establishment.

A snail leaves a silvery trail at the back of Ivy's chair, and I roll my eyes. "I'll be back in a moment. Just heading to the bar."

She whips her head around, gripping my wrist. "You're not leaving me here, are you?"

A lump catches in my throat when I meet the desperate gleam in her starburst eyes. Maybe bringing her here was a mistake. These Fae would wear her skin like a coat.

"I won't be too long. Just remember what I said—avoid eye contact. By the way, happy birthday. This was the surprise!"

The human female gawks at me, speechless. I try for what I hope is an encouraging smile, but she only looks even more confused.

"Oh. Thank you..."

I chuckle. "Remember, faeries may not be able to tell a lie, but they still have silver tongues. So, don't go unintentionally accepting any more bargains, princess. If it sounds too good to be true, then it probably is."

Definitely the wrong thing to say.

She scowls, and it looks as if my attempt to make light of our bargain just blew up in my face. Well, you can't win them all.

With a nervous sound, I hurry to the bar, hoping she has the sense not to talk to any of these creatures. They really will eat her.

I tug my hood over my face as I wade through a crowd of angry patrons. They hiss and jeer—so much for making more friends.

"*Traitor,*" a hob seethes.

"*Dung-fucker,*" snarls a winged puca, spitting at my boots.

A cloud of wisps swarms me, sticking out their long tongues, and I waft them away, eager to get to the bar.

Finally, I reach the bar and pull up a stool. Stannog, the sour-faced barkeep, pays me no heed. Instead, he towels a drinking horn made from mammoth's tusk, pretending he hasn't seen me.

I cough to get his attention.

The ogre grits his crooked teeth, almost cracking the prehistoric ivory in his meaty hand. "What the hell d'ya bloody want, *dung*?"

A wry smile bites at the corners of my lips. "And a *hello* to you too, Stan."

"Go away. Ye stink of *dung*..."

Dung meaning *human*, of course.

All the Fae likens humans to heaps of manure, yet Ivy is different. She smells like honeysuckle and freshly baked biscuits straight out of the oven.

I drum my fingers noisily on the chipped countertop. "I do have a name, you know."

He crushes the horn, and the bone-white ivory turns to dust in his fingers.

Next: my skull.

"Well, it's more satisfyin' to address ye as *dung*. So, what'll it be, *dung*?"

I heave a breath. "Two tankards of that disgusting gnat's piss you call ale—and a favour..."

The barkeep plods towards an oversized keg, slamming a hand onto the tap. He pours a black, frothy substance the consistency of tar into two tankards.

Stannog says over his shoulder, "Ye know, I don't bargain with the likes of ye, right, dung?"

"Well, that's a crying shame. I was really hoping you would be interested in bartering with this golden dagger. Forged at the Gilded Rose Court."

One of the most prestigious Seelie courts in the faerielands—close to the Pool of Light, the birthplace of all Fae magic.

That makes this dagger one of the most valuable objects in this bar right now—or so it appears. In reality, it's just an ordinary bronze butter knife.

It's enchanted with a cloaking spell to make it resemble gold, complete with a fake Gilded Rose Crest on the hilt.

Stannog practically drools when I set the dagger on the sticky bar. Looks like he's taken the bait. He's barely got any magic left in his old bones these days, so he fails to spy that the dagger is, in fact, a fake.

The ogre leans over the bar, showing me his magnificent yellow teeth. "Fine. I'll take the damned blade."

I give a charming smile of my own, reaching my hand out to officiate our bargain, and the air ripples the moment his large hand swallows mine.

Once our deal is made, he slams the tankards onto the bar, and his gnat's piss soils my favourite cloak.

That'll leave a stubborn stain.

"So, what favour can I grant ye, dung?"

My eye twitches. That's the fifth time he has called me by that insipid name. "I need you to get me an appointment with your cousin. There's a waiting list, and I know you can help me jump it."

He wipes the bar with a dirty rag. "Finally decided to give up being Rogue and live among the humans, have ye?"

A susurration of disgruntled faerie voices echoes through the tavern like a cursed song, and that's when all eyes fall on me. My ears burn at the tips.

Most of the Rogue in this bar don't believe in glamours or cloaking spells. They choose to live a modest life along the fringes of the human realm like vagrants or vagabonds.

Most of them have no choice. Most are dirt poor where their magic is concerned—so poor that they can barely maintain a glamour long enough to deceive even the most gullible of humans.

That's why I resorted to thievery and trickery. It was better than being persecuted—better than living in rags.

But Bannog's glamours are permanent.

There are some who consider him blessed by the goddess, and others who think him cursed. It just depends on who you ask.

My eyes fall on Ivy. She's still hiding beneath her hood, but she sticks out like a sore thumb in that damask-blue cloak.

Several Fae eye her viciously, and from the way she hunches her shoulders, she couldn't be anything *but* human. Gracefully awkward, like a budding rose yet to bloom…

She plays with a strand of her golden hair, and even from the bar, I catch those gilded strands glinting beneath the hushed lights of the tavern.

The patrons keep a wide berth for now, and good. Ivy is my ward. We made a bargain the day she gave me her necklace, and that includes my protection, too.

Sometimes I just wish I knew what was going on inside that pretty blonde head of hers.

She truly is an enigma.

What circumstances brought her north? And what reason does she have to be so afraid of soldiers?

She catches my gaze, pleading with me to return to the table with those big eyes, and my heart skips a beat.

I hold up five fingers, turning back to Stannog. "Not that it's any of your business, but yes, I require a glamour."

Stannog shrugs his broad shoulders. "So, just make yer own glamour, then."

A low growl emits from my lips. "You and I both know that isn't an option. Glamours require too much magic, and I need to conserve mine."

It seems I finally got through to the ogre. It's been years since he so much as stepped a toe into the human world. So, he forgets how rough it can be at times.

These pocket worlds are all we have left—forgotten fragments of the faerielands. They're islands, basically, the human world our wild, treacherous sea.

And that is why I need to secure safe passage aboard a ship.

I drum my fingers on the counter again. "So, will you speak to your cousin?"

The barkeep grunts, wiping at the same stubborn stain. "I'll have ter think about it."

Well, there's no point in sticking around. Time to return to my human ward.

Before I leave, Stannog grabs the dagger, skewering me to the sticky counter by the sleeve of my coat. I meet his bloodshot eyes. "What?"

He shows me his *lovely* teeth again. "The ale isn't free. Pay up."

I chuckle, trying to play it off, yet Stannog isn't messing around. He digs the knife in deeper, twisting it into the wood, and I roll my eyes. "Put it on my tab."

He growls, hovering inches from my face. "That tab has already reached its limit. *Pay. Up.*"

I charm him with a debonair smile, hoping he takes the bait. I even throw in a fang for good measure. "For the two tankards, or the last six months?"

"*Both*," he decides.

Well, looks like he got me. So, I reach down, pulling out a leather pouch that I keep inside my pants.

The ogre doesn't even look the least perturbed that I just plucked a pouch of gold from my ass.

No. All he wants is his money.

When he gets his payment, he pulls the knife from my sleeve, and when I spy the tear in the leather, I *tsk*. "This was my best coat."

"Get lost!"

Finally, I move towards Ivy, but then I stop, having yet another brilliant idea.

Stannog curses when I return to the bar, and someone's certainly very cranky. "I thought I told ye ter get lost!"

I purse my lips. "You know, you really ought to brush up on those customer service skills, Stan. As a punter, I don't feel valued."

His eyes pop menacingly. Not a fan of sarcasm, I see.

I extend a finger at Ivy. "See that female there?"

The ogre follows the direction of my finger, a deep growl thundering in his chest. "Yes. What were ye thinking, bringing the likes of her *here*? Ye may as well just serve her up on a platter and be done with it. These bastards are lethal." He tips his head at the bar patrons.

I wave him off. "She'll be fine." I throw her a cursory glance, checking if she really is fine. She's still pissed that I've abandoned her, and her disappointment in me is almost palpable.

I point at Stannog next, mimicking a gabbing mouth with my hand, and she shakes her head. Another one who's not a fan of sarcasm, and I return my attention to Stannog. "Am I right in assuming that Bannog has contacts inside the king's court?"

King Corvis has many glamoured Fae at his court. It's how he makes himself and his courtiers appear human to the rest of the kingdom.

"Aye. That he does."

The ogre seems proud of that fact. Most Fae respect and follow the king. After all, he managed to trick a whole nation of gullible humans into believing that he was human, too.

Well, there's some truth to the lie. King Corvis was the illegitimate child of the former king, borne of a Fae mother, and his rise to power is an admirable tale—faerie bards will be singing about his exploits for years to come.

I can still feel Ivy's gaze. Something akin to shame flushes down my neck and spine, but I push the sensation aside, looking the ogre straight in the eye.

It must be done. If Ivy won't tell me what happened to her, then I'll find out through other means.

"I'm looking for information. About an event that happened in a place called Charstown." I read Ivy's letter when I first brought her to the mountain. The one written by her dear mother.

It seemed she didn't leave by her own choice after all. Something happened to her back at home, and I bet it has to do with the king.

Stannog nods his head at Ivy. "It got anything to do with the girl?"

My words turn to ash in my mouth, and I lose my silver tongue.

I think I've just tossed Ivy to the wolves. If word gets out that she's hiding with me, then she's dead.

King Corvis is a merciless despot.

Stannog heaves a gritty sigh. "I won't say nothin.'"

Well, then, in that case, "No. It has nothing to do with her whatsoever."

The ogre sees through the lie, one that will cost me my soul, no doubt. I've known him for five years; he would sooner stab you in the front than the back, but I won't take any chances.

Ivy's secrets die with me.

I return to the table, and all the tension leaves her body the moment I rejoin her side.

"Thank goodness. I was starting to wonder if you would ever return. I want to go back to the mountain. Everyone is staring at me. That winged creature won't stop licking his *teeth* at me."

Confused, I peer over my shoulder, growling when I spot the puca. His tattered bat wings drag across the floor like worn leather, and when he regards Ivy like she's something good to eat, I bare my fangs, making sure my eyes glow with bloodlust.

If he so much as breathes her air, then I will tear his wings from his spine and use them as tarp for my next camping trip.

How I *hate* puca.

Nasty faeries...

That white fluff that grows on wild berries? The puca did that. They taint everything with their *filth*.

Well, he won't be tainting Ivy tonight.

The winged faerie takes the hint and returns to his deck of cards, gambling with a redcap—another bloodthirsty heathen.

Ivy eyes the tankard warily when I slide it across the table. "Is it safe?"

"Yes. Merry birthday!"

She shakes her head, skin pale. "N-no..."

I roll my eyes. "It's fine. It's not poison, I promise."

Ivy crosses her arms. "Well, if it's safe, then *you* drink it."

I narrow my eyes. Is that a wager on her tongue?

All right. I guess this is just me living up to my end of the bargain. She paid for my protection, and that means protecting her from faerie beverages, too. Though her plan is quite flawed, since the spiked ale wouldn't have any effect on me.

I pick up her tankard, downing Stannog's gnat's piss in one gulp. The most repulsive taste fills my mouth, yet I still swallow every last drop to prove my point.

Fuck, it's *disgusting*...

Ivy presses her hand to her mouth, and she's *laughing* at me, the swine.

"Are you all right there?" she teases gently.

My head swirls as it appears I drank a little too quickly. "N-never better..."

She leans closer, and her honeysuckle scent fills my nose. "Are you sure? You're sweating."

I chuckle, pushing the other tankard towards her. "Ha, good one. Now it's your turn, *princess*. You won't regret it."

Oh, I'm sure she will.

The human bites her bottom lip, and her teeth leave indentations in the plump, red flesh.

Finally, she grabs her drink and swills it down her throat, and I see the moment it goes to her head.

She hiccups, palming her mouth. "That tastes..."

"Like gnat's piss."

The poor thing looks like she's about to vomit. I hear several titters around the bar, but Ivy isn't here for their amusement.

If there's one thing faeries love, then that's the sight of a drunken human making a fool of herself.

"It's awful. Why would you give me this?" she asks, genuinely curious, and I toss her a sceptical look.

"You're asking *me* that question? The faerie who tricked you into trading your necklace for a room in his mountain?"

She gives me a deadpan expression, and it looks like I took it too far again. One day, maybe we can look back on that exchange and laugh.

Honestly, this is the most time we've spent together—things are pretty tense between us most of the time. We still act like strangers, and I'm quite certain she loathes my entire being. But sometimes, her eyes wander, and I wonder... *Does* she like me? Humans are naturally drawn to Fae, and the feelings are certainly mutual. After all, human females are ephemeral. So, they fascinate us Fae males. Their beauty will fade one day, as it only reminds us of how short and precious life can be. I, myself, have a long life in store, and truth be told, the sheer weight of it disturbs me. All that life, and for what?

She smiles sweetly, stroking her finger around the rim of her tankard as she whispers, "Room? Try cave."

Now she's just toying with me, speaking to me in a voice like dripping honey.

Well, two can play at that game. I slip my finger beneath my shirt, and her eyes flicker when she sees the necklace.

"A cave it may be, *princess*, but it still cost you greatly..."

Ivy presses her lips into a line, keeping her emotions in check. But I know she's resisting the urge to slap me.

She chooses her next words wisely. "You may have won the battle, but you haven't won the war."

Wow.

Did she come up with that all by herself?

I snicker. "Well, it's a good thing I have plenty of fight in me."

Ivy smirks, batting her eyelashes, and the sight of her deviant smile goes straight to my cock. It seems this budding beauty has finally discovered her greatest weapon, and I really am no match.

She just won all the wars.

"Me too."

We stare at each other for some time, and I'm not sure what is happening. The air between us is thick with electricity, making my hair rise on end, and I keep stealing glances at her lush, red lips.

Losing the war...

"Tegwyn?"

My eyes travel upwards again, and I take note of the way her eyes shine. "Yeah?"

She sucks in a breath. "Why...why did you save me? Back then..."

It takes me a moment to realise what she's talking about.

She's talking about the time I saved her from the kelpie. Now she's *definitely* left me tongue-tied.

It's as if she robs me of my ability to speak, and I keep finding that I'm not quite so silver-tongued when I'm with her.

She waves me off. "It's okay. You don't have to tell me. I was just...curious."

I can't tear my gaze away from her. The whole tavern seems to vanish, and now it's just the two of us.

Why *did* I save her? I'm no white knight; I don't even possess a sword. But I shot an arrow right through that kelpie's skull. I killed one of my own, but truth be told, I would do it again and again if it kept her alive.

My palms sweat, and thank goddess she can't see beneath the gloves.

"Thank you, anyway. Even though you saved me only to trick me later, I'm still grateful."

Yes. That *is* the reason why I saved her, so I could get my grubby hands on her pretty necklace.

Let's leave it at that.

Before I can open my mouth to respond, a shadow looms over our table, and then the awful stench of blood and death finds us.

And I thought the puca was the most vicious creature in this tavern tonight.

In the end, nothing could compare to the monster that has just graced us with its presence.

13

Tegwyn

WITH A CRIMSON DOUBLET embellished with golden thread, brown leather boots, and a longsword at the belt, the creature resembles a handsome prince from a prestigious court.

Or a *knight,* even.

But I won't be fooled so easily, and I'm not the only one. Everyone inside this tavern knows what he is, which is why they keep their distance.

Ivy can't take her eyes off him, naturally.

Her mouth hangs open, and a vapid expression comes over her lovely face. It's *happening*...she's losing herself.

She can't be blamed, though. The faerie presents a beautiful façade, one with the most devastating locks of shining sable.

With a bone structure carved as if from the finest diamond, how could she not be smitten? As a mortal, she won't be able to see the heady cloud of scarlet that surrounds him like a wisp of smoke, the one that completely enraptures her and robs her of all common sense.

My claws peek from my gloves. If he thinks he's getting his hands on her, he can kiss my ass.

He places his gloved hand on the crescent-moon pommel of his longsword, shooting Ivy a dashing smile filled with brilliant white teeth.

She blushes beet-red. It's best I get her out of here. I won't have her falling prey to this predator.

"My, you're certainly a sight for weary eyes," he whispers, his voice like silk. "For many weeks I have travelled, yet I have stumbled upon no maid so fair. What is thy name, sweet lady?"

Ivy's pupils bloom like rose petals, dominating her starburst eyes. "I...can't remember..."

I pinch the bridge of my nose, heaving a gritty sigh.

I need to end this.

Rising from my seat, I move around the table, getting a good look at our new *friend*. His mask may be foolproof to a naïve human like Ivy, but I know better...

His white skin has a powdery texture like chalk, and his glacier-blue eyes are rimmed with red, and don't forget the overly sensual lips, either.

He makes me want to vomit.

"We're leaving," I announce, keeping my eyes on the loathsome creature. "Come along, Ivy."

The faerie's eyes dazzle at the sound of her name. "Ivy? A most befitting moniker for a beautiful maid." He bows low, bending his body at the perfect angle. "I am Lord Valent, High Lord of the Onyx Crescent Court. It is an honour to be graced with your presence, my lady."

Ivy's skin deepens with lust, and a feminine giggle escapes her lips. Shit. *Losing* her...

I don't care if this bastard holds his own court; I will send him back to the Unseelie Lands in bite-sized pieces.

He shouldn't be trespassing in Rogue territory, but as a High Lord, it's obvious he thinks himself above us. We should be honoured that he deigned to grace our humble little tavern with his presence.

It's why most of the bar's patrons keep a wide berth. He's a powerful Fae and *rich* in magic, as his castle is situated right beside the Pool of Light.

Power ripples from him in waves, and I am simply no match. But I don't need magic to fight this pompous prick.

Lord Valent bestows me with a courteous bow, and his stench of blood grows ever stronger. "I'm sorry to have troubled you, simple Rogue, but I was simply awestruck by your beautiful maid."

I hiss through clenched teeth, "She is *not* my maid. And don't call me *Rogue*..."

He cocks a brow, straightening once again. "I dare say. I did find it rather peculiar that a female of her standing would be taken with someone so..." he stops, searching for the right word to describe a Rogue like me, "*alarming*."

His lordship regards my fangs, horns, and claws, and I toss my head back, barking a laugh. "And I could say the same about you. You're not so glamorous yourself."

Lord Valent palms his chest, feigning indignation. "Well, I never, but I do think we should leave the debate up to this sweet female." He turns to Ivy, "Tell me, Ivy, do you find me charming?"

He winks, and once again, she turns beet-red.

"Yes, your lordship, I...I do," she gasps, chest heaving, "very much."

This time, she bites her lip.

I frown at her. I know it's not her fault. These creatures are masters of seduction, but does she have to be so goddamn obvious?

"Why are you still sitting? We're leaving."

She tears her gaze away from Lord Valent at long last, and it's like I no longer exist. All she sees is the vile predator.

I finally understand the human expression of *chopped liver*... because that is what I've just become.

"Did you say something?" she asks absentmindedly.

Before I can reply, Lord Valent gets down on one knee, taking her dainty hands in his fingers.

A low sound reverberates in my chest, rising from the darkest pits of my soul.

He dares lay a hand on her...

"Please, not yet. Stay a while longer."

Ivy's face warps with guilt, and she has never looked more conflicted. But then she produces another hazy smile, murmuring, "Well...I could always stay and finish my drink."

Before she reaches for her tankard, I pick it up and chug it back. Once again, Stannog's gnat's piss taints my bloodstream, yet like the stubborn shit I am, I continue.

Anything to save Ivy from a wretched fate. I'm losing her to this monster, and if I don't do something fast, then she'll be gone forever; I can already hear the bar's patrons placing bets on her life.

They can bet on my *ass*.

I burp close to Lord Valent, hoping the stench melts the skin right off his creepy face, and his mask cracks for the briefest moment.

"Most commendable, *Rogue*..."

I can't help but feel proud of myself. He may act aloof, but deep down, I know he's seething.

Wiping my lips, I slam the tankard down on the table, giving Valent an impish smile—except now I see *two* Lord Valents.

Fuck.

"*Now* we leave... Ivy?"

She shakes her head, finally coming to her senses. "Erm...sure," she stammers, joining me.

My shoulders sag with relief, and we head for the door.

His silken voice projects through the bar, so confident, so self-assured. "Goodbye, sweet Ivy. I'll never forget you."

Ivy stops, gazing back over her shoulder. Sadness shimmers inside her big starburst eyes, and it looks as if I was wrong.

She's already so far under his thrall. Now the poor thing will pine for him day and night until she's driven to the brink of insanity.

I never should have brought her here. Unarmed, helpless...

In the end, this tavern is a writhing nest of vipers.

And I'm the worst viper of all.

"Ivy, what are you doing? Let's go," I whisper.

She can't take her eyes off Lord Valent, and again, her pupils explode, leaving nothing but a bright ring of sea green.

"We're staying," she intones, inhaling his red smoke.

Mumbling echoes through the bar, followed by the clinking of coins, and I spy Stannog shaking his head in disappointment.

"No. We leave," I reply desperately now.

Ivy completely ignores me as she saunters back to Lord Valent's side, taking her cloak off at his request. The rest of the bar watches the show unfold; it's not every day they get to see a master at work.

Ivy will belong to Lord Valent by the night's end, and there is nothing I can do to stop it.

It looks like I failed to keep my end of the bargain.

I did not protect her.

Lord Valent orders honeyed wine for the entire bar, and Stannog begrudgingly obliges.

Now Ivy will become drunk on faerie wine, a drunkenness the likes of which she will never wake from.

Beautiful girls materialise from thin air, floating around the tavern like neat swathes of silk as they hand out shimmering goblets.

These must be Stannog's 'nighttime' staff. Some of them possess bright wings of gossamer, and others bear horns and antlers, yet they all have one thing in common—they've shared my bed.

One with the peppered wings of a moth approaches Ivy's side, pouring a generous amount of wine into a silver goblet, and the human tries her hardest not to stare at the large appendages sticking out from her back.

"Fermented for one hundred years for the lovely girl," the female croons, her voice as clear and resonant as the pealing notes of a wind chime.

Ivy takes the goblet from the faerie's long, slender fingers, and the moment it vanishes down her throat, she giggles like a happy idiot.

Just as I thought... *Spiked.*

The Fae female smirks, whirling back towards the bar with all the lethal grace of a feline.

On her way through the gate, I grip her wrist, whispering into her pointed ear, *"Don't."*

She bats her yellow, cat-like eyes. "Whatever are you talking about?"

"Fuck you. You know *exactly* what I'm talking about, Mellow. Leave her be."

As far as faeries go, Mellow was pretty average in bed. Let's just say that desperate times call for desperate measures.

Mellow bares her straight white teeth. She's always been a jealous, petty bitch. She must think that Ivy and I are courting. We're not, but Mellow won't see it that way.

"You made a mistake bringing that *dung* here, and my name is *Minnow*, prick."

Who cares what her name is? I didn't care when I was fucking her, and I sure as hell don't care now that we're no longer paramours.

I tighten my grip on her frail wrist, flashing my eyes in warning. Then I let her go once Stannog growls at me to stop.

Milda, Merrow, or whatever her stupid name is, is one of his best workers, so he doesn't want me to ruin her face.

A face that's as forgetful as her name.

The winged female rubs at the red mark that I left on her wrist. Then she whacks me across the back of the head with her tray, making me spill my gnat's piss.

I refuse to participate in honeyed wine; I won't touch anything that Unseelie bought with his gold.

Lord Valent can't take his cold, glacier eyes off Ivy as she dances just for him, and I hope her death will be quick and painless.

All I can do is brood at the bar while Ivy makes a fool of herself, dancing for the amusement of these wicked creatures. She will wear down the soles of her feet before Valent is through with her.

Everyone cheers her on, and someone even starts to play the flute for her as she twirls and twirls, and whenever she trips or stumbles, I die a little inside.

The bar erupts with cruel laughter.

Mildew caws the loudest, and I growl when the bitch grabs Ivy's shoulders, spinning her faster and faster.

The human falls into the arms of the puca, and the two toss her back and forth, turning it into a game.

Ivy titters the whole time, and she thinks she's having the time of her life.

But faeries like to play with their food first. It makes their suffering taste all that sweeter...

"Enough!" Lord Valent bellows, coming to her rescue at last.

The patrons withdraw once the lord makes his presence known. Moola returns to serving punters, while the puca resumes his card game.

Me, on the other hand... I stare down into the bottom of my empty tankard, hoping I'll find the answers I seek.

The world tips on its axis. Then my vision distorts, making it hard to tell fact from fiction. A small part of me just wants to head home. Why should I care? Ivy made her choice.

Still, I turn on my barstool, my heart plunging to the deepest depths of my soul when I spy her there.

Lord Valent plays with a lock of her beautiful blonde hair, and a giggle pours from her sweet lips, chasing away the darkness, like the pealing notes of a Yule bell... a bell that will soon stop forever.

I can't bear to watch. Time to head home to my dark mountain.

Yes. Run away, coward.

Rosemary's taunting voice swirls through my drunken mind, but I ignore her nasty comments, rising from the stool.

"Are ye really going ter leave her trapped in that spider's web?"

I peer across the bar. Stannog side-eyes me with that familiar disdain, and for once, I deserve his hostility.

Yes. I *am* going to leave her with the spider. What more can I do? She's already gone.

"*Well?*" he demands.

I put up a strong front, hoping he doesn't notice that I'm dying inside. "Pretty spider... Wouldn't you agree?"

I go to swig the dregs of my disgusting drink, but Stannog snatches it from my hand, showing me his crooked teeth. "Get that lass home before it's too late."

I sigh. "It's already too late..."

"No. It's not. Just this once, I'll help."

A smirk curves my lips. "Since when did *you* start loving *dung*?"

Stannog growls, "I don't. But I'm not about ter let that poor girl die. Ye brought her here, now ye take her back."

I groan, rubbing my eyes. Then I twist around in my stool, listening to their conversation.

"You poor thing," Lord Valent cries in dismay.

Ivy pauses, and it takes me a moment to realise.

They're talking about *me*...

"He's...not so bad," she replies bashfully, and it's clear she's having a hard time trying to find something nice to say about me.

She continues, "Sure, he's crude and selfish, but I'd be dead if it weren't for him."

Lord Valent shakes his head, black locks shining with the movement. "Yes, but not at the expense of your necklace. I hate to be the one to tell you this, but that Rogue is not your friend. He only meant to deceive you, and it looks like his gambit paid off."

I glower at him from the corner of my eye. Such a way with words.

But why do I have a sick feeling in my gut? One akin to shame?

Ivy actually has the stomach to look sad for me. Maybe she doesn't hate me as much as I thought.

"My mama taught me to see the good in everyone, but... I do really have to try with him."

My world crashes around me. I am not *good* in her eyes.

Lord Valent chuckles, "Well, I can think of one good thing about him. If he hadn't brought you here tonight, then we never would have met."

Ivy laughs shyly, and I stick out my tongue. Looks like we've got a smooth talker here.

"You can't continue this way," Lord Valent announces. "He's a monster, pure and simple, and he only means to hurt you. I have my charger outside. Let us make haste before anyone notices we're missing."

The blood crashes through my head like the waves of an oncoming storm, and I kick my stool out from beneath me as I finally face the enemy.

"No!"

14

Ivy

I JERK MY HEAD towards the bar, feeling the hair pricking at the back of my neck when I catch sight of Tegwyn.

Pure, unadulterated fear courses through my veins, yet I don't run. I gawk at the horned faerie, the one whose eyes glow like the dying embers of a hearth. If this is the true wrath of the Fae, then I don't want to see it.

I sober up immediately, rising from my chair in a bid for escape, but Lord Valent wraps his long, slender fingers around my elbow. "No. Stay put, sweet Ivy. I will deal with this fiend."

Fiend? Is that what Tegwyn has become now? I just don't know anymore.

Who is friend and who is foe?

My heart races, yet all I can do is put my faith into the male beside me. He's the only one displaying any calm right now.

Yet a part of me knows that Tegwyn wouldn't hurt me. We're friends... right?

"Is there a problem, *Rogue*?" Lord Valent asks, looking at Tegwyn.

I yelp when Tegwyn suddenly appears before the high Fae lord, gripping him by the buttons of his brocaded doublet.

I'll never get used to the way these creatures move. One place one moment, and another the next.

I cast my eyes around the bar, finally seeing them for the first time. How they all *snarl*. They deceived me, every single one.

When I drank the honeyed wine, I could have sworn these faeries were my friends. I hardly seemed to notice the way they licked their lips, or the way they sneered at my shame. I can't believe I put my trust in them.

Tegwyn brandishes an iron cross, holding it up to Lord Valent's throat, and wait...that's *my* cross.

What is *he* doing with it?

Several Fae gasp when they see what he's holding, and they no longer look so pleased with themselves. Tegwyn came to this tavern armed. They better not piss him off.

The cross hovers inches from Lord Valent's throat, and there's no missing the spark dancing inside his curious eyes as he studies the iron.

Tegwyn, on the other hand, doesn't fare so well. Sweat drips from his face, and it's obvious the iron is having a far more adverse effect on him than Lord Valent. Still, he never loses his composure.

Mama always told me how iron repelled the Fae, but I never really believed it was true until now. To see it in action...it's pretty alarming.

His breathing becomes laboured, and for the first time tonight, I truly *see* him.

Tegwyn is sick, and he needs my help.

"Stay *away* from her," he growls, never breaking his hold on my father's iron cross.

Lord Valent chuckles. "Do you really think that scant bit of iron can harm me?"

Tegwyn bares his teeth, gripping the cross tighter, and even with gloves, the iron is hurting him. "Why? You're Fae, aren't you?"

The high lord's smug smile becomes almost serpentine. "Yes... But not in the way you are, I'm afraid, *Rogue*."

Tegwyn growls, "You think you're so much better than the rest of us just because you live in a fancy castle by the Pool. The thing is, I've lived amongst humans my whole life. So, I think I can speak for myself when I say that I can handle a bit of *scant* iron..."

Lord Valent peers at the cross again, and a silent gasp escapes me once a bead of sweat drips down his alabaster face. He *is* afraid.

"Ivy, head to the door," Tegwyn orders, never taking his glowing eyes off the high Fae lord.

What kind of high Fae lord? I couldn't say. As far as I'm aware, he's Unseelie. But one thing I do know for certain: Lord Valent is not a friend. I really was a fool to trust him.

Finally, I rise, joining Tegwyn on the other side of the table, and his wrath is almost palpable. I can taste it on my tongue.

He leans closer to me. "Go. I will be right behind you."

I glance towards the door, hoping no one will try to stop me. All the other faeries keep their distance. The moth-winged female from earlier regards me as if I'm pond scum. What did I ever do to evoke her wrath?

The ogre behind the bar flaunts a bronze mace, and I make my decision, backing away to the door.

Tegwyn lets go of Lord Valent's collar, shielding me from view as he backs me to the door, and warmth trickles through me when I realise he is protecting me.

The door materialises, and Tegwyn nods towards it. "Through the door. Quickly."

My heart thumps, and I grip his hand, squeezing his fingers tightly. "Don't leave me, all right?"

I feel the eyes of the beautiful moth-winged female from the other end of the tavern, and I'm sure she can hear everything we're saying with her Fae ears.

And I bet she hates me even more for it.

Tegwyn's eyes flick my way. Before, his pupils were black slices cutting through the gold of his burning eyes, but now, they're soft and rounded.

"I promise," he replies, his voice sincere. "Now go."

With a deep breath, I push through the door, eager to put the tavern behind me.

But then Lord Valent's smooth, lilting tone carries across the room, making me freeze mid-step. "So long, Ivy sweet. Maybe one day, when this Rogue is finally bored with you, you can make your way back to me."

Wind brushes at the back of my neck, and when I turn around, a scream bursts from my throat.

Tegwyn presses the iron cross against Lord Valent's cheek, his eyes ablaze, and I swear I'm looking at the devil.

He's absolutely insane, vanishing behind a cloud of smoke as he burns the Lord's cheek, and soon all I can see are those yellow eyes.

"Try seducing beautiful women now with a face like charred meat, you fucking bastard!"

Lord Valent roars in pain, and I watch helplessly, wishing I could do something to stop this madness, but I'm frozen.

Forever the helpless damsel.

The smell. It's *indescribable*... Iron truly is lethal to the Fae.

Finally, I muster some strength, shouting from the top of my lungs, "Tegwyn, stop!"

To my relief, the faerie yields at the sound of my voice, and that's all the time the high lord needs. He wraps his cold fingers around Tegwyn's throat, throwing him down onto the table to choke the very essence from his lungs, and Tegwyn succumbs—quickly.

One squeeze from those cruel fingers, and he will leave this world forever.

The rest of the Fae cheer Lord Valent on, and several even exchange gold. They truly are awful. How can they take delight in this?

That's when a mace swings across the table, almost lopping the head clean off Tegwyn, and I jump, gazing up at the hulking barkeep.

Lord Valent glares at him, irritated, but the barkeep merely sneers, indicating his head at his weapon. "If ye don't clear off right now, Your *Lordship*, then the next swing will aim for yer head!"

Lord Valent bares his teeth, eyes burning a deep, hellish red. "Do you have any idea who I am?"

The ogre shrugs, "Some posh Unseelie twat who's far from his castle? That much I can gather. Don't fuck around with us Rogues. We won't take ye shit here."

Lord Valent weighs up his options, glancing around the bar. The other patrons have found their courage now that their barkeep has taken his stand, and His Lordship is greatly outnumbered.

Finally, he peers down at Tegwyn, letting go of his throat. Then he straightens, wiping at an imaginary piece of lint on his doublet as he heads for the door. "Well, I know when I'm not wanted."

I freeze when he brushes past me, yet he doesn't spare me a second glance. Instead, he summons the door, vanishing into the night.

Tegwyn remains on the table, breathing heavily as his lungs grasp for air, and I don't think—I rush to his side, gripping his cheeks. "Tegwyn, are you all right?"

Dread slithers down my spine when I spy the state he's in. His cheeks are gaunt, and his skin is wan and glossy with sweat.

Yet at the sound of my voice, he stirs, opening his eyes. I gaze into a pair of gleaming slits, and when he grins that vulpine smile, exposing his fangs, I almost weep.

"Still breathing, I'm afraid, princess."

Something between a laugh and a cry escapes me, and I never thought I'd see the day I would be relieved to hear his voice. At least someone in this tavern cares whether he lives or not. Faeries can be so cruel, even to their own kind.

Tegwyn sits up straight, clutching at his throat, but before I can inspect his injury, a cough interrupts us. We look up at the same time to find the barkeep hovering above us. "Hate to break up this touchin' moment, but it's time ye buggered off!"

Tegwyn gives a half-hearted laugh, sliding off the table. He sways, unbalanced, and fear lances through my chest.

"Save your breath, Stan. We were just leaving."

He hobbles towards the door, and I shuffle behind him, keeping close.

Stan stomps after us, and the ground shudders beneath his sheer weight. "And don't even think about coming back. Ye're barred, ye hear me? I never wanna see yer face in me tavern again!"

Tegwyn opens the door, and he doesn't even bother looking back. "I'll be crying myself to sleep."

Stan mumbles more expletives, glad to see the back of us, I bet, and now we finally leave his accursed tavern.

The moment we're outside, I round on Tegwyn, placing my hands on my hips. "What on earth was that outburst all about?"

He doesn't look at me again, keeping his eyes ahead as he ambles towards the trees. But he hardly makes it two steps before he trips, face-planting the ground. "Fuck! That floor comes up fast."

I kneel beside him, offering him my hand. The faerie regards it strangely, peering up at me with raised brows. "What is that?"

I sigh. "My hand. I'm helping you to your feet. You know, being *kind*...unless kindness is a foreign concept for you?"

He sniggers, gripping my hand, and my heart hammers when his claws prick my palm. "Ha, clever."

I help him to his feet, but he stubbornly pushes me away, insisting on walking himself. "I'm fine."

"No, you're not. What happened in there? What did he do to you?"

Tegwyn leans against the trunk of one of the giant redwoods, the mighty behemoth dwarfing him.

He eyes me curiously, a smirk growing on his impish face. "Why? Were you worried about me?"

I stammer, "N-no. I just—"

Before the sentence leaves my lips, he's upon me, pinning me to the tree behind me. I don't think he means to corner me; it's a genuine misstep. Off-balance, he can barely walk straight.

Now, as close as we stand, I can smell the pine and woodsmoke on his breath. "Don't fear, little Ivy. I'm Fae, I heal fast."

We gaze into each other's eyes, and I can't rid the image of him dying from my mind. I don't know what he must see on my face because his own countenance cracks, and then he moves away. "I'll be all right. Luckily, that bald bastard stopped him in time."

My eyes sting, and I can't explain the emotions that come over me. I almost saw him die, and it disturbed me.

Even now, his eyes have lost their wicked shine.

"What did he do to you?" I whisper.

Tegwyn narrows his eyelids, scrutinising me carefully, looking for the right way to explain.

"Please, I can handle it."

He sighs, breath clouding as he stumbles through the forest. "He stole my lifeforce."

My heart cleaves in two. "Your lifeforce?"

"That's right. If I had been human, I'd have died in seconds. He only took a few centuries from my lifespan, so there's no need to worry. Fae live an awfully long time. *Far* too long, for my liking."

I pause, and he glances over his shoulder. "Ivy?"

My heart pounds. Lord Valent can steal someone's lifeforce by merely touching them? But he had touched me...

Does that mean...?

I shiver.

"W-what *was* he?"

The faerie gives me his full attention, and once again, he falters. But then he answers, his voice crystal clear on the cold wind, "He was a leannán sídhe."

My blood runs cold when I hear the strange name. Dare I ask what a leannán sídhe is?

"They feed off the lifeforce of their victims. Usually humans, but they have been known to turn on other faeries, too. As you witnessed."

My stomach sinks lower and lower, and I throw my arms around myself to shield my skin against the biting wind.

"Would he have fed from my lifeforce?"

Tegwyn cocks his head, weighing up his next words. "Yes. But he wouldn't have done it so quickly. Your suffering would have lasted weeks, months, maybe years. You would have died when he was tired of you."

A frigid claw scratches up the length of my spine, and I shudder, wishing I could bury myself in the ground.

How easily I had fallen under that monster's thrall. I have never felt so ashamed.

Mama would be so disappointed with me. And to think I had told him my darkest secrets, my most wanton desires...

Something passes through Tegwyn's eyes. If I'm not mistaken, it almost resembles guilt.

He steps forward, going to place a hand on my shoulder, but then he thinks better of it, shoving it into his pocket, instead.

I don't meet his eyes.

"You wouldn't be the first human to have fallen prey to his kind."

I inhale a shaky breath, lifting my face. Tegwyn's eyes glow like embers once again.

"Yes. But he almost succeeded. At one point, I truly was prepared to leave with him."

The memory flashes through my mind, and I grip myself tighter. I don't have to explain. Tegwyn was there.

What terrifies me the most is that a large part of me actually did consider leaving with him. He promised me endless riches in his expansive castle, a place where I could paint to my heart's content. He even promised he would make me famous beyond my wildest dreams, a world-renowned artist in all the realms, and I almost took the bait.

Tegwyn stands close, and he's at a complete loss for words. I bet he doesn't even know how to say anything kind, but it's okay; I know he cares deep down. It was why he lashed out and attacked that monster. He was protecting me. I guess in his own messed-up way, he has always been protecting me. I just had to make a bargain with him first—my necklace for his protection.

But there was truly something primal about him tonight. The way he went for that creature, eyes burning with lethal rage. He went above and beyond the terms of our contract.

Finally, I try to change the subject, smiling tightly. "So... how long have you been carrying my iron cross?"

The faerie blinks, distracted for a moment. Then he scoffs, turning back towards the forest. "What iron cross?"

He can't be serious? I saw it in plain sight—the whole tavern did. I'm pretty sure he left a scar on Lord Valent's cheek.

Well, I guess that's one thing I can be glad about. The Unseelie lord didn't leave completely unscathed, and I can make peace with that gruesome fact.

I just hope I never have the misfortune of meeting him ever again.

The moment we return to the mountain, I head straight for my room/cave, hoping to get some sleep. No doubt I will be waking in the middle of the night in a cold sweat.

"And where are you going?"

I stop, peeking over my shoulder. Tegwyn leans against the arch of the main chamber, bathed in shadow. If it weren't for his glowing eyes, I wouldn't even know he was there.

"To bed. I'm tired."

Tegwyn gives me one of his crooked smirks, and his fangs glint in the faded light. "The night's still young, princess. And it's still your birthday..."

Somehow, I get the feeling he doesn't want to be alone. I know he has trouble sleeping; I hear him talking to himself at night.

Unable to bear the thought of him being alone, I finally join his side, letting him lead me into the kitchen for a night of merriment.

I thought I'd sobered up, but it turns out that I'm still pretty drunk. We *both* are, and I would have assumed that Tegwyn would have had at least some level of tolerance where alcohol consumption was concerned.

He throws me down into a splintered chair, disappearing into an alcove inside the wall. He curses inside, tossing out various pots and pans of shining bronze, and when he re-emerges, an impish smile etched on his face, he lifts a bottle of blood-red wine.

My head swirls just looking at it. "No. No more *Fae* wine."

He chuckles, grabbing two ceramic cups despite my protests. "Relax. It's just human wine, unfortunately."

While that does make me feel better, faerie wine or not, I'm still too drunk to drink any more, still too sick.

"I stole this bottle off a cargo ship two years ago. Imported from the *south*. So, it should be good."

I raise an eyebrow. "Is there anything you own that isn't stolen?"

He barks a laugh, leaning down to poke my nose. "My, you really are on fire tonight."

Tegwyn pours the wine into a cup, handing it over to me. I meet my reflection inside.

The wine almost reminds me of the red of Lord Valent's eyes, and I whimper, spilling my drink.

Tegwyn steadies me by wrapping his gloved fingers around my wrist, and he doesn't pry or judge. He actually appears... *angry*. But not with me.

His teeth grind, as if he's trying to restrain himself a great deal. His claws are drawn, yet they never cut me.

"Ivy...he won't ever find you again."

I shut my eyes, and I can't help it this time. A tear slips past my lashes, and I wipe it away, not wanting him to see me cry.

"How...how do you know that?"

He looks at me pointedly, yellow eyes boring into my soul. "Because if he does...I will *kill* him..."

His irises glow at the word *kill*, making the breath whoosh from my lungs.

And he would, too, and I dare not think about what those claws of his are truly capable of.

As if sensing my thoughts, he lets go of my wrist, raising his drink. "A toast to Lord Valent. May his face be forever charred..."

The faerie goes to sip his wine, but I take his hand, squeezing it tightly. "Thank you for fighting for me. No one has ever stood up for me like that before. You were so brave, so...selfless."

He blinks in utter confusion, and if I'm not mistaken, his cheeks redden. Then he yanks on his silly cravat and mutters, "Just holding up my end of the bargain."

I smile this time, grabbing my own drink. "If you say so."

Tegwyn hikes a brow. "What are you implying?"

I give a discreet shrug, and soon the cave starts spinning as I sip the wine.

We laugh at nothing, and at one point we twirl around the kitchen, crashing into various things. It turns out that faeries really are as useless as humans when drunk. Tegwyn can barely function.

By the night's end, he's tucking me into bed, placing me down onto the soft mattress. The heather twigs crunch beneath my weight, bringing up a lovely smell, and I sigh.

The bed is really comfortable.

When I shut my eyes, drifting off to sleep, I swear I hear the ocean.

"Go to sleep," he demands, sounding far away.

Panic leaks through my veins, and I open my eyes, searching the cave. "Tegwyn, come back!"

"I'm right here! Holy shit, Ivy..."

His face swivels into view, and I'm so happy to see him again.

Tegwyn's face shines buttery gold beneath the soft light of the flickering lamp, and I can't look away from him. He's breathtaking.

Once again, he's the beautiful Fae from my mural, and I reach up, brushing my fingertips along his sculpted cheek. His skin may be coarse, yet he's still a work of art. Smudged watermarks and charcoal... one day, I will paint him again.

I smile. "Don't listen to a word they say, Tegwyn."

He exhales, lifting yet another brow, and for someone so otherworldly, his facial expressions are rather human.

"And what do they say?"

"That you're evil and you like to eat small children, but you're not evil. You're... beautiful..."

He stares at me in stunned silence. Then he throws his head back and guffaws. "Fuck! You really are drunk."

He rises to his feet, but I yank on his sleeve, bringing him back to the bed. "No. Don't leave..."

No smart comebacks this time. The faerie gazes at me wide-eyed, lips forming the words that his brain so desperately seeks. His pupils dilate, and he almost looks sweet when they swell up like that. I lose myself in his yellow eyes, and they're so full of life. This Fae male has enchanted me from the very moment he appeared in my dreams, and one day, I really am going to capture his likeness on canvas.

My eyes rest on his lips. He still has that prominent Cupid's bow, and I wonder what it would be like to kiss him.

I tug gently on his cravat, bringing him closer, and as our lips brush, he jerks away, increasing the ever-growing distance between us.

For a moment, he looks at me baffled, a myriad of expressions flickering across his face. But then confusion soon gives way to anger, hurt, and finally, regret.

Before I can call out his name, he vanishes into the shadows, leaving me totally bereft.

My heart breaks. He *rejected* me...

And I only have myself to blame.

I was a fool to think he would ever feel the same, and I bury myself beneath my blankets, hoping I never wake again.

15

Tegwyn

I'm halfway down the mountain by the time I stop, digging my claws into the wall to slow my momentum.

My heart slams against my ribs, as I can't rid the smell of her sweet honeysuckle from my skin, and she's already so deep in my veins.

The memory of her drunken face swims up before me, and I scrape my claws down the cave wall, leaving prominent grooves inside the ancient stone.

She tried to kiss me, and I ran.

I've never rejected a female's advances—human *or* Fae—what the hell is wrong with me? Have I lost my stride?

There's just something about her that makes me so nervous, and I become tongue-tied whenever I'm in her presence.

My lungs heave like a pair of bellows as I scratch my claws down my face this time, hoping the pain will knock some sense back into me. This was never supposed to happen; I was never supposed to become *invested*.

Ivy was just a means to an end. I wanted her pretty necklace so I could pawn it off to the highest bidder and leave this godforsaken country. I can't develop feelings for her.

My heart still bangs against my chest, and it hasn't stopped pounding since she leaned in for that kiss.

I'm sure this will pass. At most, it's my *prick* that's developing feelings for her.

Yet, I saved her life from that leech back at the tavern, and the memory of his smug face still sets my blood ablaze. I'll char the face of any bastard who lays their hands on her porcelain skin. Ivy is my ward, and I will continue to do everything in my power to protect her.

Now, I make a silent vow to never take things further—no matter how tempting it may be to run back up the tunnel and plant my own kiss between her legs.

We made a contract the day she handed over her necklace, and I won't break its terms. I may be wicked, but I won't take further advantage of that naïve girl.

I guess there's nothing more to do than to stew in my own self-loathing. It's going to be a long, lonely night.

With my right *hand*...and Rosemary's judgmental tone.

Pine needles crunch underfoot—needles coated with a thick layer of hoarfrost—as winter fast approaches. The forest is eerily quiet this morning, heavy boughs dusted with a smattering of snow as I trek my usual hunting grounds, embracing the newfound chill. The chill helps clear the mind and the irksome headache that pulses between my eyes. I wish I hadn't got so inebriated last night. The cold grounds me, reminding me that I have endless responsibilities. Winter is coming, and it's time to stock up on meat.

It's funny how accustomed I have grown to the seasons. After all, there is no changing of the seasons back at the faerielands. At the Seelie Court, it is eternal summer, and the Unseelie experiences a permanent winter. There is no spring or autumn, because such change only occurs in the human realm.

The Fae are practically frozen in time.

My breath plumes like a cloud as I search the ground for one of my traps.

I've trained my stomach to go without food for weeks. One of the many advantages of being Fae, but now that I have Ivy, I'm hunting for two.

I just hope she likes rabbit.

My pantry is running short. Ivy has already depleted two bags of oats, and it looks like I'm going to have to teach her a thing or two about rationing.

I just don't know how I'll face her again after last night. A ghost of her warm breath still lingers, and I reach up, brushing my finger over my lips. If only I hadn't been such a coward, I could have...

A shuffling sound alerts my attention to a nearby thicket. That's where I laid one of my traps.

Creeping closer, I pry the thorny branches apart. A rabbit hangs from a wire snare, its soft toes grazing the snow-covered ground, and a lump sticks in my throat.

It's always the same; I always get choked up whenever I take one of their lives.

Yet I need to eat. Maghelena will forgive me.

Its body is still warm when I cut it loose from the snare, and then I lift it by the scruff, gazing into its jewel-black eye. I hope it died quickly. I set the trap in a way that made death quick and painless.

"I'm sorry," I whisper, tying the deceased cottontail to my belt.

I still have another twenty snares to go.

I don't return until dusk.

In the end, I only found five rabbits, but their meat should suffice for several weeks if I apply salt.

I'm greeted by a sickly-sweet stench as I march up the tunnel, covering my nose. When I stop at the kitchen, I find her standing over the hearth, waving at a cloud of smoke with an old rag. Something burns in the pot, and whatever it is, it needs to be condemned into the nearest pit.

My heart thuds as a fleeting memory of our almost kiss returns, but I push it away, addressing her clearly, "What are you doing?"

She gasps, yet doesn't meet my eyes. Her cheeks redden, and it looks like she's remembering last night, too.

Will either of us forget?

"I...I'm making porridge."

I hike a brow, stepping closer to inspect the contents of the pot. She moves aside quickly, crossing her arms as she looks the other way.

Normally, she makes delicious porridge, yet today the oats are stuck to the pot. Maybe she was distracted?

I roll my eyes. "You need to add water."

"Oh, right, of course. I knew I was missing something." She laughs nervously.

I hiss through gritted teeth, but rather than reprimanding her, I move to one side so she can salvage her meal.

In the end, she gives up, tossing the pot in the basin with a heavy sigh. "It's hopeless."

The room falls quiet now that the sizzling of burning porridge has gone. It appears she is regretting last night after all, and I try to think of something to say, anything to fill the void.

I pluck one of the rabbits from my belt, flinging it across the table. She has not once offered to join me on a hunt. She has never so much as asked to skin a rabbit.

And I think I know why... She doesn't eat meat.

The only thing she seems to eat is porridge, and the occasional nuts and berries when she's foraging in the woods.

Well, that's just not going to suffice.

"Want to learn how to skin a rabbit?" I smile, exposing my fangs, but she only has eyes for the dead lapin—the one spilling its blood across the table.

Now she looks as green as I do. I bet she has never skinned or gutted anything in her life.

"No, it's fine. I'll go." She makes a start for the exit.

"But *insist*, Ivy. The days are growing colder... and shorter."

She shakes her head, trying to leave again. "I said, I'm fine."

I reach out, gripping her by the wrist, and she freezes like a cornered animal. I thank the goddess that I had the foresight to wear gloves, because I don't think I could have coped with the sensation of her skin against mine.

The way hers glows a soft, buttery gold in the candlelight is enough to make my imagination run wild.

"I really think it's best you watch."

She closes her eyes, breathing steadily through her nose. "N-no."

My claws prick her ever so slightly, just enough to get the message across. "You can't expect to survive the winter on nuts and berries..."

Ivy remains mulishly steadfast.

She doesn't have to give up on her love of animals if she decides to hunt with me. It's a matter of survival out here.

Her breath whooshes from her lips, "I can't. If I do, then... I'll be giving up."

I narrow my eyes. "Giving up on what?"

"On myself. I don't want to let go of my old self. Of the girl I used to be... Carefree and innocent. So, for that reason, I choose not to partake."

She makes a move for the exit, but I'm in front of her before she can so much as blink.

Ivy yelps at my sudden appearance, yet I back her up towards the table, caging her in with my arms so she can't escape.

My claws splinter the wood.

"Sit down and learn how to skin a rabbit like a *good* little huntress." It's an order, not a request.

I'm still seething at her ridiculous confession. Giving up on herself? What good is there holding on to her past if she's dead?

Strange female...

Ivy looks me straight in the eye, and my heart flutters like the wings of a moth when I recall how we almost kissed. Any affection she may have harboured for me is long gone now, though. I hate to ruin her perfect illusion of me, but I am no fairytale prince. I'm an evil faerie. One who hunts and kills bunnies.

"Move out of my way."

I lean closer until we're inches from another kiss. "No. You've seen the rations. We're running short. So, you're going to learn how to hunt and skin a rabbit. Do I make myself clear?"

She holds up a haughty chin. "That wasn't a part of our bargain."

My jaw ticks. She's got me there.

Yet, it doesn't stop me from digging my claws in that little bit further, creating grooves in the old wood.

I hate to be proven wrong, but she's right. I've already taken so much; I would be overstepping a line if I expected anything more from her.

Plus, I would be breaching the terms of our contract. It's bound in magic.

But fuck magic. I'm not about to let her starve herself.

It's unlikely, but anything could happen to me out here. I may have a long life ahead of me, but I can still die. Ivy would be on her own if I perished, completely and utterly helpless, and that thought doesn't bode well with me.

She cocks her head, regarding me curiously. "Why do you care so much if I starve?"

My mind empties of all rational thought. Then my mouth moves, trying to form words, but nothing comes.

My silence seems to say it all, and she closes her eyes, giving me a silent nod. "All right. I will join you."

Thank goodness. I withdraw my claws from the table.

I step aside, giving her back her personal space, and she finally makes her way to her room.

I address her back. "Meet me outside at first light. We have a long day tomorrow."

She stops, peering briefly over her shoulder. Then she nods quietly and vanishes up the tunnel.

With a huff, I fall into a chair, massaging my temples.

Teaching her is going to be hard work.

16

Tegwyn

I FIND HER WAITING outside at first light, bundled up in her blue velvet cloak.

Her teeth chatter as she gazes at the snow, her breath fogging the frigid air. She really isn't made for the north at all. Thank the goddess she came to her senses and finally decided to join me on a morning hunt. I know I'm insufferable to be around, but she needs to do this.

Gentle flurries drift from an overcast sky, coating the slope in a fine frosting of snow. Winter is coming quicker than I expected.

I hand her my quiver, and she looks at me, puzzled. "Why are you giving me this?"

I shrug. "Thought you would appreciate the honour."

Her eyes find the longbow slung across my shoulder. "Well, how about the longbow? Can I hold that, too?"

I cover the longbow with my fleece. "You most certainly can't. You're not quite there yet, princess. So, it's just the quiver for you, for now."

She tosses me a withering look, then marches out of the cave with her chin held high.

A snigger escapes me. She hates it when I call her *princess*.

I follow her after a moment; I have a long day of teaching her how to be a self-sufficient being.

I release the arrow, hitting the mark I carved into a tree, and it's a perfect aim, as usual.

I toss her a smirk over my shoulder, but to my frustration, she's not even watching.

Instead, she watches a murder of crows cawing in the trees, and I roll my eyes, beckoning her forward. "Ivy, come here."

She glances up, cheeks rosy with the cold. When I raise a questioning brow, she rolls her own eyes, joining my side.

I help her with her posture, kicking her legs apart when she doesn't move fast enough for my liking.

She huffs a breath. "I can move my own legs, you know."

"I suppose you can, but you seem to be stuck in a world of your very own choosing right now, princess, so it's the only way I can teach you."

She regards the longbow. "So, does this mean I can finally hold the bow?"

"No. You will learn the proper steps before I give you my pride and joy."

She crosses her arms. "Fine. So, what's next, *teacher*?"

I grit my teeth at her snarky attitude. "Determining your dominant eye."

Ivy puts her hands on her hips. "And how am I supposed to do that without holding the bow first?"

With a smirk, I form a triangle with my gloved fingers, moving it towards my eyes. "Whichever eye the triangle is most drawn to, that's your dominant eye. Mine's my left, see?"

She gives me a scathing look, then forms a triangle with her hands, bringing them to her eyes.

I chuckle, "Left eye dominant, like me. Lucky you."

She perks up at that. "Does this mean I can finally hold the bow?"

I tap my chin. "Hm, all right. I guess you're ready."

Her grin widens, and I ignore the fluttering in my chest when I spy the childlike wonder in her eyes. She's so green, it hurts.

Taking up my place behind her, I take an arrow from the quiver, then position her fingers around the bow.

"See the groove at the end of the arrow? That's the nock. You attach it to the bowstring, just below the marker point, ensuring that the fletching is aligned correctly with the cock vane facing outward."

She nods, following my instructions.

"Then, hold the arrow in place with your index finger above the arrow and two below."

She adjusts her fingers around the arrow, turning to face me once again.

"Now, point the arrow at the target, keeping your elbow parallel to the ground. Can you see down the spine of the arrow?"

Ivy gives another nod.

"Now, pull the bowstring towards you." I place my hand over hers, guiding her movements with my fingers. "Arms relaxed, elbow raised, and keep pulling until the bowstring is anchored against the side of your jaw."

She follows my directions, tugging the bowstring until it presses against the side of her jaw.

"Is the target in sight?"

"Yes."

"Good. Now release."

She releases, and the arrow hisses through the air, hitting the very heart of the target.

I stare, impressed.

Not bad for a beginner.

When I face her again, she's grinning from ear to ear, and I go completely still at the magnificent sight.

We're standing awfully close.

My heart beats on my tongue, and I get lost inside the endless sea of her eyes, forgetting myself for a moment. What were we doing again?

Ivy looks at me the same way, and when her rounded pupils fall on my lips, I don't run. This time, I stay.

Her breath ghosts my lips once again, and when she leans closer, closing her eyes, my own shut.

A branch cracks behind us, and we both stop, whirling around.

The blood rushes back to my head, and now the spell between us breaks, our almost kiss forgotten on the wind.

A beautiful red doe watches us from the trees. She stands beside a spruce just fifteen yards away, and it's a perfect shot. I don my hunting hat, trying to ignore the creature's curious gaze. She's young, so she hasn't learned to fear us yet.

A shame.

"Ivy, draw..." I whisper.

She stares at the doe helplessly, blue-green eyes wide with wonder.

I grind my teeth, whispering a little louder, "Ivy. Draw. *Now.*"

Her arms shake as she can't stop staring at the beautiful deer.

The animal steps out from the trees, and I have never seen a more innocent creature. The sweet doe has absolutely no idea of the real danger she's in, and it almost seems unfair.

But Ivy needs to learn.

"*Ivy...*" I growl.

Her lip trembles, tears gleaming inside her big, starburst eyes. Then finally, she lowers her arrow, shaking her head.

"No. It's wrong. It's just so..."

Her voice trails away, but I don't need to hear the rest of her sentence. Because I see it, too. It's wrong because the deer is still so young and curious, and to kill her would be cowardly at this stage. It should be a fair fight at least.

But meat is meat, and I can't afford to get sentimental.

After all, I'm hunting for *two* now. Ivy will not starve on my watch.

Tearing the weapon from her grip, I point the arrow at the deer's sweet brown eyes, aiming for a clean shot.

My throat constricts, and I struggle to breathe. Why won't she run?

Instead of fleeing, the doe steps closer, sniffing the tip of the arrow with her shiny nose. Her ears prick, and then she cocks her head.

I...can't kill her...

The doe trusts me because I'm Fae. A so-called friend of the forest.

Ivy waves her arms, and the deer startles, making a beeline for the trees with a flash of her white tail.

I round on the human immediately. "Do you have any idea what you've just done?"

She's still gazing at the spot where the deer vanished. "I-I'm sorry. I couldn't..."

I grip her shoulders. "That deer could have seen you through the winter!"

Ivy whimpers, and I look down at my hands. My claws are drawn, cutting into her arms, and when I remove them, they drip with blood.

Shit.

She staggers away from me, looking at me like I'm the monster under her bed.

Guilt shreds my insides when I realise...I *hurt* her.

"Ivy..." I whisper.

"Stay away!" she shrieks, tripping over snow in her haste to get away from me.

The look of betrayal on her face sends me spiralling into the abyss, and maybe this time, I won't ever crawl back out. With a wretched sob, she disappears into the forest, turning her back on me, but I don't go after her.

Instead, I stare at her blood. It drips from the tips of my claws, staining the snow at my feet.

Hurting her was never my intention. I'm *definitely* going to hell after this.

Nothing will ever make this right again.

I find her in her room, cleaning her wounds with a wet cloth.

She doesn't see me watching her in the shadows. Nor does she see me when she presses the cloth to her shoulder, hissing in pain, and guilt tears me apart yet again.

I really never meant to hurt her. Maybe all those kids back in the village were right about me, after all. Maybe I *am* a monster.

Ivy stiffens. Then she spins suddenly, the colour draining from her face when she sees me.

I probably look like a horned demon from the bowels of hell, especially with the way my eyes glow.

She whimpers, gripping her blankets like a child. "Stay away..."

She's terrified of me now, and rightly so. For her sake, I don't use my speed. I move at a languid, human pace, raising my hands as a sign of peace—I even make sure that my claws are back inside my gloves. "I'm not going to hurt you, Ivy."

She grips the blankets tighter, and I finally realise that she's undressed.

The blood burns hot in my veins. Then my mouth dries, and the room spins in circles.

But as always, I get a hold of myself. I'm already on thin ice, and I need to regain her trust.

Ivy wrings the blankets with her fingers, worrying her bottom lip. Her terrified eyes don't leave me, and shame gouges deep beneath my skin again, leaving permanent marks on my soul.

I will never forget the way she looked at me, as if I were some type of monster hellbent on vanquishing her. Still, I want to help.

"Here, let me..."

As I dare a step closer, she holds the blankets higher, tensing her shoulders. But when she realises I mean no harm, she relaxes her posture, offering me her wounded arm. I assess the wound, trying my best not to touch her. It's worse than I thought.

These deadly claws of mine really are capable of so much damage. I block away the painful memories, focusing on the present. These cuts are going to scar her beautiful skin.

Well, not if I can help it. For the pain I've caused her, I will give her something in return. It's the least I can do.

I squeeze my eyes shut, and she asks quietly, "What... what are you doing?"

It doesn't take much to make me cry these days, but there are some things buried deep in my past that would make even the bravest of knights soil their armour.

Finally, a tear drips from my eye, and Ivy watches me mesmerised. "Are...you crying?"

I don't answer her. Instead, I wipe the tear from my cheek, dabbing it gently on her wound. It heals with a flash of light, and when it's over, she stares at the smooth skin of her bare shoulder, fascinated.

"It's healed. How?"

Again, those big, guileless eyes leave me spellbound. My magic depletes, and already I can feel my reserves draining.

"I...*healed* you, Ivy..." I rasp, trying to ignore the pounding behind my eyes.

She blinks. "With...your tears?"

"Yes. Fae tears have healing properties."

Her chin drops, and that's when my vision tunnels, making her my sole focus. I'm fading away, but it was worth it.

At least I can make it up to her now.

It's rare for a faerie to give so freely, but it had to be done. I took something from her, and as a result, I gave her something of my own. Magic is equal to blood for the Fae.

"Are you all right?"

My eyes droop. "I-I'm *fine*, Ivy...you...you can pull up your dress now."

Ivy gasps, remembering that she left her bodice open. She ties up the strings quickly, turning as red as a poppy, and I do the honourable thing and look away. The mounds of her breasts are far too tempting, and the last thing I want to do is unleash my beast on her. She's seen enough of my beastly side today.

When she's decent again, she pushes the blankets aside, eyeing me curiously. "Why would you heal me?"

I cock a brow. Is that a trick question?

"How do you mean?"

She shakes her head. "Normally, you're not so...*giving*... What's the catch?"

I smirk lazily. "No catch, princess. Blood for blood, or *magic* for blood. What I did was unforgivable, so it was the only way I could absolve myself."

Her eyes shine with something I can't quite decipher, and that's when I realise she's shedding tears of her own. They drip down her fair cheeks.

My eyes narrow. "What are *you* crying for?"

Ivy sniffs, and how odd—she's even prettier when she cries. She truly is a rarity.

"I'm...sorry..."

"Sorry for what?"

"For scaring the deer. I just...couldn't..."

She doesn't finish, burying her face in her hands, and I watch on, speechless. "There's no need to cry. I'm not mad at you."

"No. You have every right to be mad at me. I scared away your chance to eat this winter. How can you ever forgive me?"

It takes a moment for her words to register. When they finally do, I release a grave sigh. "Actually, I wasn't hunting that deer for *me*, Ivy. I...was hunting for you. I don't need to eat as much as a human. Winters here are harsh, and, well...food is scarce."

She looks up from her fingers, her bottom lip trembling. "You were mad because you were worried about feeding me?"

I don't know how to tell her without making her feel worse, so I keep my mouth shut.

Nice going, idiot.

Now she throws her face back into her hands, and I really don't know what to do with her. I'm clueless around crying females.

"I'm so useless. I'm never going to survive out here."

I run my fingers through my hair, right between my horns as I laugh nervously. "N-no...you're not useless. Just...*gentle*. This world needs more people like you, Ivy. It's just unfortunate that it's riddled with cold-hearted creatures like…well, *me*."

And that goes for both humans and Fae. We're as bad as each other.

But this girl is different. She's far too kind. This world will eat her alive, but that's okay. Because I will be protecting her every step of the way. I'm no chivalrous knight, but I will still uphold my duty, ensuring she's safe.

She gazes at me, bewildered, fat tears rolling down her cheeks. "You're not cold-hearted…"

The tension eases from my shoulders when she speaks those words, and I can almost believe them.

A dry chuckle escapes me. "Trust me, you've no idea of the things I've done."

She regards me peculiarly, and my heart hammers in my ears.

Then she smiles and says, "I don't care about any of that. In fact, the more time I spend with you, the more I'm starting to think that my mama was wrong about you. You're not like all the other Fae, Tegwyn."

My heart skips a beat, but I maintain my decorum, acting as if her words have no effect on me. Truth be told, they're making me nervous. It's as if she's cutting me wide open, baring my soul for all to see.

"Then what am I like?" I chortle, trying to lighten the mood.

She grins, reaching across to palm my face with her warm hand. I freeze, the breath fleeing from my lips when she circles her thumb around my cheek.

"That, I'm still trying to figure out."

A tense silence follows, the only sound my raging heart. What is this female doing to me?

Her mere touch alone is enough to make me do her bidding. Maybe I'm not as cunning as I thought.

"Well...when you're done figuring it out, Ivy, let me know. Goodnight."

I could do with some sleep. I need to replenish my magic.

As I rise, she grabs my wrist, whispering, "Thank you for healing me."

I meet her gaze. This is the part where I usually run away. But I stay put, merely accepting her thanks. "You're welcome."

Finally, she lets go of my wrist, lying down beneath the furs and blankets. "Good night, Tegwyn."

"Yeah, you...you too..."

She snorts at my lackluster response, rolling onto her side.

Once again, I vanish into the shadows, but I decide to wait until she falls asleep. Watching her sleep is rather pleasant.

When did I become so perverse?

Well, time to get some rest, myself. I'm going to need all the magic I can muster these next few weeks.

17

Ivy

I wake one morning with a cramping in my gut as I assume the foetal position.

Wonderful. My monthly bleed.

Oh, how I wish I had one of Mama's healing tonics right now. Anything to rid myself of the nausea and pain and fatigue.

I'm too tired to get up. I must drift off again because it's later when I become aware of a presence, one that wasn't there previously. His gaze burns into me.

"You're still in bed."

A shiver courses down my spine at the timbre of his voice. He always sounds as if he's singing. How a voice can be rough yet melodious still astounds me.

I groan, throwing the blankets and furs over my head. He can't see me like this. No wonder I was so weepy last night.

Worst of all, he witnessed my crying.

"Normally, you're bright-eyed and bushy-tailed by dawn. It's midmorning. Are you sick?"

I shake my head, too ashamed to look at him. "I'm fine, just...tired..."

A brush of wind at my back, and soon he's standing right above me. He tugs the furs and blankets away, and I roll onto my stomach, covering my face with my hands.

"Ivy. What in the name of Mag—?"

He pauses, inhaling deeply through his nose, and the hair rises at the back of my neck. He falls still.

Too still.

It's unnatural.

"You're *hurt*..." he growls.

I cringe at his words. This can't be happening.

"Why are you bleeding?"

My heart pounds, and then I finally find the courage to look at him. His eyes flicker like the flames of a sconce, his teeth bared in preparation of an attack.

Does he really not know?

"Has someone *hurt* you?"

I grab my pillow, using it to cover my face.

"Describe them to me, Ivy, and I will hunt them down and present you with their head."

My heart splinters at the gory description, and I rise, meeting his shuttered gaze.

At least he appears to be in better health. The moment he used his tears to heal my wound, he seemed to decline.

Still, his eyes don't glow as brightly, and his gold-green skin exhibits a sickly hue. He looks dreadful, just as he did when he touched iron.

I sigh. "Tegwyn, I'm not hurt."

His jaw ticks. "Then explain the blood."

My skin blanches when I spy the glint of a claw peeking out from his gloves, and it finally occurs to me that I have never once seen him without them on.

Is he ashamed?

Tegwyn follows my gaze, muttering a curse. Now he sheathes his claws, searching my face again.

He really is worried about me. It's heartwarming, I suppose, *sweet* even. He truly is a paradox.

"Tegwyn. No one has harmed me. I'm just..."

His brows jump to his horns. "You're *what?*"

I stare down at my hands, cheeks burning red with shame. "I...have my bleed..."

He blinks. "*Bleed?*"

"As in my *monthly* bleed. I've had them every month since I turned twelve. Well, twelve and a *half*..."

A nervous sound escapes me, and I cover my face, wishing the ground would just swallow me whole and be done with it.

It takes him a few moments, but when the realisation finally hits him, he stumbles, tripping on a stalagmite. "S-shit!"

I burst into a fit of laughter, slapping my hand over my mouth to stifle the sound. It's nervous laughter, but I just go with it, letting emotion override my senses.

He just looks so ridiculous.

"Fuck! I should... I need to..."

He makes a beeline for the exit, but I reach out for him. "No! It's okay, you... weren't supposed to know..."

Another giggle escapes me, and I just can't help myself now.

Silly, clueless faerie.

"Of... of course..." he mutters. "How could I not have realised? A human female's monthly bleed is *legendary* after all."

Legendary?

He catches the confusion in my gaze. "Erm, Fae females aren't quite so regular... Many of them don't bleed at all. Others never bear young."

His voice trails off, and I'm not used to seeing him this way. He really can be an odd creature at times.

Tegwyn runs a hand through his hair. "So...w-when it's over, you...you are...?"

I lower my gaze. "Yes."

He's talking about the possibility of my becoming pregnant once my cycle is over. It seems such an alien concept for him, but I can't meet his eyes.

Not again.

I'm afraid of what I may find inside them.

He chuckles awkwardly, backing towards the exit again. "Commendable. Truly. Well, when you're done *bleeding*, Ivy... I'll be in the kitchen."

And with a flash, he's gone.

I don't get up for some time. In the end, I throw the furs and blankets back over my head, wishing I could erase that entire conversation from my mind.

These next five days are going to be rough.

Tegwyn

I dig my claws into the wall, keeping a reasonable distance from Ivy at the other end of the tunnel.

I'm *aroused*, and every instinct in my body is telling me to run back up to her so I can fuck her brains out.

The thought of her sweet, fertile body has my mouth salivating, and my heart thumps faster and faster.

No matter what, I must resist. Even when my pounding heart drowns out all common sense, I will keep away.

Faeries fuck with wanton abandon, and I am no exception; I once bit the wing off a dryad during one particularly steamy climax, and her satisfied screams still echo in my depraved mind.

We lasted five whole days.

The Fae can go at it for a while, and we never tire.

But I cannot have those lewd thoughts about Ivy. She would never survive. I would *kill* her...

Her heady scent fires up my bloodstream, though, and I can't rid the image of her flushed cheeks from my mind.

With a snarl, I yank on my cravat, using it to dab my face.

I must get a hold of myself.

I finally make it outside, veering right where I once spied her bathing. The memory of her milky skin swivels up before me, and I don't bother removing my clothes. I slip right under the water, ridding my body of her heat and her scent. My need vanishes instantly. Thank the goddess for making mountain water so frigid.

Living with her is going to be torture, but no matter what, I must have restraint.

I know exactly what has got me so hot under the collar...There's a reason why a human woman's bleed is legendary amongst Fae.

Human females are highly fertile, and it messes with my hindbrain, giving me the ridiculous notion of filling her with my seed so she can bear my young.

Mating with humans is how the Fae sustain their numbers. It prevents us from going extinct.

Pure-blood faeries are quite the rarity these days; Rogue Fae, in particular, like to interbreed with the human race, and the aftereffects are never pretty.

For *humans*, that is.

In fact, they're catastrophic.

Hence why I seldom sleep with human females these days, and the ones I have bedded, I've had to be careful.

Half-blood faeries don't have it easy in this world, and I'll be damned if I'll have a helping hand in creating one.

My own childhood was rough enough as a pure-blood Fae.

Besides, the urge to mate was just never there. Those girls had just been a quick, easy fuck.

Ivy, on the other hand... She's something else, and I know it has something to do with why I find her scent so addictive. It's the reason why mine has hints of musk lately. I'm going into a rut.

Fae have killed humans in the throes of passion, so no matter what, I must keep away.

Besides, I'm growing rather accustomed to her presence, and it's been nice having another living, breathing creature to talk to.

So, it looks like I'll be visiting this quaint little brook for the foreseeable future.

Should be fun.

Ivy

I finally emerge from my blanket cocoon by late evening.

Tegwyn is nowhere in sight, and for a split second, my heart aches for his presence. It looks as if that faerie is starting to grow on me.

Considering how we got off to a prickly start, I find it rather heartwarming. Maybe we really can become friends one day.

There's water waiting in the pot, so I make myself a bowl of porridge, stirring the oats with the spoon until I get them the way I like them.

If only I had some berries...but that's okay; you can never go wrong with plain old porridge.

I take my seat at the splintered table, blowing into my bowl to cool it down, and once the warm porridge settles in my stomach, I exhale deeply.

The cramps have subsided. Thank the heavens; I thought they would never end.

When I blink, Tegwyn is standing at the threshold, eyes glazed and ringed with shadows.

His clothes are dripping wet, and I drop my spoon. "Tegwyn, you're soaking."

He chuckles, a strange, mirthless sound. "Am I?"

I shake my head in disbelief, coming around the table to check on him. If he's not careful, he's going to catch a cold.

"Come on, let's get you out of that coat."

As I go to help him out of his long, drenched coat, he flinches, making me pause.

"What's wrong?"

It's as if he's afraid of me touching him, and I don't understand. Was it something I said?

"I'm fine, Ivy...f-finish your porridge..."

I re-settle myself, trying to pretend that I'm not a little wounded by his reaction.

Maybe he was worried about accidentally cutting me with his claws, but I know he would sooner cut off his own fingers than hurt me again. I trust him wholly.

Tegwyn's boots squelch as he claims the other chair at the table, and not once does he look my way.

I think he's still horrified about what happened earlier.

It's understandable. He's Fae; he wouldn't know the first thing about human biology.

I know he's been with girls in the past, but they were most likely Fae like him.

Do Fae females truly not bleed as much as their human counterparts? I don't recall my mother ever telling me so.

She just warned me of their deception and trickery.

Tegwyn's coat drips in the silence, and I chew my lip, trying to think of something to say.

I peer up. "Tegwyn. Why are you wet?"

He glances in my direction, yet his eyes go straight through me. I may as well be a ghost.

"Wet?"

"Yes," I huff. "Did you go for a swim?"

Another heartless chuckle, and then he whispers, "Something like that."

My brow furrows at the strange remark. "With your *clothes* on?"

He sighs, closing his eyes. "There wasn't enough time to take them off..."

Silence stretches between us. Something is *definitely* off with him today. He's standoffish, whereas before, he was caring.

This creature, who I once considered callous, healed my wounds with his very own tears. I will never forget the kind thing that he did for me.

He acted selflessly, giving up his own magic to ensure I was healed, and my heart hiccups as I remember the sensation of his fingers on my skin. They weren't sharp or prickly, but warm and gentle.

I return to my porridge, wishing again for some berries. We have no honey or sugar in the mountain, and I shove my spoon into my mouth, trying my best to enjoy the bland taste.

That's when he drops a cloth onto the table, and there I find an assortment of round, juicy berries.

My heart flutters. He must have hand-picked them just for me. There are a few nuts in the mix, too, and a smile curves my lips when I look at him. "Thank you, Tegwyn."

The faerie doesn't meet my gaze, but I do spy a similar smile curving his mouth. "Don't mention it, princess."

Now I add the berries to my porridge, noticing that they taste much sweeter than usual. Did he pepper them with magic?

Nonetheless, I'm grateful, and maybe I will just make it through these next few days.

Finally, he speaks, his voice husky with something I can't quite decipher. "When your...*bleed* is over, Ivy...we'll head east. There's a market where you can stock up for the winter. People travel far and wide just to sell their wares there. All the berries you could eat and more..."

His voice ends on a slight growl, one that goes straight to my core, and that's when I notice the change in his scent—sharp, potent, and musky.

His claws are drawn, digging into the wood of the table, and my heart flaps like the wings of a bird.

Now his strange behaviour makes sense.

I gaze down at my berries, muscles trembling as his scent smothers me like a warm blanket.

I must get a hold of myself. He's Fae; I'm human. We would only destroy each other.

He comes back to his senses, turning my way. His scent vanishes instantly; did he use some kind of cloaking spell?

Now he tries his best at an amicable smile, and I can't help it now. I snort at his silly expression.

What on earth has come over me?

His fangs gleam in the candlelight. I really am becoming accustomed to his grin.

Once upon a time, his fangs scared me, yet now, I look forward to seeing them every morning.

"I can't wait," I reply.

His heated gaze never leaves me, and I return to my porridge, hoping he doesn't spy the colour my cheeks have turned.

Something has changed between us, and life inside the mountain really won't be the same again.

18

Ivy

FIVE DAYS LATER, I wake to a pair of glowing eyes hovering in the corner of the cave, startling me for the briefest moment.

But when I rub my eyes, letting my vision adjust, I finally make out the horned silhouette of Tegwyn watching me sleep.

Yeah. That's not unnerving at all. I roll my eyes, curling up under the blankets.

I'm so used to him by now that I can just tune him out. If he wants to watch me sleep, then so be it.

His lilting tone carries across the cave. "When you're done snoozing, Ivy, you can make a start on getting ready. We leave in thirty minutes."

I turn my head, finding his gleaming eyes in the corner again. "That depends on the time."

A smirk stretches his lips. "Way too early, I'm afraid."

With a huff, I roll onto my back, staring at the stalactites, and my eyes shut closed.

"We have a long day ahead of us, princess. So, the quicker, the better."

"But it's cold," I remark. I'm really not a morning person.

It seems I'm wearing his patience thin because I'm pretty sure his left eye twitches. "Well, tough shit. You want rations for winter, then you get out of bed."

I toss the blankets aside, swinging my legs over the bed. "Fine, I'm up. No need to bite my head off."

He makes no attempt to leave. He just waits in the corner, and I angle my head. "Do you mind? I need to dress."

The faerie regards me strangely at first. When he cottons on, he hides his eyes, moving towards the exit. "Of course. I'll be outside."

I blow a frustrated sigh.

Honestly.

Once he's out of sight, I remove my nightdress, shivering when a cool breeze wafts against my bare shoulders. It's like living on a glacier.

I slip on a simple cotton dress, tying up the bodice with shaking fingers.

He coughs for attention outside. "You *may* want to reposition your lamp. It's casting your shadow across the wall."

I turn towards the wall in question, and there I spy my lengthened shadow dancing across the ancient stone.

My exposed breasts bounce, and I cover my chest. "Tegwyn! Go! Now!"

There's no missing the smirk in his tone as he meanders down the tunnel, a laugh reverberating in his chest. "With pleasure."

I can still hear him laughing when he's halfway down the mountain, and I finish tying my bodice, cursing under my breath.

That peeping Tom. Wait till I get my hands on him.

Once I'm dressed, I march out of the cave, finding him waiting at the foot of the mountain.

He's covered in flecks of snow, gazing up at a darkened sky as he welcomes the flurries onto his face, and the sight takes my breath away.

It's so peaceful and quiet, there's barely a sound to be heard for miles—not even the fluttering of a bird's wings up in the whitened branches.

My eyes fall back on the faerie. If he thinks he's getting off that easy...

Tegwyn glances my way, a wry smile tugging his lips. "You took your time."

I grit my teeth. "Are you really going to play dumb with me?"

He tilts his horned head. "Sorry, you've lost me, princess."

My cheeks flush bright red. "You watched me undress!"

He blinks at me, nonplussed. Then he guffaws, vanishing down the slope.

Shaking my head, I stomp after him, but as soon as I lose my footing, he's there, holding his arm out. It's his olive branch, so to speak, and with a sigh, I take his arm, letting him lead me the rest of the way down the slope.

Horrid one moment, and then chivalrous the next. It's hard to keep up with him.

At least the night is beautiful. The snow reflects the full belly of the moon, brightening up the shadows of the forest. Rocks and twigs glitter with hoarfrost as Tegwyn guides me with ease, helping me around difficult patches of ice.

I have to be slowing him down, yet he continues at my languorous pace, and I can't help but soak up his delicious warmth and his rich, earthy scent of pine and woodsmoke. Maybe today won't be so bad after all.

Five hours later, we finally reach our destination—a long, winding stretch of road that bisects the sprawling forest.

A sunken road sign made from blue slate reads: "*Twenty mi to Est.*"

It's the first sign of human life I have seen in weeks, and the sight takes my breath away. How something as trivial as a road sign can leave me speechless, I'll never know, but I've become so accustomed to the wild, treacherous lands of the north these last several weeks that I forgot how simple the human world could be.

The forest is much tamer on the other side of the road. Thick blankets of moss no longer cling to the branches or trees. The canopy reveals patches of grey sky, and even the birds seem to chirp louder.

Ferns have shrunk in size, and tree roots no longer twist up from the ground to trip you on your feet. The mist has cleared, too, and now I can see further than ten feet ahead of me.

The faerie wilds truly are primitive. It's an ancient world untouched by humans—untouched by *time.*

Tegwyn shrouds his face with his hood and scarf, taking up a position behind a tall spruce. I slump on a tree stump overgrown with toadstools, grateful for the chance to rest. I even take off my right boot so I can remove a stubborn stone; it's been annoying me for miles.

"And who gave you permission to sit?"

I meet his luminous eyes. They burn brighter beneath the dark of his cowl, and I can tell by the way they narrow that he's smirking at me. Nothing new there.

"I did. I needed a rest."

He sighs, blowing the scarf on his face. "If you insist, *princess.*"

I really wish he would stop calling me that.

I'm not a princess.

A breath loosens from my own lips, unconsciously mirroring him. "So, twenty miles? Will it really take us that long to reach the market?"

The faerie snorts. "No. We'll be hitching a ride."

I look up and down the barren road. "A ride from *whom*?"

Tegwyn ignores the question, unfurling his map on the ground before me. He kneels, using rocks and twigs as paperweights. There are marker points for each town and city, and it appears this Fae likes to get around. He points his gloved finger on a small peninsula along the eastern coastline, and my heart flutters in my throat.

"This is where we're heading—the Eastern Market. Or in other words, the *lion's mane*..." He scoffs, "I don't see it, do you? This shitty kingdom looks nothing like a lion."

I barely hear his rambling as I stare at the peninsula, the one surrounded by a blue expanse.

Could it be?

After all these years, will I get to see the sea?

"You're pulling a very strange facial expression right now. What's on your mind?"

I meet his gaze, and whatever he must see in my eyes, it's enough to catch him off guard.

My vision fogs, and before my eyes betray me, I reach up, wiping away a traitorous tear. "The...sea..."

"Yes. What about it?"

I inhale a shaky breath, wondering how I tell him that my dream of seeing the ocean is about to come true. I've been dreaming of this day since I was a little girl. Ever since I first opened the pages of a book, learning how big the world truly was outside of my tiny cottage. It almost doesn't seem real, and I wish my parents were here to experience this moment with me.

Tegwyn pulls off his scarf, and a small, knowing smile curves his lips. "You've never seen the ocean before... have you?"

I lower my gaze, giving him a subtle nod. For some reason, I feel vulnerable exposing myself to him like this. But I'm starting to think that I can trust him, and he has proven himself more than enough times.

There's a good heart beating inside that chest of his.

I've spied small glimpses of his soul, and the more time I spend with him, the more I'm starting to believe that my mother may have been wrong about the Fae. Some Fae, at least.

I can't believe it's been a whole month since I last saw her. My dreams had to take a backseat for a while.

Life just became a game of survival, and hoping and praying that I would reunite with my parents again.

Since that awful night, I've forgotten how to dream, how to have hope. That sweet girl who used to love painting died the night those soldiers came. But just maybe I will get to reunite with her once again.

"My parents were going to take me to see the ocean for my birthday..."

My voice cracks, and I look away.

He doesn't speak for a while. He just continues to stare at me with an ambiguous expression.

Sometimes, I don't know what to expect when I gaze inside those glowing orbs, but right now, I'm afraid.

Will he be mocking or dismissive?

Will he laugh?

"Well...if that isn't the sweetest thing I've heard."

Surprised, I meet his eyes, and I can't help it now. A laugh escapes me. "*Sweet*? I'm shocked you know that word."

He chuckles, "Yeah, me too, but after hearing your sad little tale, I couldn't help myself. Thanks, by the way. My reputation is surely in tatters."

A louder laugh loosens from my lips, and the sound rings across the gloomy forest, brightening up the dull day.

Tegwyn watches me with those strange eyes again, and I'm pretty sure his pupils dilate.

Silence befalls us, and that's when he casts his gaze to the ground.

I sense the downward shift of his emotions, tilting my head. "Tegwyn? What's wrong?"

He heaves a sigh, unable to meet my eyes. "Unfortunately, I can't make any promises. The market is heavily patrolled."

My heart dips like a sinking ship, and the world becomes a colourless place once again. "Oh."

"The king has his men stationed at every major port. So, we must be as quick as possible. There may be no time to see the ocean. I'm sorry."

A stray tear slides down my cheek, and I brush it away.

"I just didn't want you to get your hopes up."

Another tear escapes, and I know he saw that one. His breath stutters, and he can't even bring himself to look at me.

"It's fine, I understand. If we get caught, there's no telling what will happen."

Tegwyn stows his map away, then stalks off down the road. I watch him curiously from my stump, wondering what he's up to.

When he stops to investigate a tree, running his hand up and down the bark, I roll my eyes. It seems innocent enough a gesture, but I know he's up to something nefarious.

And then when he withdraws a heavy axe from his belt, it only confirms my suspicions. "What are you doing?"

He sniggers, running a finger along the axe's sharp edge. "You'll see."

I raise a brow. "See what?"

A maddened gleam invades his eyes, and then he swings his axe, making me jump. He ploughs the tool into the trunk, sending a spray of pine needles across the forest floor, and I can't take my eyes off him. His arms are so strong, and I'm simply mesmerised by his sheer strength. There's power behind every blow of that axe, and I have to catch my breath, reaching up to wipe the sweat from my brow, as I watch him.

"Why are you cutting that tree?"

Tegwyn stops, panting for air. "Why? Did you want to say a few words first?"

I purse my lips, ignoring the jibe. "No. I was just wondering what this has to do with the market?"

He smirks, exposing his fangs. "You just wait."

With a final swing, the tree topples forward, landing across the road to form an obstacle, and I knew it—something *nefarious*.

I shake my head. "I get it. You're going to steal a carriage from an unsuspecting civilian. The tree's merely a diversion. *Classic*."

His chest is still heaving, mist pouring from his lips as he uses his scarf to dab his face. "Jumping to conclusions yet again. *Classic...*"

My eyes roll for the umpteenth time. "Now what?"

"We wait."

I throw my palm over my face.

I'm about to take part in a road heist. Mama and Papa would be so proud.

Yet I should see what he has in store first before I judge too harshly. He seemed rather wounded when I accused him of thievery. Maybe I should apologise.

But before I get my chance, he positions himself behind a tree, motioning at me to do the same. Reluctantly, I follow his example, taking up my place behind another tree.

An hour passes. Then two hours.

Snow melts around us, creating a beautiful, dripping melody of sweet notes throughout the forest. Tegwyn has his eyes closed, and it almost looks as if he's meditating.

He's in his own little world, and I wonder if the pealing notes of the forest are just as enchanting for him as they are for me.

The faerie tenses, and I jerk my head towards the road, heart slamming against my ribs.

His eyes open, and then his voice takes on a sombre tone. "They're coming."

It takes me a while to hear them, but shouts soon echo up the road, chasing the heat away from my veins. A horse whinnies, and then they round the bend, a band of seven men hauling carts filled with goods. Their merry banter reverberates through the thick, mossy trees, a strange, alien sound after spending so many weeks in the perilous wilds.

It's odd to hear human voices again after so long, and I have this disembodied sensation, like I'm floating above the trees, observing my own kind from a different perspective.

Is that how *we* sound to the Fae?

So...*listless*?

They lack cadence. Their voices bear no melodic lilt or resonance, and maybe I sound just as lifeless.

Tegwyn whispers beside me, counting down the moments before they stop by the felled tree, and *there's* a voice with cadence.

His voice seems to vibrate through the earth, and when he speaks, his words suck you in, like he's reciting you a lullaby.

The party comes to a complete halt, and all I can do is hold my breath.

Satisfied that his nefarious plan has finally come to fruition, Tegwyn glances my way, a smirk besmirching his face.

I shake my head in disappointment. He should be ashamed.

A man shouts at the back of the group. "Oi! Why've yer stopped?"

I can't bear to listen. Those poor men are about to be robbed before my very eyes.

And I am just as despicable for allowing it to happen. So, I cover my ears, waiting for it to all be over.

"There's a bloody big log on the road!"

"How're we supposed to get to the market now?"

"We're going to have to move it. Come on, lads!"

They all get off their carts, and soon an argument breaks out.

"No, you get there!"

"Don't lift it yet!"

"Ow, me toe!"

I startle when someone taps my shoulder, and that's when I gaze into the otherworldly eyes of Tegwyn, momentarily surprised by their brightness.

A vibrant ring glistens like real gold around his pupils, and maybe this was a mistake. He may be able to cover his horns and face, but those amber eyes could never pass for human.

We shouldn't do this; I don't want him to get caught.

"It's time," he says.

I close my eyes, exhaling deeply through my nose. "No. We should rethink this. Those men. They will see what you are right—"

The faerie leans closer, and now our faces are inches apart. I forget how to breathe.

Those eyes simply arrest me in place.

"Just trust me, Ivy. We won't get caught."

It must be something inside those gilded eyes, because my fingers curl around his gloved hand as he guides me to my feet, leading me to the road.

The men don't even so much as glance our way. Is he using some kind of cloaking spell to shield us? I don't sense any magic.

Tegwyn approaches a pony near the back of the party, and I've never seen a sweeter creature.

With big, shining eyes of obsidian and a dappled grey coat like pebble-stone, all I want to do is pet her.

"Why, hello there," Tegwyn croons, reaching his claws towards the frightened pony.

She pulls at her fastenings, trying to get away from the ominous faerie with the glowing eyes, and I round on him.

"Stop, you're scaring her!"

He takes me entirely by surprise, whispering sweet nothings into the frightened animal's ear. "It's okay. I mean no harm. That's a good girl..."

He brushes his knuckles down the pony's cheek, very conscious of his sharp claws, and the pony finally shuts her eyes, relaxing at his touch.

My throat closes up at the pure, wholesome sight, and he truly is captivating with the way he calmed that frightened animal.

He had the same effect on the deer in the woods. Are animals drawn to him somehow?

Tegwyn has a true gift.

Finally, he glances over his shoulder, waving me forward. "Come. She's at ease."

I look back at the men. They're still debating how to move the log.

Quickly, I join his side, offering the pony a little pat. I don't know what Fae magic he cast over her, but she undeniably trusts us now.

Tegwyn unfastens the canvas on the back of the cart with quick, deft fingers, tossing it aside once he's finished. "Get under."

There are heaps and heaps of apples, and I look his way curiously.

I genuinely thought he was going to steal the cart and the pony, but I was wrong.

I jumped to conclusions, and guilt for doing so floods my veins. "I thought you were really going to steal it. I'm so sorry, Teg—"

"Never mind that now. Inside, quickly," he hisses, peering over his shoulder.

I follow his gaze. The men have finally figured out how to lift the log, and we've run out of time. So, I duck under the canvas, wincing when the apples poke into my ribs.

Tegwyn climbs in after me, re-fastening the strings of the canvas.

"Not the most comfortable," I note.

He turns my way, eyes gleaming as bright as torches in the dim light. "You're supposed to hide under the apples."

My brows furrow. "Under?"

"Yes. The guards check every cart upon entry. If we hide, all they'll see is apples."

And so, he buries himself beneath the apples to demonstrate, leaving only his eyes exposed. They blink at me for a few moments, and I cover my mouth, resisting the urge to laugh. But then he rolls a few apples over his face and finally disappears—a true master of stealth.

I follow his example, and now apples poke me all over the place. Heavens, do they smell wonderful.

My stomach rumbles, and I just remembered that I skipped breakfast.

Tegwyn's head pops up again, and I spy that juicy red apple inside his mouth. He holds out another for me. I gaze at the offering, mouth dripping in hunger. I've never seen one so round...

He waves the apple under my nose, and I snatch it from his grip, giving in to temptation at last. "You really are a bad influence on me."

He chuckles, vanishing under the pile again, and just as I bite into the forbidden fruit, savouring its sweet juices, the cart rolls forward.

We're moving.

I just hope our gamble pays off.

19

Tegwyn

DISTANT VOICES REND THE night air, and I hold my breath.

We've been on the move for eight hours, and with every bump on the road, I curse a little bit louder. This trip would've been far easier if I could have used my glamour, but that kind of magic would only drain my reserves. Besides, I'm still making up for the loss back at the roadside. Glamouring myself and Ivy simultaneously took its toll, and it's still costing me dearly. A good night's rest should do the trick. We just have to find an inn willing to take us in. Fortunately, I know just the place.

Ivy is silent beside me. We haven't spoken since we left the roadside.

I know it's not the most dignified way to travel, but it was the only way I could smuggle us into the city without wasting magic.

We shouldn't be too far now.

The voices grow stronger, and Ivy stirs uncomfortably. I feel my way through the apples until I find the warmth of her cloak. "Not long now."

She sucks in a breath. "Okay."

The cart rolls to a stop, and my claws retract of their own accord—a reflex reaction. It's fight or flight mode now.

The canvas unfastens above us, and then light pours into the cart. The veiled face of a king's guard enters my line of vision, and I lie perfectly still, hoping Ivy has the sense to do the same.

His beetle-black armour shines before the flickering sconces on the fortification behind him, and I spy the silver-eyed crow on his breastplate.

King Corvis's seal.

If only these humans realised they were swearing fealty to a Fae of all things, they'd be beside themselves with rage.

Ivy swallows audibly on my left. I hope the guard doesn't pick up on the sound.

Luckily for us, he's human, and human beings have shit hearing. Meanwhile, I can hear every thump of his heart behind his breastplate. Ivy's heart beats like the wings of a songbird, and I focus on the sound, letting it soothe me as it has done these last few weeks.

I won't let anything happen to her. If these men spot us, then I will gladly fight in her honour.

Finally, the guard drops the canvas, and I loose a breath as he urges the driver onward. "Lift the gate!"

The knot vanishes in my chest, and I wipe the sweat from my forehead, smiling victoriously.

Our gamble paid off. We passed the inspection.

An iron portcullis screeches upward, and the cart moves once again. The light fades as we pass through a tunnel that reeks of damp, but the smell has nothing on what comes next.

Excrement.

Human excrement, to be precise. I cover my nose, bracing for the worst. The Eastern Market is the most crowded in the kingdom, and it's going to be a real challenge to remain unnoticed.

Mindless chatter reaches my ears, and I roll my eyes, wondering how these creatures became the dominant race. They absolutely have nothing of substance to say.

The cart parks along a cobblestone street, and I pick up on the sharp scent of ale. It looks like we've stopped outside a public house.

Typical.

"When I say run..." I announce, getting to my feet.

Ivy sits up beside me, eyes gleaming brightly as she nods. "Got it."

We'll have to move fast. If we're caught, the driver will report us to the guard, and I'll tear them all apart if they dare lay a hand on Ivy.

There's something I've always wanted to try. And I think it may just work. But it could be costly...

I just hope she doesn't throw up on my boots.

Well, here goes nothing, I tell myself as I grip her arm.

"Run!"

Ivy

One moment, I'm leaning on a heap of bumpy apples, and the next I'm flying through space and time.

Everything flashes by. The sky becomes the earth, and the city lights become the stars as I shut my eyes, listening to the rhythm of my own pounding heart.

Tegwyn is my only anchor in the chaos, and I hold onto him tightly, thinking I can hear the rapid beat of his heart.

Then it all stops, and I gulp as if I'm drowning, hands shaking as my head spins like a globe.

My vision warps and folds, and I don't know my left from my right, which way is up, and what way is down. Tegwyn has his arms wrapped around me, and I hadn't even noticed I'd been gripping his coat like a lifeline.

His breath tickles the shell of my ear as he chuckles lightly, holding up my entire weight. My body trembles, and I cling onto him tighter, hooking my knees around his waist to secure myself in place.

"You can let go now, Ivy. It's over. We're safe."

Safe?

"Wh-what happened? Why did the world move so fast?"

He's still sniggering down my ear when he pushes me against a hard surface, and the sensation of cool stone brings me back to earth.

"Because, princess...I rippled us away before that bumpkin could realise we were inside his cart. Look..."

I peer over his shoulder, finding the 'bumpkin' in question. He picks up a chewed apple core, pinching the stalk between his fingers as he investigates its mysterious origins, and a nervous giggle escapes me.

Of course. Now it all makes sense.

I just travelled at *Fae* speed. At least I have a name for it now.

Rippled. Tegwyn *rippled* us away to safety, and it was one of the most thrilling experiences of my life.

He studies me carefully beneath his hood. "Do you feel all right?"

I'm still laughing when I meet his gleaming eyes. "That was amazing! Can we do that again?"

His mouth parts, and I can't help myself now. It's like I'm drunk on his magic.

"You don't feel sick at all?" he continues, brows knitted in confusion. "I took a huge risk just now. I wasn't entirely sure how you'd fare."

I continue to chortle, my mind heady from his lightning speed, and I'm neither here nor there. I think I left my head back at the cart. Now I'm away with the *faeries*... Literally.

Tegwyn still holds me, and it appears he's afraid to let me go. We're tucked away safely inside a back alley where no one can see us, and it's like we're the only two souls left in the world.

Somehow, I see the world in brand new colours, and everything is so much brighter than it was before.

What has come over me?

Tegwyn tucks a gloved finger beneath my chin to investigate my eyes, and I'm still tittering like a crazy fool.

"Oh... It appears there *were* some side effects after all. Your pupils are enormous."

"As are yours. I can see myself inside them."

And I can, too.

I spy two little versions of myself inside the black holes of his yellow eyes, and they suck me in, consuming every little part of me.

He huffs and steps away, taking his glorious body heat with him. Then he grips my upper arm and drags me further into the alleyway, leaving the hustle and bustle of the thoroughfare behind us.

I can barely walk on my own feet, and I'm still giddy from moving at his Fae speed. "Where are we going?"

He exhales, creating a cloud of vapour. "To find a place for the night. There's an inn this way where they don't ask questions. It should suffice."

We soon arrive at a crooked, two-storey shack that appears to have been built into the masonry of the wall.

A scrawny black cat watches us on the front step, but unlike the pony or the doe, it doesn't gravitate to Tegwyn.

It hisses when he steps too close, but the faerie rips off his scarf, hissing right back in the same language. Alarmed, the stray scampers off once it spies his fangs, and I look after it sadly. "Poor cat."

Tegwyn tsks, "It had it coming. Now come. Let's get you inside."

He leads me into the building, and we arrive at a battered front desk. The hunchbacked man barely glances up from his deck of cards as Tegwyn checks us in. "One room, please. Two beds."

"We only got single beds, kid."

Tegwyn's eyes shift towards me, and a light blush takes over his gold-green face. "You must have something. Surely…"

"He told you there were no twin rooms left, shithead. So, take it or fuck off."

A shrill, guttural voice responds this time, and I peer over the desk, spying a small, wrinkled creature with tattered bat ears carrying his own deck of cards.

He glares at me with bulbous red eyes, and I hide behind Tegwyn.

Now I notice the underbite of the *concierge* of sorts, and to my surprise, he has tusks. Large ones.

He's Fae.

They're *both* Fae.

No wonder they don't ask questions. This place must be riddled with magic, and they want to keep it that way.

I bet the humans don't know about this adorable little shack tucked away inside this alleyway. Tegwyn pinches the bridge of his nose. Then, with a defeated sigh, he accepts the single room with the single bed, muttering to himself as he leads the way up the rickety stairs.

It looks as if we'll be sharing, and now I understand his blush because I have one of my own burning up the sides of my cheeks.

This is going to be awkward.

We arrive at our room on the second floor, and it's overrun with cockroaches.

Tegwyn chases the insects away with a flick of his magic, then passes out into a moth-eaten chair by the fireplace, shutting his eyes.

He points at the bed. "You take the bed..."

I creep towards the bed in question, finding that it's surprisingly clean when I lift away the linen sheets. They're fresh, soft, and smell like daisies. Tegwyn's magic, perhaps?

"But where will you sleep?" I ask, peering his way.

He waves his hand down at the chair he's lounging on. "On the chair, of course."

No. He should sleep comfortably. He needs a good night's rest to replenish his magic; he's used far too much already.

I shake my head. "No. You should—"

His eyes snap open, and then I meet that burning amber. "Just take the bed, Ivy."

I'm overcome with something, and I have no idea what's coming over me. I just don't like the idea of him sleeping on that stiff chair.

Well, if he insists on sleeping rough, then he should at least get a fire going.

As if reading my mind, he clicks his fingers, and then flames appear in the hearth, flickering and filling the room with heat. Unfortunately, his energy recedes further, draining the colour from his face.

I gasp, "Tegwyn, stop! I could have started the fire."

He regards me with unseeing eyes, his gaze clouded over with fatigue. "No. You sleep..."

The faerie gestures towards the bed for the umpteenth time, and I worry my lip, regarding him on that tattered chair.

It's not as if I can force him at this point, so I approach the bed, shaking my head. He really is a stubborn mule. He's determined to spend the whole night on the world's most uncomfortable chair, but truth be told... I just want him beside me. I'm a little terrified of this place. It's new and strange, and bitter cold.

As I lay on the straw-filled bed, gazing up at the rafters on the low-hanging ceiling, I wonder how I should coax him. We would just be sleeping. Nothing more.

"Tegwyn?"

"Yes?"

I shut my eyes, preparing for his imminent rejection. "Will you just get on the bed? I know you're trying to be a gentleman, but it's fine. It's big enough for the two of us."

He tenses, and I don't dare look up. I just wait for his inevitable *no*.

But then, to my surprise, the chair squeaks beneath his weight, and I stifle a smile once the mattress sinks beside me. Finally. All is right with the world.

He doesn't get under the quilts. He merely lies on his back, gazing up at the ceiling as he twirls his thumbs. It's obvious he's uncomfortable, and I'm rather surprised.

He never struck me as the *shy* type.

I bet he has been with a lot of females. That beautiful Fae with the dappled moth wings comes to mind. She seemed to be quite smitten with him. I could tell by the way she looked at him; I could tell by the way she looked at *me*. Her buttercup irises had been green with envy.

Well, at least she can sleep easier at night when she finds out that there is nothing between us. I'm not sure what Tegwyn and I are to each other, but it's not much more than casual friendship. He's my keeper, and I'm his ward. As per the terms of our contract.

"Tegwyn?"

"What?"

A smile curves my lips. "Thank you for joining me. I feel much safer now."

He snorts, rolling his eyes. "Whatever makes you happy, princess."

I peer across the bed, glancing at his horns specifically. I always wanted to know how he slept with them, but it doesn't look like he has any trouble at all. Yet, he doesn't remove his boots or his cloak, and I think I spy the glint of a bronze knife in his hands.

Heavens. Does he ever relax?

But I appreciate the gesture. The knife's not just for him, it's for both of us. He's really going above and beyond the terms of our contract.

Carefully, I reach across, placing my palm around his right cheek. His slitted pupils explode, and soon that faerie glow returns to his skin.

Thank goodness.

My gaze moves to his lips, and I'm so glad he removed that scraggly old scarf.

Tegwyn shouldn't hide his face.

Again, I'm tempted to discover what his mouth feels like. I must still be a little high from the rush earlier, but before I do something stupid, I shut my eyes, letting go of his face.

Then I turn onto my side, facing the peeling wallpaper. "Sleep tight, Tegwyn."

I don't think he ever gets any sleep. I feel his gaze throughout the night, even long after I fall asleep.

But I still sleep like a baby. Just having him close is enough.

I wake up a few hours later to the sight of Tegwyn's luminous eyes. I don't even flinch, a testament to how accustomed I've become to his presence. He really doesn't scare me anymore.

"Tegwyn, what's wrong?" I ask, a yawn splitting my lips.

He whirls towards the door, cloak sweeping in the breeze behind him. "Just come along, and no questions."

I climb out of bed, grabbing my boots. Then I drape my cloak around my shoulders, following him out of the room and down the creaky stairs.

The inn is far too silent. Even the foyer is devoid of life once we reach the ground floor.

We step out onto the cobblestone, winding through the backstreets of the city—a massive labyrinth of alleyways that seems to go on and on. A low mist hangs in the air, the chill permeating the material of my cloak.

Meanwhile, Tegwyn is undeterred by the cold, his gaze dead set on wherever we're going.

I don't dare ask. My sheer trust in him really will be the death of me.

We tread several more side streets before he comes to a stop, pointing towards a high wall.

A gasp draws from my lips. I've never seen a wall so tall. Its turrets stand proud like sentries, silhouetted against the starry night sky. The entire structure stretches for miles.

I wonder how long the stonemasons took to build this battlement.

The faerie slinks through more streets with ease. Unfortunately, I'm not so graceful, but the occupants of the wattle and daub houses are fast asleep.

Soon, we reach our destination, craning our necks as we gaze up at the wall.

My head spins. It must be at least thirty feet.

Tegwyn walks perpendicular to the wall, stopping before a tunnel that's big enough for us both to squeeze through.

A strong, putrid smell invades my nose, and I cover my face. "Ergh, what is that?"

He replies, completely unaffected by the stench. He must have one strong nose. "Brine mixed with sewage. The people of this city dump their waste into the river, so it flows out to sea. Observe." He directs his finger towards a small stream that guzzles into the trench. "The city has hundreds of these channels."

My stomach roils, and I glance away from the stream before I turn even greener than Tegwyn.

He sniggers, "Just try to keep to one side of the tunnel, and you should be fine."

He steps into the tunnel. Breathing sharply, I follow him inside, keeping my hand over my nose. The stream runs the length of the tunnel as we traipse along a small ledge, but despite the rotten smell, my heart thumps with excitement.

The sea is mere feet away, and I almost topple into the stream.

What if it doesn't live up to my expectations?

The stream falls from a grate ahead, and there I spy the open sky.

Tegwyn pauses, peering over his shoulder. A distant crashing can be heard on the other side of the grate, and my heart rate spikes. Unfortunately, the ledge doesn't go any farther.

"You won't be able to see much from here, but if you crane your neck far enough, you may just catch a glimpse."

My hopes are quashed, and now the grate reminds me of a cage. All I see is star-kissed night, and several white birds that hover like kites. Laughing gulls.

I hear them too, and I close my eyes, savouring the sound they make.

Now I peer into the murky water. It's not too deep. At best, it would reach my ankles.

Before I think too much about it, I swing my legs over the ledge, then jump.

"Ivy!" Tegwyn shouts.

But it's too late. I'm already ankle-deep in water, lifting my dress as I wade towards the grate.

All the breath leaves my body when I finally glimpse that large expanse, and it's better than I imagined. There are no words.

It's breathtaking.

The moon reflects along the surface, rippling and flowing with the waves, and when I cast my gaze further, I spy a solid line where the sky meets the sea. The horizon.

When I look at the waves below, my head swirls, and then I grip the barnacled grate tighter, pressing my face between the bars. They're as sharp as knives, roaring and crashing into the rocks below, and I gasp when a fine mist sprays my face. Some of it gets into my mouth. I taste the salt on my tongue, and a sudden laugh escapes me.

Sea spray drips down my cheeks, and I rub it into my skin, savouring the ocean chill. Tears prick my eyes.

Sure, it's not as blue as I imagined. Maybe dark indigo. It's still one of the most beautiful things I have ever seen. I could never thank Tegwyn enough for this. He gave me a wonderful gift tonight, and I will cherish it forever.

"I finally made it to the ocean, Mama...Papa."

20

Tegwyn

I DON'T GET MUCH sleep.

Ivy just looks so perfect beside me, an expression of pure bliss on her angelic face. How could I even contemplate closing my eyes?

So, I stay awake the whole night, remaining on high alert. My fingers clasp the knife tightly as I listen out for every minuscule sound, like a rat scurrying behind the walls, or the other guests of the inn checking in and out throughout the night.

In the never-ending void, my mind wanders back to the moment she caught her first glimpse of the sea. The way her eyes sparkled made my black heart thump twice as fast, and now I rest my hand against my chest, feeling the organ beating within.

Except, it beats only for *her* now... I risked everything just so she could wade through that river of shit. I've never been the self-sacrificing type, as it's not in my nature to give so freely. What is this human doing to me?

The one thing I know for certain is that I'm in big fucking trouble. My own dreams are becoming a distant memory the more time I spend with her.

Do I even still want to leave the kingdom? All I've ever wanted was to make enough money to leave this godforsaken place, but if I left... Who would take care of Ivy? She would be defenceless. The thought of leaving her alone opens up a sinking hole in my gut, and I tighten my leather grip around my knife, keeping an ear out for the slightest sound.

It's almost dawn. Gilded light pours in from the dusty, leaded windows, painting her face in a fiery glow, and the sight of her leaves me breathless.

It's best we make a move, and soon. I just don't have the heart to disturb her. The sunlight brings out the velvet texture of her rosebud lips, and I yearn to feel them pressed against my own.

How would she feel about kissing the lips of a cold-blooded monster?

I caught the way she used to stare at me when she first moved into the mountain. The girl was truly alarmed by my appearance, yet her eyes have softened lately.

She smiles at me now.

But it's all probably in my head. A woman of her grace should be with a dashing prince or a knight. Not a horned, impish faerie who looks as if he were forged in the burning flames of hell.

Her eyelashes flutter as she begins to wake, and I finally meet those starburst eyes of blue-green.

A crooked smile tugs at the corner of my lips. "Sleep well?"

She yawns, rubbing the grit from her eyes, and even of a morning, she's as precious as a newborn fawn.

"What time is it?" she asks.

"Too early..."

Ivy peers at me blearily, a small smile teasing the corners of her own lips. "How about you? Did you sleep well?"

I shrug. "Not complaining."

Her eyes widen at my response, and then her blonde eyebrows furrow. "Was it me? Was I snoring?"

A laugh spills from my throat as I rise, tucking my knife into my pocket. "Trust me, princess. It wasn't your snoring keeping me awake..."

"Then what?"

I meet the spectacular light of her eyes, deciding it's best to keep that information to myself. I'd probably just make her feel worse; she can't help being beautiful after all.

I don't need to dress, as I never took my cloak or boots off to begin with. So, I lean against the wall, waiting for her to gather her things.

Once she's finished, we head for the door, yet before we depart, I grab my scarf, wrapping it around my face. "We're going into the market today. No matter what happens, you mustn't leave my side. It can get... overwhelming..."

Her skin pales, and I hate to paint that awful expression on her face, but she needs to be forewarned. There will be a lot of people where we're heading.

"And don't be alarmed if I suddenly turn invisible. That'll just be my glamour."

Her eyes waver. "Your glamour? As in a *cloaking* spell?"

"Yes. All Fae possess the ability to glamour themselves to a certain degree. It's just harder for some of us."

"How come?"

"Rogue Fae have limited abilities. Sadly, we have to budget our magic in order to survive. As you probably witnessed last night."

I'm referring to the pitiful state I managed to get myself in. I need to be more careful. However, I would do it all again if it kept her safe.

Sorrow glimmers inside her jewel-like eyes, and she really does have a heart of gold. "That's so sad. I couldn't imagine having that kind of magic and hardly getting to use it."

I roll my eyes, tossing my hood over my head to hide my horns. "The perks of being *Rogue*... Don't worry. Not all of us are so unlucky. Fae like Lord *Valent* have unlimited magic and resources. He can glamour himself whenever he so much as desires."

Ivy flinches at the name. Maybe I shouldn't have brought up that leannán sídhe.

She's nervous as it is, and she stays close to my side when we climb down the rickety stairs and out onto the cobblestone, leaving the inn behind us forever.

Good riddance. It's an awful place.

The bed was *far* too lumpy.

We wind through endless alleyways until we make it to the main thoroughfare, and just as I anticipated: crowded. Horse-drawn carriages plague the filthy streets, and humans bump into one another, cursing and spouting insults.

I steer Ivy through the throngs, keeping my head bent low. Even with my hood, there's no hiding my glowing eyes, so it's best I don't look at anyone too directly.

I grip her arm, trying my hardest not to extend my claws in case I hurt her. Her muscles are tense beneath my fingers, and I spy the way a few men ogle her.

I resist the urge to rip out the throat of one male who looks a little too pleased to see her. I'm strangely possessive of my ward.

Shadows dance in my peripheral vision as the darkness threatens to override my senses. It's only exacerbated when we pass by the Temple of Myr—the humans' answer to a god.

There is only one God in my eyes, and that is Maghelena, the mother herself. Not the heathen whom these humans blindly revere.

Hordes of homeless people hover along the steps of the temple, hoping for some respite from their pestilence and hunger, but as always, their God doesn't heed their prayers.

We pass a mother with young children. The children are dressed in old rags, and at this time of year, they will surely freeze.

Ivy stops and stares at the small family for a moment, tears shimmering in her green eyes. It's not a sight for the faint of heart.

Even I can't stomach looking at those freezing, starving infants.

I sigh.

Just this once...

I approach the mother, dropping alms into her pot. Her eyes widen the moment she spies the coins inside.

"May Myr bless you, kind sir!"

Thank goodness for the scarf. At least then she can't see the face that I'm pulling.

"You're welcome, miss."

She continues to praise me, sending more blessings from her false god. Her smallest daughter hands me a pebble in gratitude, and I stuff it inside my coat pocket, deciding I will glamour it later. I can make it look like a gold lion or something.

We finally leave the place of worship. From the corner of my eye, Ivy stares at me, flabbergasted.

"What?" I grouse.

She shakes her head, smiling strangely. "Nothing... You just surprise me sometimes."

I'm not even going to entertain that with a response.

So I give to the poor. *Sometimes...*

When I can.

We make it to the market at last. It's located inside a gated region, and we enter with no problem.

So far, so good. No one seems to notice the Fae in their midst, and let's hope it stays that way.

Merchants occupy stalls, selling their wares to curious onlookers, and as I predicted, the lanes are crammed with bodies.

Walking at this languid, human pace is boring me to death. *Why* do people feel the need to stop right in front of you? *Irksome.*

Various accents fill the air as men from far-off places sell their exotic foods. Ivy's eyes nearly pop from her sockets as she gazes in wonder, and all these new scents and sounds must be so new for her.

I would find it sweet if not curious. Her parents kept her sheltered her entire life, and I'm still itching to know the exact details of her past. Hopefully, I will hear news from Stannog's cousin soon. That's if the big, dumb oaf bothered to pass on my message.

Ivy laughs at a swordfish in a fishmonger's stall, and I suddenly grow queasy. I was never a fan of seafood.

Too fishy.

Instead, I direct her to the fruit and vegetables, and soon we stumble upon a colourful lane of yellow, pink, green, and orange. The smile on her face says it all. "My goodness. I've never seen so much fruit."

I give her a toothy grin beneath the scarf, hoping she catches the gesture in my eyes. "See? Told you that you'd like it here."

Ivy tugs me along, and warmth seeps through my veins as she picks up fruit after fruit, laughing like an eager child, and she's just too pure for this wretched world.

Something so pure could easily be killed, and I ball my fists, piercing my palms with my claws. No matter what, I will protect her.

Ivy stops beside me, carrying a pair of mangos, and her honeysuckle scent overrides my senses.

"Are you all right?" she asks.

"Never better," I lie. "Come on. Let's get you more fruit."

I lead her down the lane, and I watch as she picks out pineapple, kiwi, and a strange pink fruit covered in spikes called *rambutan*.

In the end, we bought six bags, and she's going to be spoiled for choice this winter.

I even decided to purchase her a bag of oats since I know how much she loves her porridge, and the sweet smile she gave me sent my heart spiralling.

Now we depart for the exit, and I didn't have to use my glamour after all. The only thing I had to glamour was a handful of pebbles, which almost nearly killed me, but the merchants were none the wiser when I handed them gravel instead of gold.

All I have left is Fae gold in my pockets, so I can't take any risks. I gave the last of my human money to that starving family.

We pass by a noisy lane teeming with animals, and Ivy begs me to stay just a little longer.

So, I acquiesce, but so long as she doesn't ask to take anything home.

Monkeys howl, some with manes like a lion, and others with painted faces like court jesters.

Luminous parrots curse in human tongue, and I'm almost tempted to take one home until Ivy stops at a cage with the most unusual animal that I've ever seen, and considering I'm Fae, that's quite the feat.

I've seen plenty of weird shit in my time, but this lizard/rodent takes number one place. It's covered in scales and possesses a long, sticky tongue that looks good for slurping up insects.

"What is it?" Ivy asks.

I read the sign above the swinging cage. "A pangolin."

Ivy giggles with delight. "I never knew animals could look like this. Look!"

I follow her gaze, spying several white bear cubs locked inside another cage, and all these captive animals are making me despondent. Humans should be the ones behind bars.

My eyes find the seven-foot man standing beside the cage. He wears the thick coat of an ice-bear. I bet that pelt belonged to the mother of the cubs.

It's a cruel, brutal world we live in.

"I really wish they didn't have to be inside cages. Those poor babies deserve to be free."

Ivy sighs, and something heavy weighs upon me. She fights back tears as the bear cubs claw at the bars of their cage, and it comes to my attention then that they're calling out to *me*...

I gaze around, noticing that all the animals have focused on me now, and it must be my faerie charms at work again.

It's a blessing and a curse, I guess.

Those bears still cry for me, and they almost sound like human infants.

I sigh. Just this once...

"When I say run, Ivy."

Quickly, I lift my hand, and with a click of my fingers, every cage pops loose.

In a matter of moments, the entire market is overrun with wild animals, and Ivy looks at me, shocked. "You set them free?"

The sky spins. I think I hit my limit. No more magic. That was the final straw.

A blue and gold macaw whizzes past us, spouting, "Run!"

I think the merchants are on to me, and I owe the bird a great deal.

Gripping Ivy's hand, I ripple us away to safety, and once again she laughs like a goofy idiot when I find a nice, quiet lane. "That was amazing!"

I barely have the energy to tell her off, wiping the sweat from my brow. "It really was... I had no idea I could do magic like that."

One or two cages perhaps, but not every single cage in the lane.

Animals are still running amok because of my folly, save for a few tamarins who join my side. They surround me like I'm some kind of messiah, and one even picks the lint from my cloak.

A bonobo joins us, and the young ape has nothing but gratitude inside his shining brown eyes. Then the bear cubs arrive, and several birds and parrots. I have no idea what is happening.

It's as if they know that I was the one who helped them.

Ivy watches me with shining eyes, and I try to take how impressed she is as a good sign.

First, I give to the poor. And now I liberate caged animals. I just hope she doesn't get the wrong idea, though. I am not a good guy in any shape or form.

I'm the villain in this story... I should be inside a cage. Not these pure, innocent beasts that have done nothing wrong.

Finally, I find the strength to stand, and the animals watch sadly as I leave. Ivy takes my gloved hand, squeezing it tightly. "Thank you for helping them."

My heart beats faster when I meet the warmth in her eyes, and I guess it was worth it just to have her look at me like that.

Though it will only be a matter of time until they're all captured again or *killed*... So, I extend my magic that little further, just long enough to give them time to escape the market and find sanctuary.

Somewhere where they don't have to live inside a cage ever again.

"The market doesn't close for several hours. We can head back to the inn or try to hitch a ride out of the city. The decision's yours, Ivy. What should we do?"

She isn't listening to me. Instead, she's focused on a pair of middle-aged women at a nearby stall.

"I hear the girl's dead," one mutters.

"Maybe it's for the best," the other replies. "I hate to think about what they'd do to her if they found her. I have a daughter the same age."

The first woman sighs. "To think she survived all this time only to perish so suddenly. I'd never have dreamed. The Princess Ivora, alive after all these years..."

21

Tegwyn

Bags drop to the ground, and I whirl around instantly.

Ivy stares straight ahead, her eyes glazed and expressionless, and I wave a hand in front of her face. "Ivy?"

She blinks, vapid eyes turning my way, and her skin is as white as snow.

The hair on the back of my neck pricks on end. "What's wrong?"

Ivy's mouth moves, but no words escape. Then she shakes her head and whispers, "I-I'm fine... We...we should go."

She bends to pick up her fruit, hands trembling as she reaches her fingers out, and I study her closely. Something has spooked her, and I backtrack, trying to ascertain the source of her unease.

But the thought leaves my mind when I peer around the market. People are watching us, and I lower my hood, kneeling down to help her pick up her fruit.

Her rambutans have fallen into a muddy puddle, but we can clean them when we return to the mountain.

The shrill whinny of a horse pierces the silent air, and Ivy falls completely still. I search for the sound.

A mounted member of the king's guard strides towards us, his beetle-black armour glistening beneath the watery light of the winter sun.

It looks like he's out on patrol, maintaining order in the city, so I hang my head, trying to avoid his steely gaze. The crowd makes way for him, and I think of a shark swimming through a school of fish.

He utters no thanks to his inferiors, his stony gaze razor-focused as he looks ahead with a haughty chin, and I've never seen a viler face. Thin lips, greasy hair, hooked nose...

His mount tramples one of Ivy's rambutans, and its fleshy white pulp bursts from within.

The horse clears the path, leaving a perfect impression of its iron horseshoe in the patch of mud, and I gaze down at the squashed fruit for a while, thinking of spilled guts.

The king really has these people fooled. Truly and utterly hoodwinked. He's as Fae as I am. Well, *half* Fae...

Yet, he sits upon a throne, ruling with a bronze fist.

What would happen if they all learned the truth? Would they rebel against him?

One would think with a Fae king in power that things would be better for the magical folk who call this kingdom *home*.

But truth be told, things are worse.

We're still persecuted for merely existing. Our old kingdom turned its back on us. There's no going back to the faerielands for many of us.

The patrol finally disappears, and my gaze falls on Ivy. She remains stock still, her vacant eyes staring at something I can't quite see.

"He's gone. You can move now," I inform her.

"O-oh..."

Slowly, she rises to her feet, picking her bags up off the ground. Then she departs for the gates, and I stare at the back of her golden head, wondering what has got into her.

I don't question it further. My only concern now is getting her away from the city.

I'm not surprised when she tells me she wants to leave. We find a peach cart parked in a quiet side street, climbing into the back as we did the day previously.

Except this time, we're caught. Before I have a chance to glamour the driver, he startles us with a laugh, and that's how we find our free ride out of the city.

Again, we bypass the guards, and when they lift the portcullis, they don't bother to inspect the cart on the way out. It's much easier to leave the city than it is to get inside, but I count my blessings. My magic is just about spent after this trip; I don't think I have a single drop left inside me.

When we return, I will rest for three whole days. If only falling asleep were that simple. My nightmares always have a way of catching up with me in the end.

Randyll—the name of our gracious rider—talks non-stop about his peaches, and Ivy manages to maintain some level of decorum throughout the whole ride.

She has far more patience than I have. If that were me in the front seat, I'd have knocked him off the cart with his very own lute.

I sulk in the back with his peaches, wishing he would shut up for just one second. The only reason why I haven't knocked him out yet is because we owe him a great debt, and I *hate* owing debts.

So, the least I can do is put up with his rabbiting.

"We grow all kinds of peaches back at my father's farm. We have furry peaches, round peaches, spotted peaches, *purple* peaches..."

"Purple peaches?" Ivy asks, puzzled.

"Yes, of course. Grown on nothing but pure magic!"

I roll my eyes. I highly doubt it. Still, I grab a peach from a wooden barrel, biting into its flesh, and maybe there *is* some magic involved. Randyll grows some nice peaches.

Ivy feigns a pleasant smile. "They sound *wonderful...*"

I snort. "They sound wonderful...."

She scowls at me from over her shoulder.

To my utter horror, Randyll passes the reins to Ivy, and now he starts plucking the strings of his lute, singing a song about, you guessed it, *peaches...*

He's not just a humble peach farmer, but a bard, too, and an annoying one at that who can't hold a tune.

By nightfall, we reach the road where Ivy and I started our journey, and I almost kiss the ground for sheer joy.

Thank Maghelena, our merciful Goddess.

"Farewell, my humble hitchhikers," Randyll waves. "Maybe one day you can come to my farm and see my family's peaches for yourself."

"We highly doubt it," I say through clenched teeth, waving a hand as the lunatic drives away.

Ivy scolds me, waving her own hand. "Don't be so mean. He gave us free peaches."

And he did, too.

A whole barrel.

I sigh, reaching the edge of the faerie wilds, noticing the stark contrast with the neighbouring woods on the left side of the road. The trees are tamer there. An owl hoots on its perch, and moonlight bathes the forest in a serene white glow.

On the right side of the road—thick, oppressive silence that presses in on all sides, making you claustrophobic. Sound seldom echoes in the faerie wilds. That's because the trees are smothered in moss and vines, making it hard for light and sound to permeate. Though sometimes, you can hear the cries of little children screaming in the dead of night—human children who've been plucked away from their homes, never to be seen again.

The wilds are more like a jungle than a humble, temperate forest, and I sure hope Randyll isn't stupid enough to venture onto the Fae side of the road. He's far too tempting a snack, and if he plays that lute, even more so. Faeries *love* music.

I shove thoughts of the musical human aside as I push aside a curtain of moss. "So? He's outlived his usefulness. Now, let us return. We still have a three-hour hike ahead of us."

As I speak, a poster catches my eye. It's been nailed to the mossy bark of a conifer, and the human who tacked it there had some nerve.

Some faeries call these trees home. Some of these trees *are* faeries...

But where I expect to see my scowling, horned face gazing back from the vellum, instead, I find a flaxen-haired beauty with lips to die for. Rosebud lips, for that matter.

The blood leaches from my veins. I'd recognise that heavenly pout anywhere.

"Tegwyn? What's the matter? Why have you—?"

The breath drains from her lungs when she stops beside me, turning as still as a statue. I can't look at her, my mind spinning with a million questions.

Why is she on a wanted poster?

She's been lying to you. How can you be so blind? As if she would ever spill her deepest, darkest secrets with you, monster...

At the sound of Rosemary's cruel taunt, I tear the poster from the tree, almost ripping it from its tack. The shadows of the forest make their presence known again, curling around me like the claws of death.

My breath comes in quick bursts, and I finally find the courage to look at her. I regret it immediately. As I thought—guilty.

She *is* hiding something from me, and just when I thought we'd turned a new leaf. Ivy doesn't trust me, and it hurts more than a hot iron rod.

"Is there something you want to share, Ivy?" I ask quietly, my tone ominous.

She pales, glancing at her feet. "I... have nothing to say..."

And then she's off, braving a step into the mossy wilds.

I burn holes into the back of her head the whole way home, and the shadows don't leave my side. Not once.

One way or another, I'm going to get my answers.

No more secrets.

22

Ivy

PRINCESS IVORA.

The name still sounds so foreign.

Could it be true? Could I really be a princess?

I've always just been Ivy—well, at least to the townspeople back at Charstown. Yet my full name has and always will be Ivora.

Now it all makes sense—why my parents told me to keep my full name a secret. Maybe that's why the king sent his men to our cottage, because someone had found out my real name and reported me to the guard.

Perhaps someone saw me wearing the necklace. It's all my fault.

Now, my parents are gone because of my foolishness. Worst of all, now I'm not even sure if they were my real parents to begin with.

If they weren't my biological parents, then who were they?

I've barely slept since Tegwyn and I stumbled upon my wanted poster by the roadside, and there was no mistaking that the girl had been me.

If only I could find my parents and speak with them again. They're gone, though, and I don't even know if they're still alive.

Tegwyn has been acting stranger than usual. From the corner of my eye, I catch him staring at me, and sometimes, I wonder if I should tell him.

After all, he has been a great friend to me. He has shown me kindness these last few weeks, and I'm pretty sure I can trust him now.

But he has grown suspicious of me. Have I lost my only ally in the world?

Well, no, that's not true. I still have my Aunt Elly, wherever she may be. I could resume my search and find her again, but I can't bring myself to leave Tegwyn.

I think the faerie was lonely before I got here, but he has a habit of pushing people away.

Yet he can't fool me; I spy the hope in his eyes, no matter how small. He likes having me around, and for that reason, I must stay.

He has come a long, long way. When I first met him, he was cruel and crass. Well, he's still crass, but he's kind, too. Most of all, he's loyal and selfless; he protected me from that soul-sucking leech back at the tavern and almost paid with his life.

And he shot an arrow through the kelpie in the marsh. He has saved my life twice...no, *thrice*, including the bugbear, so I owe him a great debt.

So, the least I can do is confide in him and tell him my secrets. And I will start with my real name.

My Aunt Elly is still a stranger. I'm not even sure if she's alive.

Tegwyn is the devil I know.

Besides, leaving the mountain would be nearly impossible. I'm wanted and there are faeries left, right, and centre waiting to gobble me whole.

I suppose it's rather poetic that we're both fugitives—Tegwyn's posters used to grace the walls of Charstown, too. We're more alike than I realised, just a couple of kids running from the law...

My mind is set. I am going to tell him *everything*.

Tossing the blankets and furs aside, I get out of bed to dress, then march down the tunnel.

The kitchen is empty when I arrive, and bitter cold. The chill clings to my skin, and with a shiver, I kneel before the hearth to start a fire.

Soon, I warm my hands before the flickering flames, closing my eyes as I bask in the fire's heat.

It puts my soul at ease, and for the first time in days, I relax.

A scroll of parchment lies inside my pocket. I've read it nonstop since I left home, and the paper has become crinkled as a result. But maybe I'll find a hidden message in my mother's scrawl. She was always cryptic in that fashion.

With shaking hands, I unfurl the scroll, straining my eyes over her handwriting for the umpteenth time.

Nothing. Just her last parting words to me.

However, one phrase does capture my attention. *"You will always be our daughter..."*

Will I? I just don't know anymore. I need answers, and soon.

"Oh, Mama. There must be something you're not telling me. What should I do? What path do I take?"

I half expect her words to shuffle and rearrange themselves, yet they remain static. With a sigh, I roll up the parchment, gazing into the flames.

Suddenly, the hair rises at the back of my neck, and I have the uncanny feeling of being watched.

"What are you reading?"

Startled, I whirl around, spying that horned shadow in the corner of the cave. His eyes glow like embers, and a shudder skates down my spine when I catch that suspicious glare.

"Tegwyn," I laugh, hoping he doesn't catch the nervousness in my tone. "You gave me a fright."

He doesn't respond. He merely keeps his narrowed pupils on me, and not once does he blink.

The Fae stalks closer, shadows trailing behind him as he repeats slowly for my benefit, "I asked you a question. What. Are. You. *Reading*?"

His eyes burn brighter to punctuate his point.

Finally, I rise to my feet, retracting my decision. It's best he doesn't know after all. He's too suspicious, regarding me like I'm some kind of villain he wishes to vanquish.

Hostility drips from him like a toxin, and when a shadow curls around him like the tail of a vicious viper, it only solidifies my decision. "Nothing of importance."

His jaw ticks, and then he whispers just low enough for me to hear, "Well, it certainly looked important."

He stops before me, disturbing the flames of the hearth when he sends a cool breeze my way, but I maintain my stance.

"Well, what is it?" he enunciates again, an unnatural lilt to his voice.

I can't look away from his eyes, and soon I'm drowning in pools of sticky honey, pulling and yanking at that tacky substance until I'm completely smothered.

But I manage to rip myself free as I turn away, whispering, "I don't think it's any of your concern."

It's a small, minute gesture, but a smirk tugs at the left side of his mouth, exposing his fangs. "I have a right to know if you're hiding something from me, Ivy. It *is* my mountain."

My cheeks blaze at his words, and now I speak with more conviction. "No, you don't. Keep your nose out of my personal affairs."

He huffs a breath, shutting his eyes. Then he raises his palms, taking his shadows away with him. "You're right. No concern of mine."

Finally, he merges with the darkness, and I'm glad we could come to some agreement.

But it shouldn't be this way. We're back to being enemies.

My gaze falls on the sputtering hearth. *Should* I tell him? If I confide in him, then it may just mend the rift between us. I don't like it when we don't get along. The world seems a brighter place when we're on the same side.

But then a brush of cool wind at my neck soon has me changing my mind, and now I turn to find him at the other end of the cave, holding my scroll.

The blood roars hot through my head. "Give it back!"

Tegwyn chuckles, waving the scroll in his fingertips, and I never should have turned my back on him. "Then come and get it, *princess*."

I grind my teeth. "No. You're being a child, and I refuse to play this game. Give it back to me. *Now*."

The faerie feigns a yawn, leaning against the wall as he starts to read my mother's scrawl. "Fine. Then I'll just go ahead and read this while you simmer in silence."

Something snaps inside me, sparking through my veins like a fork of white-hot lightning, and then I spring forward, jumping onto his back before he has a chance to ripple.

Once again, I'm dragged through space and time as he moves at Fae speed, and I hold on for dear life.

He will not get away from me.

The world resumes its normal pace, and then we're back inside the cave, standing right before the crackling flames.

My vision warps and folds, and I can barely think straight, yet I seize my chance, reaching for my mother's scroll.

But before I can get my hands on him, he flips me onto my back, and soon I'm lying on the cold, hard ground, gazing up at his enraged face.

Déjà vu hits me full force. Why do I feel like we've been here before?

Back at the cottage. He's pinning my arms and legs to the floor of the kitchen as he gets the better of me, just as he does now...

He breathes down at me raggedly, and the flames of the hearth dance in his eyes. "You bitch... You fucking *bit* me!"

I did?

I thought my mouth tasted of copper.

Now I glance at his bloodied ear, and a desperate laugh escapes me. "Then you shouldn't have taken my scroll!"

I wiggle the parchment in my fingers, and his eyes widen with shock. I'm surprised myself; I don't know how I managed to sneak it from his grip.

A shadow crosses his eyes, and then he becomes a thing of nightmares, fangs bared as the darkness materialises around him, wrapping him up in its cruel tendrils. "What are you hiding?!"

"Nothing!"

Snarling, he tries to rip the scroll from my fingertips, but I hold it close to my chest, far from his prying claws. But then my heart stops when a ripping sound rends the air.

No...

One of his claws has torn right through the parchment, and I kick him away. "Get off me!"

When he doesn't budge, I kick him in the groin.

I try to salvage what's left of my scroll, but a breeze sweeps up the tunnel, blowing the fragments towards the flames. "No!"

I drop to my knees before the hearth, but it's too late. The flames engulf my mother's final words to me, and it's hopeless. Truly.

Tegwyn gets to his feet, and I round on him quickly before he has a chance to escape. "Are you happy? It's gone!"

His face is unreadable as his gaze lingers on the flames, and I have no idea what's running through his mind. But I don't care; I don't care if he's having an existential crisis or if the guilt is tearing him apart. I get off the ground, stumbling forward to grip his shirt. "Well, *say* something!"

His empty gaze finds mine, and I'm not sure what comes over me. Maybe the darkness has gouged its way inside of me, and now it's festering inside my soul, turning me as evil as he is.

"You piece of shit!"

I punch his chest with each word, but when I aim for his face, his gloved hand shoots out, seizing me by the wrist, and his claws finally make their appearance. "Don't. Do. *That...*"

I can't help it anymore. The darkness spews from my lips, and that's what he does: brings out the *darkness* in me.

"I hate you. I fucking *hate* you!"

The faerie freezes instantly. His grip tightens on my wrist, and I flinch when his claws prick me, threatening to draw blood.

Before the scream leaves my throat, he pushes me away, and I almost land on my ass. When I look up again, he's already gone.

Dropping to my knees at last, I cry out in despair. How did it come to this? One moment, we're friends, and the next, we're enemies...

I can't stay.

I have to leave.

I wake at the crack of dawn and gather the few meagre possessions I have left in the world.

When I'm finished, I depart for the tunnel, taking one last look before I leave.

This cave was mine for a while. Despite the lonely nights I spent inside its cold, grey walls, there were still some good times.

For a moment, I thought I could actually grow to love him... But not anymore. This is for the best.

I tiptoe down the tunnel as the contents of my bag jostle dangerously, and I hope he doesn't hear me somewhere. One peek inside the kitchen confirms it's empty, and with a heavy heart, I take several jars of honeyed fruits and pickled vegetables from the cupboard, then meander down the tunnel again.

Now the next thing on my mind: my necklace.

Forget our bargain. It was a load of horse crap, anyway, and I will never allow myself to be tricked so easily again.

I soon find the fissure in the wall and slip inside. I hold my lamp out before me, expecting to find him lurking in the darkness, but like the kitchen, he's nowhere in sight.

Odd.

Tegwyn never spends the whole night out of the mountain, especially in the cold of winter.

I hope he's okay.

Shaking the thoughts away, I start searching for my necklace. My eyes land on a padlocked drawer, but when I tug on the handle, it stays put.

Typical.

There must be a key somewhere.

So, I move my hands around his desk, shuffling aside various rolls of parchment and feathered quills, yet my search proves fruitless.

Losing all hope, I start rummaging through boxes, tossing aside bric-a-brac until I find a sewing kit.

If I can't find the key, then I will *make* a key. Bending several sewing needles, I get to work on the padlock, biting my lip in concentration. I don't expect to have much luck, but when the tumbler clicks, my eyes widen, and then I open the drawer.

To my great disappointment, it's annoyingly empty.

However, I get an idea and begin to knock on the bottom with my knuckles. The sound reverberates.

I should have known...

Pushing the bottom of the drawer aside, I stagger back when I finally find what's hidden beneath.

There, on a stained, yellowed parchment, lies my necklace.

The diamonds shine brightly once again, greeting me like an old friend, and I don't think twice—I stuff the necklace inside my pocket and scurry out of the cave.

It doesn't take me long to find the exit, and I soon arrive at the slope. The cold takes my breath away the instant I step outside.

Dawn peeks over the mountains, painting the snow blood red, and I'm running out of time. Bypassing the main trail, I find a lesser-used path. Loose scree clatters in my wake, and I slip several times, spreading my arms out for balance. I must be losing my mind, but if it means avoiding that faerie, so be it.

I tread carefully, trying not to make any sudden movements. Rock rattles underfoot, and every time they make a sound, I think it's *him* following me...

The ground soon levels out, the forest directly in my line of sight, and I breathe a sigh of relief.

Finally.

A hooded figure appears suddenly in my path, and I almost slip the rest of the way down.

With a face veiled in shadow, he's death forged in flesh.

I backtrack, never taking my eyes off him.

"Going somewhere?" he rasps, lifting his face into the watery light, and I finally meet those yellow eyes.

They shine no longer, and he's a mere reflection of the Fae he was.

I wet my lips with my tongue, trying to find my voice, "I...I was..."

He stalks closer, tendrils of darkness hissing in his wake, and I almost stumble on a rock. "Go on."

My heart pounds, and I shut my eyes, whispering, "I was going for a stroll."

The faerie studies me for a long time, his once flaming eyes reminding me of shards of ice. Then he bares his fangs, a low growl reverberating in his chest. "Don't *lie* to me...I know you were trying to run."

I finally find my voice, meeting his cold, lifeless eyes. "Trying? I was succeeding."

A cruel smirk taints his lips, and then he takes another torturous step closer. "And how far did you think you would get before I found you again?"

I bare my own teeth. "You talk as if I'm your prisoner... Was that what I was all along to you, Tegwyn? Your *prisoner*?"

His eyes flash, and then the shadows slink closer, waiting to consume me whole. "Give it back."

I raise my chin. "Give *what* back?"

"You know what I'm talking about."

Trees rustle in the wind, yet I stand my ground. He will never get it back. The necklace was never his.

He chuckles. "Tread carefully, Ivy... You don't want to break a bargain with a faerie."

His eyes glow in warning, but I don't care anymore. I'm not afraid.

"No. You tricked me. The necklace was never yours to take. So, move out of my way."

In one fluid motion, he grabs his longbow, the one concealed in shadow, then points his arrow at me.

A manic glint dances in his eyes as he draws the bowstring, displaying his fanged smile. "The necklace. Now. Before it gets ugly."

I don't take my eyes off him, refusing to show fear. My heart punches against my chest. How could he threaten me over a piece of jewellery? Is the necklace really worth that much to him?

I'm no idiot. I know this has nothing to do with the necklace. He's just trying to hold on to something, *anything*, because he knows that he's already lost. This necklace will be all that he has left of me once I'm gone.

I squeeze my eyes, and a tear slips down my cheek.

Fine. If it means so much to him.

I dig my hand into my pocket, throwing the necklace down at his boots. "Go on. Take it. You obviously need it more than I do."

He doesn't speak. He just lowers the arrow, keeping his penetrating gaze on me the whole time as he bends to pick up the necklace.

Tegwyn crushes the pendant inside his gloved hand once he has it in his grasp, and a maelstrom of emotions storms through his golden eyes so quickly that I barely see it...

The heartbreak.

His eyes find mine, and a cloud of white escapes my lips when his face finally cracks.

I flinch when he drops the necklace at my feet, turning his back on me forever as he heads up the mountain.

My heart shatters with every step he takes away from me.

We're done here.

I guess it really was never meant to be.

Fumbling, I grab the necklace, never looking back. There is nothing left for me here, so I run as fast as I can, my world spinning into utter chaos.

Yet through the chaos, there was still some beauty and light. I had that with him.

But now, it's over...

Stones pelt the back of my legs, but I don't stop. Even when the stones turn into rocks as big as my head, I don't hesitate.

I just run, run, run, down into the pits of despair.

A rock nearly twice my size rolls past, and I realise...far too late.

I'm caught in an avalanche.

If I could just outrun—

Someone shoves me aside, and then a thunderclap splits the mountain in two.

I roll the rest of the way down the slope, and the moment I stop, I get to my feet, finding him lifeless beside me. He's not moving.

And that wasn't the mountain cracking in two.

That was Tegwyn's horn, *shattering*...

His blood pours from the broken stump, staining the perfect snow vermilion, and a strangled cry rips free from my throat, echoing through the woods and into oblivion.

He's gone.

23

Tegwyn

The beast spread its fingers far and wide, threatening to plunge the world into total darkness, but despite how terrified he was, Tegwyn closed his eyes and drew in a deep breath.

It's just a tree. It's just a tree...

When he opened his eyes again, it wasn't a beast he found himself gazing at, but a tangle of twisted branches that stretched towards the sky, hiding its perfect blue from sight. The tree stood along the edge of his grandpa's farm, and today would be the day he finally climbed it.

After all, he was six years old now, one of the big kids, and big kids don't get scared.

So, he lifted his hands, digging his claws into the first branch. When the beast showed no sign of protest, he grabbed the next branch and then the next until he reached the top.

The sight took his breath away immediately. A gilded sea of barley swept towards the horizon, and as he breathed in through his nose, savouring the warm smells of bread and distant may blossom, he smiled.

Grandpa's barley field was loved by all in town; Tegwyn had spent many summers running barefoot through its long, yellow stalks, but now it looked even better from above. He closed his eyes, enjoying a sweet, gentle breeze that rippled across the land, making the barley undulate like a wave of pure gold.

Summer was by far his most favourite season. He loved everything about it, from the lush green grass to the sizzling heat.

Through a blurry haze on the horizon, he spied the farmhouse—the only home he'd ever known. There, he helped his grandpa out on the farm, and right now, he was learning how to milk the cows.

Tegwyn had always had a way with animals. It was as if they trusted him on some intrinsic level, knowing he meant no harm, despite his alarming appearance.

One day, he would get to assist his grandpa with the shearing of the lambs. The only thing he was dreading was the dehorning process.

Every time the farmhands pinned down a ram to burn off its horns, a sharp pain burned through Tegwyn's skull. The process looked extremely uncomfortable. As if they were stripping the young ram of his identity somehow. How could the ram hope to defend himself without his horns?

Instinctively, he reached his hand up, rubbing at a pair of fledgling nubs above his hairline.

He wasn't sure what they were or where they'd come from. Perhaps he had bumped his head too hard.

Tegwyn did receive enough beatings from the local boys in town, after all.

His eyes landed on a distant cluster of chimneys, and he gritted his teeth, wishing he could set them ablaze with his glare.

The quaint little town of Tillyfold...

How they always stared and pointed whenever Tegwyn so much as graced its muddy lanes with his presence. Mothers shielded their babes from him whenever he passed by, and old ladies spat at his boots whenever he offered to carry their bags.

The only reason why they tolerated him was because of his grandfather. His grandpa's farm was the staple of the town, and many of the townsfolk worked on his sprawling fields. But Tegwyn wished that they could just be a little nicer to him. Mother always told him to never stoop to their level and to prove them wrong. He was not a monster, but a boy with a big heart.

Still, he could happily stay up in the tree forever if it meant that he never had to see a single person in that town again. They only picked on him because he was different. Tegwyn was Fae *after all, with skin of bright green gold.*

Shouts echoed below the tree, and his heart beat faster when he recognised the voices.

It was the butcher's three sons—Duke, Earl, and Marque.

The Pigsworths were always giving him a hard time. Their father's abattoir was right next to the farm, so they passed by often.

Duke, the eldest, was eight years old and nearly twice the size of Tegwyn. He liked to throw stones at him whenever he saw him in town, yet the boy received no punishment from his mother.

In Rosemary Pigsworth's eyes, Duke was the perfect prince. All three of her boys were royalty where she was concerned. Which was why she bestowed them with such grand names.

Duke was jealous of Tegwyn because he could read and write much better than he could. As a matter of fact, Tegwyn was the best in his class at the local schoolhouse, and as a result, he had no friends.

As cumbersome as Duke was, though, he still had a girlfriend—seven-year-old Milly Shoehorn, the cobbler's daughter. She was the most beautiful girl Tegwyn had ever seen. With soft golden hair, bright sapphire eyes, and cheeks as pink and round as apples...

His insides squirmed whenever he glanced her way, and he could never quite understand the hot feeling he got under his skin whenever she walked by, smelling of nothing but sweet lilac. Tegwyn had often seen it described as love *in some of the books he read, but how could that be possible? He thought only grown-ups fell in love.*

He would never get a girl like Milly, even if he lived to be five hundred. Only the Dukes of this world got girls like Milly...

All three boys walked beneath the tree, and he held his breath. Hopefully, they would just leave and go on their way.

Tegwyn didn't want any trouble today.

"What the hell is that?" Duke exclaimed in disgust.

"Ergh, it's a worm!"

That was Marque. The middle child.

It took Tegwyn a moment to realise what they were talking about, and when it finally dawned on him, his insides turned cold.

They had found Henry... His pet caterpillar.

Henry was the larva of an Elephant Hawk moth, and Tegwyn supposed that he saw a kindred spirit in the ugly green caterpillar, hence why he saved it from a carrion crow the other day.

"Kill it! Kill it!" the boys started to chant, and Tegwyn had no choice but to be brave. He would fight, for Henry's honour.

Sliding down the tree with his claws, he landed like a cat before all three boys, and the look of pure shock on their faces almost made him caw with laughter.

No one else in town could move quite like Tegwyn, and to think he was still a kid.

How would they look at him when he was fully grown and could utilise his magic to its fullest potential?

That was the real reason why they were afraid of him. The Fae could glamour and trick humans, and many had succumbed to their twisted ways.

Yet Tegwyn wasn't like those faeries. He had never even made a bargain before...

But now, he may have to bargain for Henry's life.

Duke, with his round, scabby face, sneered when he looked at Tegwyn.

Tegwyn puffed out his chest, repeating the mantra in his head—no teeth, no claws. *He didn't want to hurt anyone.*

"Give him back, Duke," he said, looking the boy straight in his beady eyes.

Yet the boy merely smirked, holding up the jar that housed Henry. "This worm yours, lizard boy?"

Earl and Marque started doing poor impressions of lizards, sticking out their tongues, but Tegwyn ignored them, keeping his gaze on Duke. "Yes. Hand him over."

Duke sniggered, tipping the jar upside down, and now the caterpillar squirmed on the grass.

Tegwyn's heart thumped hard, yet no matter what, he would not hurt Duke or his brothers.

He would not let them incite him. It's what they wanted. To bring out the monster *in him...*

Marque and Earl seized him by the arms, making him watch, helplessly, as their elder brother crushed Henry beneath his boot.

When they finally let him go, Tegwyn dropped to the ground by the caterpillar's remains, and they circled around him, calling him cruel names.

That was the exact moment he felt it. The darkness creeping deep beneath his skin, spreading its poison far and wide.

Tegwyn narrowed his eyes, glaring up at Duke, and were those shadows *slithering out from the trees like snakes?*

Not possible...

Shadows don't move.

Nor were they sentient.

But Tegwyn could have sworn they emerged when he got mad just now.

"You bastard,"he growled, only having eyes for the bully who insisted on making his life utterly miserable. "He was my friend*!"*

Like a hot bolt of lightning, he knocked Duke off his feet, pinning him to the ground, and the boy's screams rent the air.

The sound filled Tegwyn's heart with pure, wicked joy, yet he still never used his claws. Instead, he punched Duke in the face, breaking his nose until his vision splattered red.

Before he could do any real damage, Margue and Earl dragged him away, and now all three boys kicked him to the dirt. When Duke swung his fist towards Tegwyn's face, stars sprinkled in the corners of his eyes, and something warm trickled from his nose.

Blood.

Then, when the boy pressed his knees down hard on Tegwyn's arms, prying his mouth wide open, he made him eat the last of Henry.

It just wasn't fair. Tegwyn never asked to be this way, yet they still bullied him endlessly.

One day, he would get them back.

One day...

Once they were finished with him, they left him shaking on the ground, and he curled up into a ball, wishing to die.

He deserved to be eaten by the carrion crows for failing to save Henry. The poor caterpillar had never even got to be a moth.

He would have made a beautiful moth...

"Tegwyn?"

His sensitive Fae ears picked up on the sound of a woman's voice. It was his mother calling his name. Yet he couldn't go to her. Why did she even love him? He was a monster...

Tegwyn's mother was human, like Duke and his brothers. Yet unlike the rest of the townsfolk, she loved him dearly, as well as his grandpa. But Tegwyn didn't deserve either of their love.

His mother still missed her human son. She never talked about him, but Tegwyn saw it in her eyes.

Six years ago, she'd sold her son to a travelling Fae merchant in exchange for his health.

Her son had been terribly ill, and it was said that only the magic of the faerielands could heal his ailments. The only price she had to pay was to never see or hear from her son ever again and to raise another in his stead.

Tegwyn had been that other...

He was what was known as a changeling: *a faerie child that steals the place of a human infant in their cradle. Except in these circumstances, the human mother willingly accepted the trade.*

His mother made a bargain with the Fae, and if she didn't uphold her end and raise Tegwyn until his twenty-first year, then there would be dire consequences to pay.

What if the merchant returned with her son and rescinded the contract? Would his mother swap him back without a second thought?

Would the merchant return him to the land of faerie? Would he even find a place in that elusive realm again?

Tegwyn had been raised amongst humans his whole life. He would be a pariah in the faerielands as much as he was in the human world.

Tegwyn would never belong anywhere...

Barely rustled behind him as footsteps approached, and then a gasp pierced the sweet summer air. "Tegwyn!"

Soft hands lifted him from the ground, and then her face swam into view. Beautiful red curls framed a heart-shaped face. His mother really was the epitome of grace.

By all human accounts of the Fae, they were often described as beautiful or terribly dreadful. No mere human could ever compare to either extreme.

But whoever spewed those silly rumours had obviously never met his mother. There was simply no one more beautiful...

A worried crease formed between her soulful brown eyes, and the way she looked at him simply broke his heart. He didn't deserve her love.

"Oh, Tegwyn. What happened to you?"

His lip trembled, and then he looked the other way, squeezing his eyes. "I'm s-sorry, Mother..."

She cradled him in her arms, shushing him. "It's all right, sweetheart. We won't let them get away with this."

Tegwyn hiccoughed. "They...killed Henry..."

His mother paused. "Henry? Oh, Henry... Oh... Tegwyn, my child, I'm so sorry. We will get you a new pet, I promise."

He shook his head. "But... I want Henry..."

Finally, he burst into tears, burying his face into his mother's cotton shawl.

She stroked his head, rubbing her fingers gently across his tender bumps, and he breathed in her scent. She smelled of lavender...

"Come. Let's get you cleaned up."

She lifted him in her arms, carrying him back to the farmhouse, and once there, she seated him on a stool, tending to his cuts with warm water and salt.

She needn't bother, though. Tegwyn was Fae—the wounds would heal well enough on their own, but she still tended to them regardless with the utmost care.

When she pressed a wet cloth to his forehead, he hissed in pain, stamping his feet on the stone floor of the kitchen. "It hurts!"

But then she pecked his head, ruffling his hair. "There, all better."

Tegwyn cast his eyes to the ground. "Please don't tell Grandpa I was fighting again."

Mother sighed, gripping his chin. "He will find out eventually."

He closed his eyes. "But...he'll be ashamed of me..."

"Listen to me. Your grandpa loves you very much, Tegwyn, but fighting is never the answer."

He blew a sigh, wafting her hair from her face. "I know."

She winced when she smelled his breath. "Ergh, what have you been eating?"

The memory returned in full colour, and then he could see poor Henry beneath Duke's boot again.

"They...made me eat Henry!"

His mother's jaw clenched, and then she had that look *on her face. The one she got whenever she went on a rampage through the village.*

She was always arguing with Duke's mother, and the two were constantly at odds.

"He did what *now?" she whispered, her voice dark and almost bordering on dangerous.*

Tegwyn scooted back on his stool, swallowing hard. Should he bother telling her about the next thing on his mind?

"Also...I said a bad word..."

Her eyes narrowed. "Which one?"

He gazed at his boots again. "The... the one you call another boy if his parents aren't married..."

Tegwyn tittered, hoping it would lighten the sombre mood, but his mother was furious.

She tossed the cloth into the bowl, placing her hands on her hips. "Tegwyn, you know you're not supposed to say words like that."

He grinned. "But it can also be used to describe a really awful person, like Duke! I read it in a book once..."

Tegwyn's voice trailed off when she gave him the look. *"That's no excuse."*

He dropped his head, and more tears slipped from his eyes. "I'm sorry."

She sighed, pulling the stool close. She wrapped her hands around his cheeks, wiping away his tears with her thumbs. "I forgive you. Just don't resort to name-calling again. All right?"

"All right."

Mother smiled, and there was no denying the affection she had for him now.

After all, she did promise the merchant that she would love and raise Tegwyn like her very own son, and Tegwyn could finally see that it wasn't just magic that bound her to the contract.

She truly meant it when she said, "I love you, Tegwyn."

"I love you, too, Mother."

And he did, too.

Tegwyn couldn't even remember his real parents or his family; he had never even met another faerie. He did love her with all his heart, and he didn't care what anyone said.

She would always be his mother...

"Tegwyn?"

"Yes?"

"Wake up."

"What?"

"Wake up!"

His mother shook him roughly, and then the small farmhouse kitchen shattered to pieces.

24

Tegwyn

I WAKE WITH A loud gasp, heart hammering, face sweating as I search the room. "Mother?"

She's gone. But where?

Slowly, I realise: I'm no longer in the farmhouse; I'm inside some poorly lit cave. Was it all a dream? No, it couldn't have been.

I can still smell her lavender perfume...

Something moves beside me, and I yelp, bumping my head against a low-hanging ceiling. "Fuck!"

I really hope Mother isn't here because I just said a bad word. I'll be grounded for sure.

"Shh. It's okay, it's okay..."

Warm hands grip my cheeks, and I finally lock eyes with the most beautiful woman I have ever seen. Blonde, blue-green eyes, and full, kissable lips. Maybe I died and went to heaven, because I swear I'm looking at an angel right now. Especially with the way the light surrounds her like a halo. The angel smiles, and my heart thumps twice as fast. Who is she? What happened to the farmhouse? What happened to Mother?

My eyes dart around the room again—no, *cave*—trying to find something familiar, yet my mind keeps drawing blanks. What is this cold, heartless place?

This isn't home. It's dark, eerie, and smells of shit. I want my childhood home back; I want my room with its bookshelves.

I want my jars of insects.

Most of all, I want my mother and grandfather back, but they're not here. That much I can ascertain, and I feel like I've swallowed lead. Somehow, I know—they're ancient history now.

Long gone. *Ghosts.*

Stalactites hang from the ceiling like the teeth of a great dragon, and I start gasping for breath. I've never felt quite so trapped, and a cold, clammy sweat sweeps over my skin, making me queasy. I'm about to be sick.

The blonde places a bowl before me, and I hack up my entrails, filling the cave with the most pleasant sounds.

Once I'm finished, I wipe the puke from my lips, meeting those big sea-green eyes. They have a beautiful starburst pattern, and my heart does that strange flipping motion again. It turns out that she's not an angel after all, but a human girl with the most beautiful golden hair, and for a split second, I think I'm seeing Milly Shoehorn—the cobbler's daughter.

But she isn't Milly at all, and that's when it all comes crashing back.

"I-Ivy?"

My voice is dry and hoarse from retching, but I still whisper her name, regardless. A reserved smile crosses her face, and my heart pounds for the umpteenth time.

That smile… It tips my whole world upside down. She's even more beautiful than Milly.

"It's me. H-hi…"

My heart flops heavily in my chest when I hear her voice, and then I stretch out my shaking hand, needing to touch her. She has to be real.

Ivy snatches up my hand, squeezing it tightly with her fingers, and all is right with the world again. She really is here. A lump clogs my throat, and then I find it hard to breathe.

Something awful transpired between us. I can't recall what, but I know that it has something to do with her guarded smiles.

But before I can get my chance to apologise, she's shushing me, placing a finger to my lips, and then she encourages me to lie back down.

She places a hand on my forehead, and I close my eyes, melting beneath her careful touch.

She presses a ceramic cup to my mouth, urging me to drink, and the refreshing water soothes my throat. When I've had my fill, she places the cup back at my bedside, wiping any residue from my lips.

Our faces are inches apart, yet she doesn't look me in the eye. She's too afraid, and I can't fathom why.

When my memory returns, I shut my eyes, and that's when a crushing blow more powerful than the rock that knocked me out cold steals my breath. Letting her go had been one of the biggest mistakes of my life.

Pointing that arrow at her *head* had been one of the most reckless things I have ever done, and I will never forgive myself. The memory of her terrified face will forever haunt me, and I deserve all the pain and suffering that this cruel world has to offer.

She brushes a gentle hand between my horns. "You just rest now. Everything will be okay."

My teeth dig into my bottom lip as I manage to croak, "I-Ivy, I'm...sorry..."

Her hand freezes. Finally, I brave a glance, and her dewy eyes glisten with tears. They stray down her cheeks, and I want so badly to banish them from her face. But I don't deserve to touch her again; I don't even deserve her kindness.

"Let's just focus on getting you better."

I shake my head, trying to rise from the bed, yet my body's spent. "Take whatever you need. I rescind the contract. The necklace is yours, Ivy, no conditions. You are finally free to leave."

She places her hand on my shoulder, and her small, sweet smile says it all. Ivy isn't going anywhere, and something comes over me. It fogs my mind, making my vision swirl.

She has decided to stay. Unconditionally. I really don't deserve her.

She gasps suddenly, reaching up to fix the bandage around my horn, and *hold on*. Why is my horn *bandaged?* Carefully, I lift my hand, and my arm shakes when I feel that warm, wet stump.

My horn.

It's *gone.*

Panic wraps its steel fingers around my throat, seizing my breath. It's like I've lost a limb...

For so long, my horns were a burden. They marked me as *different*, but now that I've lost one...I feel like I've lost half of myself.

My vision swivels, but then she takes my cheeks in her hands, forcing me to gaze into her eyes. "Tegwyn, look at me."

Her face undulates, and once again, she resembles a mirage. I focus on her starburst eyes, and they remind me of the blue-green of the Aurorae. Yet the Aurorae could never compare.

"Stay with me, Tegwyn. Everything will be fine, I promise."

I concentrate on her sweet honeysuckle scent, breathing her in.

"You've lost quite a lot of blood. I've tried everything to staunch the flow, from yarrow leaves, bandages, scarves, but it's taking its time to clot."

Figures.

My magic is pretty much gone. Whatever spark remains is just enough to keep me alive. I swallow, my voice thick when I ask, "Where is it?"

She releases a shuddery breath, and I turn my head. "The broken end of my horn."

Ivy shuts her eyes. "On... on the table..."

Right where I eat my breakfast.

Shudder.

She continues, her words almost incomprehensible. "I'm sorry. If only I hadn't tried to...you'd still..."

Anger simmers through my veins, and I sit upright, fixing my blazing eyes on her wilted form. "Don't you dare blame yourself. The fault is *mine,* Ivy. I was the prick."

Yet she's adamant, covering her face with her hands, and a growl slips from my throat. I won't have her taking the blame for this.

So, I wrench her hands from her face, gripping her wrists as gently as I can. "Don't ever let me hear you taking the blame again. You are guiltless, Ivy."

More tears pour down her cheeks, and I track each movement with my eyes, feeling helpless to stop them. I was never the kind to be a shoulder to cry on. The best I can do is crack a joke.

"Hey, cheer up. It might grow back..."

Ivy shakes her head. "Goat horns don't grow back."

Goat? Is she serious?

I chuckle. "Are you calling me a goat?"

Despite my poor attempts at humour, a sweet laugh still spills from her lips. "Maybe."

"Well, you did a splendid job. Thank you."

I go to tap my bandage, but she bats my hand away, and I guess that's the end of that conversation. Silence passes between us, and when she chews her lip, I raise a brow. "What is it?"

She settles those enormous eyes on me again, and they really are big. I'm convinced she has faerie blood at times, yet it's only human blood I smell pumping through her veins. Ivy is all human. Just a ridiculously beautiful one.

"Thank you. For saving my life."

And there goes my heart again, skipping its beat. Yes, I saved her life, and I would do it again and again. I'd take a thousand rocks to the head if that's what it took to keep her alive. What is this sensation I'm feeling?

Love?

Faeries rarely love, but when they do find their fated soulmate... Well, they would move entire mountains.

Sometimes in the literal sense, too.

I push the silly notion aside, watching her curiously. Her eyes are shut, as if in prayer.

"Ivy?"

She sighs. "Tegwyn? There's... something you should know."

I smile lazily, dozing off once again. "Yes?"

"I'm... I think I'm the missing princess, Ivora. The one from the poster," she finally whispers.

I take a moment to contemplate. "I know."

I mean, it was pretty obvious. The resemblance was just *too* uncanny. But am I surprised that I've been harbouring a princess this whole time? Quite frankly, I couldn't give a shit. It doesn't change a thing. She will still always be Ivy.

Her breath stutters. "You...you do?"

My shoulders shrug. "Lucky hunch. I mean...*Ivy?*"

"Yes?"

My lips stretch with a wicked smirk. "I'm Prince *Charming*...in...in disguise..."

I don't get to hear her response as sleep consumes me at last, and I'm going to be out for a while.

Still, let her mull over my words for a while. Might give her something to think about.

25

Ivy

I shiver before the hearth, bundled up in several furs.

Winters in the north are truly something else. Hoarfrost coats every rock and tree; lakes and rivers are laden with ice; and animals have disappeared for hibernation.

Even the sky has turned into a perpetual cloud of grey.

It took Tegwyn several weeks to recover, and I stayed with him the entire time.

He'd slept a lot, and I'd taken those rare moments to appreciate his exquisite features; I would run the pad of my finger around his face ever so slightly, then sweep along the bridge of his nose, then across his sculpted cheekbones, the ones limned with flecks of gold. Tegwyn is a beautiful work of art, and I want to paint him someday.

Though coarse, his skin is enticing to touch, and when I traced his Cupid bow lips, I wondered, not for the first time, what they would be like to kiss…

He hadn't been all that surprised when I confessed my identity, and he was more than happy to indulge me and tell me everything he knew about the old kingdoms.

It turns out that the sigil on my necklace belonged to the Seaworth Dynasty, and that I'm the granddaughter of the late Lord Renfred Seaworth.

There were the Roseblood and the Cadstone kingdoms, too, which are now extinct—their sigils had been a blood-stained white rose and a snow-capped mountain range, respectively. Godwyn's had been a great, fiery comet on a collision course with the planet's atmosphere. I am part Seaworth on my mother's side, and part Godwyn on my father's.

According to Tegwyn, King Mervyn Godwyn had been a cruel, merciless man. He cared far more for his own wealth and power than he did for his people. He imposed heavy taxes, took away land and food from the most vulnerable communities, and killed anyone who dared to oppose him.

The Fae were no exception.

He made life harder for Rogues, especially, permitting hunting laws up and down the country, and I think about the punters I met in that stone tavern. How miserable and wretched they had all been.

They vilified me because I was human, but after what I've learned, I'm not at all surprised.

If they had known that I was the missing princess, would they have killed me? Or worse, imprisoned and tortured me?

King Mervyn had been my father, and I felt sick to my stomach to learn that I was related to such a man. I am nothing like him, but that makes no difference in the eyes of the Fae.

They won't see it any other way, and I thank my lucky stars that Tegwyn saved me in time.

Even though he's Fae himself, he cares about me deeply, and I must thank him once again for his kindness upon his return. I have no interest in the throne whatsoever; I just want my mother and father back, which is why I vow to fight the present king.

King Corvis is no better than my birth father. In my eyes, he's just as cruel. He chased me away from my home. He took my parents, and for that injustice, he will pay. After all, isn't that why he wants me? He sent his men to the cottage to retrieve me. I am a threat to his throne, and thus, it's in his best interests to have me killed.

But it's fine. I don't mind a good fight. I will be ready for him.

With a heavy sigh, I secure the furs around my shoulders, smiling down at the necklace in my hand.

The diamonds glisten before the firelight, and I stare at the bejewelled sea serpent of the Seaworth sigil yet again, mesmerised.

This necklace had once belonged to my birth mother, Rowenda Seaworth—the daughter of Lord Renfred Seaworth.

I gaze down at her photograph, the one I found inside the music box, trying to find some similarities. I do have her eyebrows, I guess.

She may have been my mother at one time, but my real mother will always be the one I knew.

The one who raised me at Charstown. The one I lost.

I just don't understand where she and Papa fit into the story. How did I manage to escape the castle and the war between Mervyn and Corvis in the first place?

I was just a baby. None of it adds up.

Footsteps echo up the tunnel, and soon I'm greeted by the sight of Tegwyn panting and sweating. He has only just started venturing outside again, but judging by his dire state, it's obvious he isn't quite ready. The faerie is out of shape. His face shines like wax as he doubles over, clutching a stitch in his side. "*Fuuuck*. That last lag was a *bitch*..."

He leans against the wall, breaths soughing from his lips.

I'm on my feet in seconds, catching him before he falls. "Tegwyn! You're supposed to be taking it easy."

He staggers towards the table, collapsing into a chair. Then he presses his face to the splintered wood, trying to find his breath.

"Had...had to clear up all the snow outside. Otherwise, we'd be trapped."

I roll my eyes, taking the other seat. "Then let *me* do it. You just focus on getting better."

He shakes his head. "No. *I* need to do it. I... must feel useful..."

I smile, taking his gloved hand. "Tegwyn, you *are* useful. More than useful. You saved my life. I'll never forget that."

He chuckles, "Which time?"

I think for a moment, grinning wider. "*All* the times."

"You do know that you are forever in my debt now, right? As Fae custom dictates."

I blink at him, stupefied. "Oh."

He lifts his gold-green face from the table, smirking like a wicked fox. "Ha, got ya. You are *not* indebted to me, Ivy. Fae don't give so freely, yet for you, I'll make an exception."

"Well, that's a relief."

His snigger lights up the room, and then he leans his face in his hand, closing his eyes.

He goes to rub along the edges of his bandaged horn, but I bat his hand away, and he glares at me pointedly.

I wag my finger at him. "No touching."

The blood has finally clotted, so the wound is healing beautifully. He just needs to keep his grubby mitts off.

Tegwyn exhales deeply. "Yes, *Mother*..."

I purse my lips, ignoring the jibe.

"It's not the same... only having *half* a horn..." he says wistfully.

A sharp lance of pain pierces my heart when I hear his sad declaration, and I take his hand again, meeting his yellow eyes. "Even with half a horn, you still have much to offer. Don't weigh all your self-worth on the length of your horns, Tegwyn."

He scoffs. "Is that supposed to be an innuendo of some kind?"

It takes me a moment to hear what I just said. When I cotton on, I let go of his hand, glancing the other way.

My cheeks flush bright red. "No! I was just..."

He guffaws, and I look at him furiously. "Well, that's the last time I try to make you feel better."

The chair scrapes behind me as I take my leave, but he seizes my wrist, dragging me back.

"No. Don't go. You *did* make me feel better. Much better, actually. So... feel free to discuss the length of my *horns* any time..."

He almost purrs the last, and my cheeks burn hotter as the sound vibrates through my spine, settling deep in my core.

I blow out a breath to cool myself down. "L-let go..."

The faerie continues to tease me. "Did you know that in some ancient Fae lore, horn length is tantamount with virility and power?"

Sweat beads on my temple, and the air in the room grows thick with tension. It's hard to breathe. I must leave. Quickly. It's *smothering* in this cave.

I wet my lips, and his eyes track the movement of my tongue. His pupils dilate, and it looks like the predator has found its prey.

"Tegwyn, let me go or... or I'll..."

He makes that seductive purring sound again, and the heat pools between my legs. "Or you will what?" he whispers, voice dark and bordering on dangerous.

I don't respond. Instead, I shove him away, spinning towards the exit.

But before I reach the arch of the cave, he's upon me, pinning me against the cold, hard ground. His amber eyes dance in the firelight, fangs bared with a wicked smile as one of his hands cradles my head, the other pinning my arms in place.

Then he lowers his face until we're inches from a kiss. "Or you will what?" he breathes against my lips, and I don't speak, don't think.

He's so close; I can see the golden flecks of his eyes, and they gleam with pure magic.

So much raw power in that single gaze alone.

My breasts pebble beneath the silk of my bodice when he rubs his pine scent along my cheek, and then his gaze drifts towards my heaving chest.

A vulpine smirk curves his lips. He knows *exactly* what he's doing to me. His eyes fall back on mine again, and I stare at a smaller version of myself inside the black of his pupils.

"Well, I'm waiting," he taunts.

I close my eyes, heart thumping beneath my chest, and it looks as if he's left me tongue-tied. I don't want my voice to betray me. Only heaven knows what sounds will come out of my traitorous mouth.

He's far too tempting.

Tegwyn chuckles. "Just as I thought. You can never win a fight against me, *princess...*"

My eyelids snap open. "Don't call me princess!"

He sniggers softly, studying my face. His gaze melts, and then his eyes turn into pools of liquid gold, drowning me in endless eternity, and now I've forgotten my own name.

Why does he have to be so frightfully beautiful? It's not fair.

We both startle once a humming blue light hovers into the cave, and I glance at Tegwyn curiously.

He mutters a curse, jumping to his feet, and I join his side, smoothing down my skirt.

"What is it?" I ask.

"Mail," he growls, glancing at the blue light irritably.

My brow furrows. "You get mail?"

He tosses me a pointed look, righting up the chair that he knocked over before tackling me to the ground. I didn't mean to offend.

The glowing orb lands on the table, and when I blink, I spy the silhouette of a minute woman imprinted on the back of my eyelids.

It's a faerie. The smallest I've seen. She has large, beady eyes like a dormouse, pointed ears, and a pair of papery wings that glisten like morning dew. Her skin is a gleaming blue, and she wears no clothes or garments that I can see.

When the small faerie catches me staring, she bares her tiny fangs, which look as sharp as sewing needles.

Tegwyn slams his hands down hard onto the table, and she loses her balance, tumbling onto her side.

I go to reprimand him for his carelessness, but he shows his teeth, never taking his incensed eyes off the smaller faerie.

"I told that big oaf not to send mail to my home address!"

That's when I spy the gilded envelope inside his hand. I didn't even see her carrying it into the cave.

Tegwyn's eyes shift in my direction, and a wide, toothy grin spreads across his face. "Could you give us a moment, please?"

I peer back and forth between the two faeries, and the little one taps her foot, clad in silken pumps—like little doll shoes—on the table, her arms crossed as she regards me impatiently.

She'd look rather sweet if she didn't look as if she wanted to stab me in the eye.

Holding up my palms, I move away so Tegwyn can converse with our visitor. He leans over the table, swallowing her up with his menacing shadow, yet the smaller faerie hardly looks perturbed. "Well, *explain.*"

She emotes animatedly with her arms, telling him her side of the story, but I don't hear a single word.

Tegwyn, however, seems to understand her every syllable, and then he sighs, palming his face.

"Tonight? Are you sure? You weren't particularly very clear on that account."

She nods her affirmative, and Tegwyn rubs his temples, groaning loudly. "Great! I'll start getting ready."

Silence drifts across the room once the pair finally stops. The smaller faerie taps her silken pump again, and Tegwyn rolls his eyes, hand vanishing into his coat pocket. "For your services."

He passes her a golden coin bigger than her whole body, and she takes it in both of her hands, examining it carefully. Then it disappears, and I blink. Where did it go?

She flitters her wings, hovering several feet in the air. He swats her away. "Now get. It's bad enough I let you *live* here…"

She blows her long tongue, drifting higher and higher until she reaches the stalactites. Then, with one final sweep of the cave, she vanishes down the tunnel, leaving me speechless. I turn to Tegwyn, and he sighs when he catches the question in my eyes. "Ask away."

I shake my head, still a little baffled. "Where do I even start?" He gives me a scathing look, so I start the first thing on my mind. "Faeries can *be* that small?"

Tegwyn narrows his eyes, and he knows exactly where my mind has gone.

Faeries are often described as minute in human folklore, but that couldn't be farther from the truth. In actuality, they come in a myriad of shapes and sizes.

"Yes, they can. That was a *wisp*. Nasty little blighters. There were several back at Stannog's tavern, floating about the rafters, but to you, they probably just resembled glowing orbs." I don't recall seeing them, but I was a little preoccupied with the bigger faeries.

However, I think I remember several wisps dancing around my head when I'd been under the influence of that Fae wine, but the memory is vague.

He smiles tightly when he spies my expression, and he must be remembering that night, too. "That one is named Thicket. She frequents my study from time to time, pulling tricks on me now and then."

"She has been here this whole time?"

Of course. Now it makes sense.

That first day in the mountain, back when I got lost and wound up in Tegwyn's study, someone had braided my hair. Could that have been Thicket?

Goosebumps prick up and down my arms. I thought it had been a ghost, which I guess wasn't all that far from the truth. Ghosts and faeries aren't unalike in that regard; I've seen both, and I can confirm that they're equally terrifying.

Tegwyn answers my question. "Yes. I paid her once to post a letter for me, and she hasn't left since. So, I let her stick around out of habit. She must be lonely if she can even stomach living with me. I don't think she talks to the other wisps."

How sad. Even though she threatened me with her tiny, pointed teeth, my heart goes out to poor Thicket.

Despite her rough edges, she still seemed rather sweet. And she braided my hair, after all.

I gesture to the envelope in his hand, noticing the wax seal. He stuffs it inside his pocket, staring nervously after the wisp.

"Is something the matter?"

Once again, an unnatural smile spreads across his face, displaying his fangs. "The... the matter?"

He keeps stealing nervous glances at the tunnel. He really can't tell a lie at all. Fae normally skirt around the truth by using impressive wordplay, but this one just stammers.

"Yes. Tegwyn, are you keeping something from me?"

He laughs, one long, ringing sound. Then he stumbles, fumbling his words. "I'm... er... I just need to... *fuck...*"

He curses, and he can't even look at me now.

I move closer. "I thought we promised to be truthful with one another from now on. No more secrets."

Shame flickers inside his golden eyes, and he sighs. "It's just a letter from an old acquaintance. Truly. Nothing nefarious."

I cross my arms, resembling little Thicket as I tap my foot against the floor.

Tegwyn steps towards the exit. "I'm going out for a while."

"When will you be back?" I enquire.

"In a couple of hours. Expect me back by nightfall."

And then he whisks away like leaves on the wind. I wait only a few moments before I grab my cloak and follow him down the tunnel and out into the blistering cold.

No more secrets.

26

Ivy

I FOLLOW TEGWYN'S FRESH tracks through the snow, treading carefully so as not to make a sound. Eventually, I come upon a clearing as I hide behind the bushy boughs of a tall spruce.

Tegwyn stands before a pair of ancient trees at the edge of the clearing. They have twisted, spiralling trunks and branches that seem to stretch like arms, and I can't tear my eyes away. I've never seen a more peculiar-looking set of trees. They seem *alive* somehow, covered in gnarls and clumps of green moss. There's definitely something *other* about them. Most trees are living in a sense, but these ones appear to be sleeping. One bears the face of an old, bearded man, and a shiver skitters down my spine.

The faerie whispers something unintelligible, and his breath fogs the cold air.

One of the trees awakens, opening a large pair of obsidian eyes, and I cover my mouth before a sound escapes.

The tree. It's Fae.

It assesses Tegwyn carefully with bottomless eyes, then extends its limbs, intertwining with those of the neighbouring tree once it deems him worthy. The branches twist and creak with the sound of snapping wood, sprouting flowers and vines along the way, and soon a gateway to another world appears. Tegwyn steps through the gate, and

I seize my chance. I spring forward, darting through the tree's branches before it can stop me, and I land on the other side with a thump.

Sharp stone grazes the heels of my palms. The ground is no longer blanketed in snow. Now it's paved with cobblestone.

I look up from beneath my hood to find myself inside a narrow alleyway with sandstone walls. Tall buildings surround me.

I'm no longer in the forest.

A cacophony of strange voices trickles my way, and I gaze at a street up ahead, spying scores of Fae of various shapes and sizes.

Quickly, I clamber to my feet, keeping to the shadows. Snow dusts my cloak, and I wipe it off, hoping none of those faeries notice the sudden chill. Somehow, I have brought winter to this quiet street, and I must be vigilant.

With a deep breath, I lower my hood, braving a step into the busy thoroughfare. I have to duck around a lumbering troll as it stomps by, nearly crushing me to death.

The Fae here aren't all so terrifying, though. Some are beautiful and slender with delicate, pointed features and flowing manes of hair. Others have wings, and several possess claws and hooves, and I spy one or two faeries that have horns like Tegwyn. Wisps hum in the air, resembling snow eddies as they flutter beneath the warm light of a lantern, one lit with pure magic. I really have entered a whole new realm.

I'm going to stick out like a sore thumb.

Luckily, no one pays me any heed as they fuss with garlands and streamers. A pair of graceful, lithe women hang red and green bunting across the street, attaching it to the chocolate box houses on either side with glowing orbs of magic.

There's a trestle table in the centre of the street filled with food, and to my relief, none of the meat appears to be human. It's mostly chicken, beef, and pork, so I'm safe, for now.

The Fae don't just like their meat; they have bowls of fruit and grains, too. Are those candied almonds?

My mouth waters, but I know better than to eat faerie food, and I walk on by.

Some of the revelers wear fancy bells and wreaths of holly, and I spot several poinsettias on the table. Of course. I thought the red and green bunting looked familiar...

They're celebrating Yule. Who would've thought that the Fae celebrated the festive season, too? It appears our races have more in common than I realised.

This will be the first holiday season without my parents, and I shut my eyes, keeping the morose thoughts at bay. I mustn't let my emotions get the better of me.

These creatures thrive off misery, yet when I gaze around the merry street, I only see happy, festive faces.

The punters at Stannog's tavern were desolate souls who could only just about tolerate each other, yet the Fae here appreciate one another, and it's easy to see the community spirit. This village is different. It's full of hope and the promise of new beginnings.

A gaggle of children rushes by, and I stare in awe. Who knew that faerie children could be so adorable?

The adults dote on them, and one troll ruffles the head of a little horned girl with shimmering eyes.

A choir sings on a street corner, and they sound like angels.

I glance ahead and spy Tegwyn vanishing into a crowd of revelers. I quicken my pace, taking note of the various storefronts on either side of the street. Bakeries, jewellers, arts and crafts. If I had the time, I would've gone inside the latter.

But the store at the end of the road really catches my attention. Tegwyn stops outside a teal shop with bright gold lettering that reads: Bannog's Whimsical Wig and Dress Store—a fancy-dress shop.

What need would Tegwyn have for fancy dress?

He grips the brass handle of the cerulean door, peering up and down the street before he slips inside. I approach quietly, spying my pale and *very* human reflection inside the glass window of the shop. There are mannequins inside the window display. One is dressed as a farmer and the other as a blacksmith. The third is a dentist.

I shield my eyes with my hands, trying to peer through the glass, but I only end up fogging it up.

My gaze lands on a narrow alleyway beside the shop, so I slip through the tight space, spying an open window ahead.

I find and stand on a crate outside the window, peering into the back of the shop. It's a simple lounge with a crackling fireplace, soft furnishings, and a fancy throw rug. The wallpaper bears a pretty floral design. What manner of creature resides here?

Tegwyn sits on a red velvet chair before the fireplace, facing a much larger seat, but I can't see who's sitting on there. Tegwyn's still wearing his hood, and he looks so unsure of himself, gazing around the ornate room.

It's a far cry from his cave. That's for sure.

"Biscuit?" a gruff, yet very gentle, voice offers.

Tegwyn declines. "No. I'm not hungry."

"But I insist. They're to *die* for. My mother's old recipe." The host tries to tempt him with a biscuit again, and I see a large, well-groomed hand.

My stomach rumbles at the sight of those chocolate-drizzled biscuits, but I steel my thoughts, telling myself that they're faerie sweets and that they're *bad* for me.

Tegwyn sighs. "If I must." He grabs a biscuit from the pretty porcelain plate, and I muffle a laugh when he melts at the first bite.

Seems he has a sweet tooth.

"Your mother was a genius," he whispers, taking another bite.

His host gushes, and a sipping sound follows. "Oh, you old charmer..."

Tegwyn balances a teacup and saucer on his knee, drumming his fingers nervously against the blue and white porcelain. I never thought I would see him drink *tea*. Judging by the aromatic flavour drifting from the pot with the knitted tea cosy on the table between them, it's chamomile.

"So, my *delightful* cousin tells me that you're after a glamour," the host drawls, and I lean in closer. A *glamour*?

Tegwyn rubs the back of his neck, tittering nervously. "You got me, but...that's not the sole reason I'm here. You mentioned in your letter about...you know..."

"Ah, yes." The host sighs, placing his cup and saucer onto the table. "I'm afraid it's not good news..."

Tegwyn stiffens, and then his eyes shine beneath the lights of the chandelier. My gut wrenches at the sight of that broken expression. I once thought him cold and unfeeling, but that couldn't be farther from the truth. Tegwyn has the biggest heart of anyone I know, and that goes for Fae and humankind.

He licks his bottom lip, clearing his throat. "What...what happened?"

The host's words are lost to me when percussion music starts playing on the street, and I look down the alley curiously. A band has set up their instruments, and their drumbeats thrum through my veins, urging me to dance. My hips are already swaying to the thumping rhythm as I make my way to the street. Tegwyn isn't going anywhere; I can return to him later.

Just after one dance...

Dancers crowd the street, completely inebriated with honeyed wine, and several are naked. Fair enough. If I had the silvery, gleaming skin of a goddess, too, then I wouldn't want to be concealed by my clothes, either.

Yet, I start to find my own clothes awfully constricting, and I'm sweating beneath my heavy cloak.

Why hide? Especially as the music pulses through me like a heartbeat, turning my thoughts wanton.

I stop myself in time, gasping for air, and to my relief, no one pays me attention. Everyone is having too much of a good time to notice the human in their midst.

It looks as if they're celebrating the unveiling of a statue, and I creep closer, forgetting all about the music and the dancers. I only want to see the sculpture now. The statue is made of shining onyx, and at first, it resembles a cloaked human male with shoulder-length hair.

I can't stop looking at his face. A slightly hooked but very human nose, but his ears are pointed, and his eyes...they shine like quicksilver.

I know *those* eyes...

Staring at me from the branch of a skeletal tree, assessing whether I am worthy enough to kill. That hadn't been an ordinary raven. Not with eyes that silver.

No. That ominous black bird had been *Fae*, and not just any Fae, too, but my mortal enemy. King Corvis regards me with the same cutting gaze, and I clench my fists, grinding my teeth. It all makes sense. Why he is so abhorrent.

King Corvis is *Fae*.

But it makes no difference to me. He is still going to die at my hand one day. And my first act of revenge? To ruin his facsimile and the festivities of the creatures who revere him.

He's a monster.

They all are.

But before I take another step towards the statue, a large, calloused hand wraps around my mouth, and then I'm dragged away into the crowd.

I never take my gaze off the statue. His eyes gleam back at me, and I send him a silent promise.

I am going to kill you one day...

27

Tegwyn

"I'm so sorry..."

I tear my eyes away from the flickering fireplace, gazing at the occupant of the mammoth-sized chair opposite me.

Bannog. Such a far cry from his surly, foul-mouthed cousin, Stannog. He truly is more than meets the eye.

Enviable culinary skills, elegant dress sense, and a cultivated manner—it's as if the ogre is telling the world that he's more than a monster. That he isn't as brutish as his kind are often believed to be, and it resonates with something deep inside me.

I can relate. The world thinks that I'm some kind of monster, too—we have that in common. Except Bannog has far more manners, and that's where our similarities end.

A heavy breath escapes me. I hadn't realised how much air I'd been holding in. I massage my temples, hoping it might knock the sense back into me. I even unsheathe my claws to help with blood flow—anything to channel my thoughts in another direction. How am I going to tell her?

"Were these people dear to you?"

I regard the dressmaker on his wingback chair, the one with the rolled-up arms and the upholstered seat of red velvet, and I don't even know where to begin.

"No," I reply, "but they were to a friend of mine."

The ogre nods his head knowingly, and his powdered wig moves with the action. "Ah, of course. The human girl you brought to the tavern. Stannog may have mentioned her."

He gives a clandestine sip of his porcelain cup, and I rise to my feet, slamming my hands down onto the table.

A growl vibrates in my chest. "What did he tell you?"

Bannog sighs, moving his fancy tea set *away* from me. "Not much, really. Only that he was so *appalled* that you would dare bring a "filthy dung girl" to his oh, so clean tavern. His words."

My left eye twitches, and then my claws slip from my gloves, creating gouges on his polished table.

"Careful. That is mahogany."

I shake my head, then retake my seat, trying to calm my erratic heart. It won't stop pounding, and I rack my brains for every manner of Fae that Stannog could have talked to about Ivy, kicking myself for my carelessness.

I never should have taken her to his shitty tavern. There's a price on her head. An *expensive* price, and I am such an idiot for trusting him.

Now all kinds of *ilk* will want to get their hands on Ivy.

"Don't fret. Your secret is safe with me. I haven't told a single soul, and I don't plan to." Bannog winks, grabbing the pot again as he goes to fill another cup of tea. "Tea?" he asks when he notices my staring.

I roll my eyes. "Fine. So long as you tell me what else you know. What has Stannog told you, exactly, about that night in question?"

The ogre's eyes flash as he twirls his teaspoon clockwise. "Ooh, do I smell a *bargain*?"

I tighten my lips, making a mental note to be more careful with my choice of words in the future.

I just made an unintentional bargain over a sip of fucking chamomile *tea* of all things. I'm such a dullard.

What more could he want from me? I've already given him my body weight in gold for one of his glamours.

That's when my charming host chuckles, waving his hand in dismissal. "It's okay. I don't require much. Only that you promise not to lose your temper."

I give him a withering look as he finally hands me my cup of tea. He really knows how to get under one's skin, doesn't he? Yet it's a reasonable enough request, so I acquiesce. "All right. What *else* did he tell you?"

The ogre lounges in his wingback chair, choosing his next words wisely. "Well, according to Stannog's *apt* descriptions, she's the exact image of the missing princess."

Another growl escapes me, and Bannog lifts his teapot away. "What did I tell you? No losing your temper."

Breathing steadily through my nose, I curb my temper long enough to take another leisurely sip of tea. It tastes like ash in my mouth.

When I'm finished, I place the cup onto the table with its saucer, speaking through clenched teeth. "So...what *else* did he have to say about her?"

There were plenty of eyewitnesses in that tavern that night. If not Stannog, then someone else could have easily reported her to the royal guard.

If I ever find them, I'll kill them.

Bannog exhales, placing his cup onto the table next to mine. "Look, Tegwyn... May I call you Tegwyn?"

I snort, "It beats *dung*..."

Bannog chuckles. "I know we're strangers, and although you have what could be described as a *strained* relationship with my cousin, he does care about you. In his roguish, offbeat way. I believe you've known him since you were a boy, right?"

"Yeah, that's right."

I first met Stannog after I left the farm. I'd needed somewhere to stay, and he had offered me a place in his basement.

For a *price*, of course.

In order to earn my keep, I had to work behind his bar every night and serve his dirty punters. The entire time, he had told me that I reeked of dung and that I needed a bath.

I was raised by humans, so it went without saying, but I suppose Bannog's right—Stannog is like the uncle I never asked for.

"He had me pumping taps, but he wouldn't let me have a single drop of ale until I came of age. I had to 'earn it' first."

Bannog smiles. "See, he does care about you. I know he's foul, and his *language*..." The ogre *tsks*. "I know he's my cousin, but we're more like brothers at times. So, any friend of Stan's is a friend of mine. It's clear you care for this girl, so you have my word."

I stammer at his comment. "Who said anything about caring? She's just a friend."

Bannog rolls his eyes. "If you say so. Look, I get it, you're young, so you have yet to recognise love when it's sitting right in front of you, but nothing good ever came from denying your feelings."

Now he's just messing with me, and it's time I cut this meeting short. I got what I came for, and I've had quite enough tea, thank you.

"It's time I headed home," I announce, getting to my feet. "Thank you for the tea."

Bannog stifles a snort as I aim for the door, and I glare at him suspiciously. "What's so funny?"

He shakes his head. "You just wait. Those feelings will come crashing out of nowhere one day, and you won't even suspect a thing."

Snapping my teeth, I adjust my hood over my shattered horn, the one I sacrificed so Ivy could live another day. I took a killing blow for her, but that doesn't prove anything. I'm wicked. Nothing more, nothing less.

The sound of cheering pours in from the window, and I glance at Bannog. He shrugs. "Celebrations for the Winter Solstice. They're a little rowdier than previous years."

How could I forget? Not that I ever cared for the holiday season. Just another insignificant day of the year.

Bannog leans closer. "I heard they're erecting a statue in honour of His Majesty's birthday."

That's right. He was born on the winter solstice. Not that I give a shit.

Bannog gazes down at his tea, a solemn expression on his face. "They're cheering extra loudly because they believe that he killed your friend, finishing off King Godwyn's bloodline for good."

I grit my teeth, slamming my claws down onto the table yet again. Luckily, Bannog rescues his teapot in time.

"If it's *blood* they want, then I'll give them plenty..."

The ogre shudders. "So violent, but there's no need. So long as you keep her safe, then we have nothing to worry about."

I have the sudden urge to return to the mountain, just so I can gaze into those wonderful starburst eyes again and confirm she's safe. But I push those feelings aside, gazing at Bannog to continue.

"There are those amongst us who haven't forgotten that she's also part Seaworth. Lord Renfred Seaworth was kind to the Fae."

I sigh. "Yeah, well, it's too bad he's dead."

The ogre raises a brow. "*Is* he?"

I narrow my eyes. "What are you getting at?"

Bannog takes another sip of tea. "If the rumours are true, then Seaworth is very much alive. He could take care of her."

My heart sinks at the idea of handing Ivy over to another, but I check my emotions, swallowing a lump.

"She is not safe here anymore. It would be for the best, Tegwyn."

He's right, but I can't bear the thought of letting her go. I suppose I could always return to my old plan. I may have a glamour in the works courtesy of Bannog now, yet would I still be willing to leave the kingdom? Find a place where I could spend the rest of my miserable life alone?

I'm not sure if I even still want that. When I think of my castle ruin now, all I see is Ivy. She has taken the place of my dreams...

"Well, I suppose I will be in touch," I finally announce, heading for the door. It's time to return home. The idea of seeing Ivy all bundled up before the hearth has me heating up with excitement.

He smiles. "It has been my pleasure, and please, do send that delightful *wisp* again."

Delightful? I think he means *insufferable*.

"I'll bear it in mind."

I'm already at the door when he decides to speak again, "The choice is yours, Tegwyn, but do heed my advice. She is not safe."

I stop, bowing my head. Soon, I am going to have to make a difficult choice. But for now, I will indulge in Ivy's company for just a little longer. That human is *mine,* and if anyone says otherwise, then I'll tear them apart.

The front door of Bannog's shop crashes open, and I reel back, unsheathing my claws. Bannog gets to his feet.

"Bannog! Where the bloody hell are ye?"

We both flinch at Stannog's grating tone, and I turn to Bannog. I didn't know he was even coming today.

The ogre sighs regrettably. "Well, well, if it isn't my lovely cousin. I wasn't expecting him till midnight. We were going to deck the tree in boughs of holly..."

That's when I spy the fir tree bejewelled with various trinkets in the corner of his lounge. It's best I leave. I'm not too fond of Yule. I abandoned all that pure, childhood wonder the day I left the farm.

"Does he know how to knock?" I gripe, slipping my claws back inside my gloves. I'm pretty sure Bannog's front door is destroyed now.

"Stannog? *Knock*?" Bannog guffaws at the preposterous thought, then proceeds to make another pot of tea.

Stannog stomps towards the lounge like a rampaging giant, but his next words stop me in my tracks.

"I know the little git's here. Who does he think he is, bringing that dung girl to the village on the night of the festival?"

Dung girl? My heart thumps, and then my claws make their appearance again. It looks like blood is about to be spilled after all.

The door to Bannog's lounge flies open, and there's no mistaking the blonde inside the arms of the ogre.

"Let me go!" she cries, kicking and screaming, but then her voice fades the moment a deathly snarl slips from my throat.

Now my world is dripped in black as I zero in on Stannog. The bastard. He *hurt* her...

The ogre drops her at my feet, and she peers up at me meekly, bottom lip shaking. "T-Tegwyn."

Yet I only have eyes for Stannog.

"What did you *do* to her?" I breathe, widening my stance as I prepare to attack.

Ivy gasps when she spies my unsheathed claws, and then her face pales five shades lighter.

The ogre scoffs when he sees my pitiful stance. "I saved her life, that's what happened. If I hadn't stepped in on time, she'd be dead. Ye shoulda seen her, staring at the king's statue like she had a death wish!"

My lip twitches, and then I expose my teeth. "That better be true or—"

Stannog caws like a crow. "Or what? You'll slice me up with your claws?"

I snicker, eyes flashing like warning beacons. "Don't tempt me..."

I don't look away from the spiteful ogre, so at odds with his kind cousin. The bastard has always had it out for me, ever since I arrived at his doorstep at the age of fifteen. And then I had the gall to bring a human to his shitty tavern, one that's in serious need of repair, might I add.

Finally, Bannog gives a dramatic sigh, falling back on his wingback chair. "All this yelling is making me thirsty. How about we all sit down and discuss our grievances like *civil* beings?"

Ivy glances at Bannog curiously, and when he catches her gaze, he waves. "Why, hello, darling. My, you're even prettier than your posters."

He chuckles warmly, then proceeds to pour that steaming honey-gold tea into not two, but *four* cups.

I don't think Ivy is in any fit state to have tea with the likes of Stannog just yet. She's still cringing in terror, sensing that raw, angry energy rippling from the big brute in waves. Ogres are legendary in human folklore; I bet she has heard many tales, ones that involve human babies and using their bones as toothpicks.

While some of those stories may be true, I don't think Stannog has ever feasted on a human infant. He's a bastard, sure, but he's not a complete brute.

Then there's Bannog, who knits tea cosies and bakes sweet biscuits—I just hope his ingredients don't involve the ground-up bones of children.

Stannog puffs out his chest when I finally look away, focusing on Ivy this time. I should have known she would've followed me. After all, I can't tell a lie to save my goddamn life. Now she is surrounded by enemies on all sides, and I close my eyes, gripping the bridge of my nose.

"Ivy... *why?*"

She wraps her cloak around her shoulders. "I'm... sorry..."

I purse my lips as I try to come up with a plan. How the hell am I going to get her out of the village?

I'm surprised the spriggan even let her through the gate. They hate humans even more than Stannog.

Ivy starts shivering, and Stannog winces at her feebleness, joining his cousin for tea at last. Yet Bannog only has sympathy for the poor girl. "Oh, my."

His gaze falls on me, and a knowing smile spreads across his face. "Here. Hand her this."

He passes me a silken handkerchief from his waistcoat, and I look at him, confused. Bannog waves his hand at the crying Ivy, and I put two and two together. He wants *me* to be the shoulder she cries on, and I grind my teeth, stuffing his stupid handkerchief into my pocket. I don't need his help; I can deal with her fragile human emotions all on my own, thank you.

But when I spy her weeping on the floor, something strange comes over me, and then the sensation grips my heart like a vise, squeezing tightly until I can no longer breathe. I have to find a way to make her stop—faeries are drawn to the scent of human despair. I suppose most of the faeries in this village are too drunk by now to notice the difference between a human and a puka, but I'm still not taking any chances.

"Come on, get up." I help her to her feet, feeling the burning eyes of each ogre on the other side of the room.

I don't need an audience.

"The... the king..." she mutters.

A breath loosens from my lips. "Yes, his statue."

She shakes her head, and a shudder wracks through her body. I stop, regarding her strangely.

Something has rattled her deeply to her bone, and that's when the hair pricks at the back of my neck.

"A few months ago...in the woods...I saw a raven..." she whispers.

It sounds like gibberish, but my throat still bobs as I swallow. "A raven?"

She nods. "Yes. One with shining eyes of quicksilver. It had been watching me."

Bannog gasps, yet I don't take my gaze off Ivy. Her heart's thumping so fast, it vibrates through her back, and I resist the urge to pull her close.

She's cold to the touch.

Bannog gets up and shuts the window, and then he pushes Ivy gently towards the fireplace. Ivy shrinks once she takes his mammoth-sized chair, and she's barely present now.

The sight of her breaks my spirit. She's so fragile, it hurts to look at her. This kingdom will eat her alive from both sides.

The humans want her dead, and the Fae want her dead, and I guess she really isn't safe anywhere.

Bannog pours her tea. "Here."

She looks at him warily. When he smiles, it reaches his kind eyes. I get her hesitation; she was taught to never accept food or beverage from the Fae, and after the time she spent in Stannog's tavern, who could blame her?

"Now, tell us what you saw, dear," Bannog says kindly, and she looks my way.

"It's all right," I assure her. "He's safe."

She meets Bannog's gaze. "The...the night I escaped the cottage...after the king sent his men to arrest my family... I saw a silver-eyed raven in the woods, and it looked at me as if it knew me."

She shudders, sipping her tea to warm her soul.

Bannog stills. "A raven with silver eyes..." It's more of a statement than a question.

He gives me a knowing glance, and I lower my hood, unsure of how to proceed. Stannog couldn't give two shits, sneaking liquor into his tea from a secret flask.

Ivy peers around the room, noticing the sudden hush. "Does that mean something?"

Bannog waits for me to explain, but when I pull my cowl down further, he sighs, doing me the honour instead. "Sweetheart, that silver-eyed raven... That was King Corvis. It's why his court's sigil is a raven. He's a shapeshifter. Fae. Just like us."

Ivy shivers, and her teacup rattles upon its saucer. "I...thought so..."

Now silence, except for Ivy's rattling and shaking. I just want to reach across and put her at ease, but I don't want to give Bannog any more ammunition. He's teased me enough already.

"And the wolf? Was that him, too?"

Bannog taps his chin. "A wolf? I don't think so. Have you had another strange encounter with an animal that doesn't seem quite of this world?"

"Y-yes. It chased me all the way to the north, the biggest wolf I'd seen. It had silver eyes, too. It would have killed me if it weren't for my horse..."

She trails off, losing herself in the memory, and I know the day well. It was the day I found her at the mercy of that kelpie.

"It coulda been one of the guards sent to sniff her out," Stannog chimes in, and so kind of him to join.

"The king's guard has already come snooping around me tavern, anyway. Relax, I didn't tell them nothin.'"

He looks at me pointedly once he spies the hate spilling from my eyes, and I draw my claws, making Ivy tense.

My heart pounds, drowning out all sound. "*Who?*"

All the faces from Stannog's tavern rush through my mind. Whoever they are, they're dead.

Stannog swigs his spiked tea. "The culprit has already been dealt with."

It doesn't look as if I'll be getting any more information from him, yet my bets are on the puka. I saw the way it looked at Ivy that night.

Now I regard Stannog curiously. Maybe he does have a heart deep down. For all his talk of hating humans, he seems eager to keep this one alive, and I wonder... He even saved her from Lord Valent, telling me to get her home.

I startle once Ivy slams her fist onto the table, and that crying, shivering girl has long gone now. "*Why* is he doing this? I was just a baby when he dethroned my father. A man I never even met. I was raised by a healer and a blacksmith, for goodness' sake!"

Her shouting bounces off the walls, and it's a good thing Bannog already shut the window. None of us know what to say.

King Corvis already has everything he could ever want. He has a throne and an entire court at his disposal.

Unless he thinks she is after his throne. It is her birthright, after all.

But if he deems her such a threat, then why didn't he kill her when he found her in the woods? Perhaps he was just seeing what he was up against.

Still, it's best we don't take any chances. We can't let him lull us into a false sense of security.

Now we have to figure out how to get her back to the mountain. Luckily for us, Bannog has an idea.

28

Tegwyn

"What?"

Bannog beams from ear to ear. "That's right. A *glamour*... My, you really do need to clean those ears out."

He titters, and I mutter obscenities under my breath, stealing a quick glance at Ivy.

Her green-blue eyes sparkle beneath the light of Bannog's crystal chandelier. "What do you mean by glamour?"

The ogre's eyes give a mischievous glint, and he rises from his wing-back chair, plodding towards a stack of boxes.

Stannog unscrews the cap of his flask, slipping another dose into his tea while Bannog's back is turned. "I can see you, Stan," Bannog utters, and Stannog gives up on his tea, deciding to drink straight from the flask.

Bannog finally grabs a box, placing it down onto the table as he peers at Ivy. "Well, come along, dear."

She hesitates, turning to me for guidance.

The kind ogre laughs. "It's safe, dear. I promise."

Making up her mind, she steps towards the box, peeking inside. I move closer to investigate myself.

"It's empty," I note, hoping that this isn't some cruel trick.

Bannog snorts, "Not quite, my friend. It only *appears* empty."

Slipping his hands into the box, he lifts a panel of translucent gossamer, and that's when I finally see the glamour.

It's woven into the thread, strings of sparkling, iridescent magic, and I reach across, running my gloved finger along the fabric. "How?"

The ogre gives a furtive glance. "A tailor never reveals his secrets..."

Well, I guess that settles that.

Now I wonder about my own glamour. Will it be just as translucent?

"I... don't see anything," Ivy announces, and I turn her way, surprised.

It seems humans are unable to see the magic. What a shame. Sometimes, I wish Ivy could see the world the way I do.

Bannog sighs. "It's okay, dear. Most mortals are blind to Fae magic."

She dips her head, and I can't bear to see the forlorn expression on her face. If anyone in this room deserves to see the magic, then it's Ivy.

Bannog hands me the gossamer, a small smirk playing across his lips. "Here, take her to the master bedroom upstairs. See how it fits." The ogre winks at me. "You can thank me later."

I ignore his asinine remark, gritting my teeth. "How much?"

He smiles. "No price."

I narrow my eyes, wondering where the catch is. "Come again?"

Bannog rolls his eyes. "It's on the house, you silly fool. My only concern is getting the princess home in one piece."

Stannog snorts behind him. "Ye could always offer him work at the shop. Let him serve some customers."

I shiver at the unpleasant memory. Stannog always made me serve his worst punters at the bar, telling me to smile the whole time, even when they were belligerent and rude. He knew I lacked the required social skills to succeed in such a role, hence why he tortured me.

Bannog shakes his head. "There is no need, cousin. It's merely a gift for Her Majesty."

Ivy blushes at the grand title, twirling a piece of her blonde hair. "Thank you for your generosity, kind sir."

"There is no need to thank me, lovely. Now go on, off you go, the pair of you."

We take our leave, and just as he shuts the door behind us, we hear Stannog telling him, "That glamour ain't gonna work, cuz. Any idiot with eyes could see that she isn't Fae."

Bannog huffs, "Oh, shush. You're just jealous because you have no talent."

"*Pah!* Tell that to all the happy punters who come to me bar!"

"*Happy* punters? I think you need to repeat that word, Stan, but *slowly* this time..."

Stannog growls, and then something smashes, followed by a loud crash.

I push Ivy towards the stairs before we get caught in the crossfire, and soon we find the master bedroom at the end of a carpeted hallway. There's no doubting who the room belongs to once we step inside, finding the large four-poster bed immediately. The wooden monstrosity swallows up the entire room, and as we approach one of the bedposts, Ivy runs a finger along a carved rose. I can't help noticing the chaise longue by the ornate fireplace, and the pincushion ottoman at the foot of the bed.

Darn. Bannog really does have good taste.

My eyes land on a changing board in the corner. I hand Ivy the gossamer. "Hurry up and dress. We need to leave as soon as possible."

She regards the gossamer hesitatingly, then sighs, taking it from my fingers so she can get dressed.

Shouts echo outside, and I approach the window, muttering a curse. The street is swarming with faeries, and I just hope that everyone is too drunk to take much notice of the human when we leave later.

One group of dancing females catches my attention, and I duck when they glance up at the window.

Shit. It's Marrow, or whatever her stupid name is again. Of course *she* would be here. Never one to pass up on a revel.

"Erm... Tegwyn?"

At the sound of her meek voice, I glance at the changing board, regretting it immediately.

The blood rushes through my head once I spy her curvy silhouette behind the canvas, and I ignore the hardness in my pants.

Fuck. Not *now*...

"Yes?" I ask, covering my eyes.

"I...need you to help me with the glamour. I...can't see it."

Yes. How could I forget?

With a deep breath, I keep my eyes closed as I step around the changing board, opening them long enough so I can see the glittering swathe of material.

I lift the glamour, telling her to turn, and she offers me a view of her slender neck.

My gaze latches onto her pulse, and my fangs ache, wishing to bite into that tender patch of skin. But then I shake some sense back into myself, focusing on my current task.

Dressing her. That's all this is.

Helping her dress...

Not *undress*.

Still, her pulse is inviting, the way it flutters beneath her neck, and *shit*...I can't do this.

She angles her head, giving me a small glimpse of her rosebud mouth. "Are you okay?"

I inhale a shivering breath, "N-never better. Come on, let's get this thing on already."

With careful fingers, I slip the gossamer over her like a veil, stepping back as it moulds to her shape.

Her ears grow at the tips as her form changes before my very eyes, but when all is said and done, I don't see much of a difference. Her beauty is pretty much unchanged.

However, her skin harbours a lucent glow, and her hair shines like shafts of sunlight. And her *body*...

The same round hips and small waist, now visible through the cut-out sections of her diaphanous dress. That gauzy dress of soft jade matches her eyes perfectly, and I stumble for words, taking her in from head to toe. My blood whooshes through my head, and I don't know how I even manage to hold it together.

I could kill Bannog right now; he gave her that fucking dress on purpose just to tease me. The dress breathes to life, leaves and vines curling around her arms and legs, and she's spring personified.

Flowers bloom in her hair, and I stagger back against the wall, unable to take my eyes off her. A goddess stands before me, and I forget how to breathe.

I'm pretty sure I'm looking at Maghelena, the mother of all Fae.

My heart slams against my ribs, threatening to escape like a rabbit trapped in a snare, and then the room spins out of control.

Ivy approaches me. "Tegwyn? Are you all right? You're gasping..."

No shit. She smells like a dream—sweet woodland flowers, draping curtains of honeysuckle, and baked goods, and that's when my claws unsheathe of their own volition.

I divert them towards the wall, raking them through the plaster, and I hope Bannog won't be too pissed.

The material of her dress whispers seductively as she glides closer, and I can't take it anymore. Any closer, and I will pounce on her and claim her neck with my teeth.

Looks like I'm about to go into a rut, so I think of something unsavory, like Stannog in the exact same dress, and that seems to do the trick. The wild beast snarls in protest as I lock him back inside his cage. My claws retreat, disappearing back inside my gloves, and all is well with the world again.

A warm hand brushes my cheek, and I flinch, finding those shining pools of sea green. They shimmer beneath the light, and I think of lush green meadows, soft and dewy after a morning rain...

"Tegwyn?"

I swallow a lump that's stuck in the back of my throat. She shows me nothing but concern, yet here I am, thinking about ripping that dress off her hips with my teeth.

"I... I'm fine..."

She smiles sweetly, brushing her thumb over my cheek, and shame cripples me instantly. If only she knew of the sordid things that I was just thinking about doing to her body.

Finally, she steps back, clasping her hands in front of her shyly, and I stare at her, perplexed. She really has no idea that she's the most ravishing creature in existence. It's her reticence that makes her all the more alluring. No one is going to be able to keep their eyes off her tonight.

The males, *especially*.

A growl starts at the base of my throat, and I swallow it quickly, moving away from the wall.

"So, how do I look?" she asks.

I cast my eyes around the room, since I can't quite find the right words, pointing at a mirror.

"Take a look for yourself."

Ivy inhales deeply, approaching the looking glass. She just stares at her reflection for a while, a small smile taking over her face. "I...look beautiful..."

My mind crashes back to earth, and then the words leave my mouth, "You've always been—"

She squeals, spinning around, and I have no idea what I'm witnessing. But that doesn't stop the smile slowly curving my own lips.

She rushes to my side, taking my hand, and a shock shoots straight down my spine. It almost feels like magic.

"Come, let's join the revel!"

The revel?

I raise my brow. "The idea is to get you *away* from the revel, princess."

"Don't be silly. We can stay for one dance!"

Actually, no. We can't. I don't dance.

"Come on!"

She drags me out of the room, and before I know it, I'm running down the stairs and right into the heart of the revel.

It's like she's cast a spell over me, but I let her lead the way, regardless, knowing that I will surely regret this.

29

Ivy

THE FRESH AIR STEALS the breath from my lungs the moment I rush outside, flashing lights dazzling me at every turn. All around, faeries dance in perfect tempo, filling the street with music and laughter, and I soak up every second of it, adjusting to the new sights and sounds.

My soul is aflame as the pulsing waves thrum through my veins, and when I sway my hips to the lilting notes, raising my arms high in the air, I suddenly feel it...

How *alive* I am.

The moment I donned that gauzy green dress of gossamer, all my inhibitions vanished. I lost my fear and my sense of survival as I willingly ran into a nest of vipers—vipers that would gladly hunt me down and torture me for sport.

A voice warns me that this is wrong: I should leave right now before anyone realises I'm here. My body keeps undulating like a wisp of smoke, though—slow, seductive, hypnotic. The music reaches places deep inside me, vibrating in the marrow of my bones until I'm utterly possessed, and finally, I tilt my head back, laughing at the swirling sky.

My dress breathes against my skin as I twirl and flex to the beat of the drums, and then I cartwheel, having no idea I could even pull such a manoeuvre. This glamour makes me even *move* like the Fae, and now I'm just as agile and graceful as these beautiful creatures.

As I land back on my feet, the vibrant lights of wisps swimming in my peripheral vision, a hand grips my shoulder, and I turn to find those glowing eyes. Tegwyn hovers close, and his pine and woodsmoke scent has never smelled so good.

Does he have any idea what he does to me? Probably not.

"Ivy, what are you *doing*?"

He's incandescent with rage, yet I merely giggle, grabbing his hand. "I'm dancing! Join me."

I tug him towards the crowd of revellers, but he's steadfast, planting his heels firmly in place. His fingers find my wrist, and then he starts pulling me away from the revel. "No. We need to leave. *Now.*"

I shake my head. "No. I want to stay. The night is so beautiful."

He yanks me close until we're inches from a kiss, and that's when my eyes fall to his carved Cupid's bow lips.

The blood rushes through my head, making me lose all common sense. What is happening to me?

He moves his mouth to my ear, whispering, "These faeries will eat you alive."

Two little Fae girls pass us, hand in hand as they dance in a circle. They both have horns like Tegwyn.

I smile, peering his way. "Even those two?"

Tegwyn glances at the small children strangely for a moment, looking at a loss for words. Then he regards me pointedly. "Yes. Even the *children* will take turns rending your flesh."

My, he really does paint quite a bloody picture.

I heed his warning for a moment, but in the end, I shake my head, making up my mind. "I don't care. I don't know what this glamour has done to me, but this is the most free I have felt in a long time, and I haven't even had a drop of faerie wine."

His unwavering eyes don't leave me as he keeps on glaring, and I take that as my cue to proceed. "Just one dance. Please? *Then* we can go."

His hardened gaze melts at the sound of my pleading tone. Then he sighs, pinching the bridge of his nose. "*Fine.* One dance. Then we go."

I bat my eyelashes, leaning closer. "So, does this mean you will dance with me?"

He gives me a deadpan look, his eyes returning to solid gold. "No."

My heart sinks, but I understand. He's shy.

"All right. I guess I'll dance by myself."

I walk right into the heart of the revel, and his groan vanishes somewhere behind me.

Hopefully, most of the Fae here really are too intoxicated to notice the fake tips of my ears. The last thing I should be doing is drawing more attention to myself, but when I jerk back and forth, trying out some new, off-kilter moves, the revellers stop. They cheer me on, even when my dancing makes no sense, but who cares?

I'm having fun.

As I dip back in a low arc, I find his heated gaze.

Tegwyn regards me, rather impressed this time, and I can almost read his thoughts from where I dance.

Not bad.

That's when I catch a flash of gold in the corner of my eye, and I find that beautiful, yellow-eyed female heading my way.

My gut clenches, and then my every inhibition returns with a vengeance. It's her. From the tavern.

Minnow.

And she still has that sour expression on her gorgeous face. Tegwyn was right; this *was* a bad idea.

She knows exactly who I am, and now she's going to make me suffer.

Finally, Minnow reaches my side, and she really is a sight to behold. That flash of gold I spied earlier was, in fact, her crown of leaves, and they match her eyes perfectly.

Her companions wear similar wreaths. A fair-skinned female with hair as white as snow wears a crown of holly berries to match her red lips, and the other wears woven branches of frosted pine. They all have beautiful wings, too.

The white-haired female has translucent wings of shimmering green, and the other has the spotted red of a peacock butterfly.

Minnow tucks her dusty, mottled wings behind her back, giving me a once-over. "My, where did you learn such a dance?"

I lower my gaze, muttering under my breath, "I... made it up."

She flutters her long, feathery eyelashes. "Come again?"

I should get back to Tegwyn; he will be waiting for me on the pavement. He was right. We should have left after all, and if I survive tonight, then I will tell him personally. He will be so smug.

Minnow leans closer, and her scent of spiced apple chokes me. "What's your name, fair one?"

That's where she's wrong. I am not fair.

I am deceiving these creatures, and when they finally discover who and what I am, they will kill me.

"I-Ivy."

Minnow hums. "Ivy? Like the parasitic plant? Most befitting."

The snowy-haired female laughs like a pealing bell, and the pure timbre seems to mock me. Minnow's smirk widens, and that's when she shows me her perfect teeth—teeth perfect for rending flesh.

"Aspen, Willow, will you help me *dispose* of this beautiful parasite?"

Aspen and Willow wear matching sneers, and soon all three faeries crowd me, gripping my arms with cruel, cutting nails.

"Maybe she could show us that lovely dance again," the pale-haired faerie, Aspen, warbles.

"Or we could gouge her pretty eyes out," Willow whispers, and I release a silent gasp when she exposes her fangs.

Now these beautiful, winged creatures turn before my very eyes, dragging me closer into the jaws of hell for daring to crash their revel.

When I blink again, Tegwyn is standing in front of me, shielding me from sight. All three faeries release my arms the moment he snarls, *"Back off."*

Minnow produces a husky laugh, flicking back her long, chestnut hair. "Tegwyn, why haven't you introduced us to your lovely friend?"

The growl rises at the back of his throat, and my heart quivers at the merciless sound. "I told you to *back off*..."

Aspen and Willow have already gone, but Minnow remains. She purrs, stepping closer to whisper into his ear, "You're highly tempting when you're like this, Teggy. Almost takes me back to that night when you kissed my—" Her words die in her throat when he grips her arm, extending his claws. Now Minnow's perfect façade cracks when he punctures her shining skin, drawing dots of blood.

"And yet, I *still* can't rid your foul taste from my tongue. You're pathetic, Mabel, or whatever your name is. So go and fuck someone else tonight."

My jaw drops at his crude words, and then I blush bright red as I imagine them together, their shimmering bodies entwined like a beautiful knot.

What was I thinking? As if Tegwyn would ever want me when he's had Mabel, I mean, *Minnow*.

I feel Minnow's satisfied smirk, and it looks like her job here is done. She may not have got to sink her claws into me, but she has still broken my spirit all the same.

I have never felt so small.

Finally, she rejoins her friends, and Tegwyn turns my way. "Ivy?"

I lift my face, and my heart cleaves in two when I spy the sorrow in his eyes. He knows that Minnow's words got to me, yet he has no idea how to offer me comfort.

"You...you were right, Tegwyn... We should have just left."

My voice cracks, and he doesn't look as smug as I thought he would. No, he looks sad and broken, and I just want this night to end.

Suddenly, he places his arms around me, pulling me flush to his chest. Our noses brush, and soon it's just the two of us, the revelers and the dancers all forgotten.

His warmth comforts me as he moves effortlessly, and who knew he could dance so well. My head is reeling, and once again, I feel as light as air.

"I didn't know you could dance," I giggle.

He looks a little affronted. "I'm not a complete heathen, you know, Ivy."

There's no missing the humour in his tone, and I laugh louder, uncaring who sees us now. Minnow can eat her heart out.

He chuckles. "Why are you laughing?"

"I'm just wondering what you will do next. Breathe fire?"

Tegwyn's eyes flash, and then his fangs glint beneath the lanterns as he whispers huskily, "Only one way to find out."

I'm not sure if he is wholly serious, but I embrace every moment, wrapping my hands around his neck.

Our hearts beat together, and I savour his proximity, breathing in his intoxicating scent.

"Ivy..." he whispers, his breath feathering my cheeks.

I open my eyes, drowning in his honeyed gaze. "Yes?"

His gaze falls on my lips, and then his pupils blow out, taking over his eyes. Then he turns his face away, sighing in defeat. "N-nothing."

Well, that's disappointing. For a moment, I thought he was going to... Never mind.

"Tegwyn?"

"Yeah?"

A frustrated huff escapes me, and I meet his black eyes, the ones ringed with gold. "When are you going to kiss me?"

His countenance falters, and then he stops spinning. "What are you—?"

He doesn't get to finish his sentence as I grip his cheek, letting our lips meet for the first time.

30

Tegwyn

My heart skips a beat as I forget how to breathe. Her kiss takes me entirely by surprise, firing up every nerve in my body, and I grasp fistfuls of her golden hair, parting her mouth with my tongue.

She makes the sweetest sound, opening her mouth wider to invite me inside. A feral growl loosens from my lips when I finally get my taste of her, and the beast is out of the cage.

How I manage to have any restraint, I'll never know, but when she presses her heaving breasts to my chest, teasing my bottom lip with her teeth, I feel myself slipping. My claws unsheathe, but with shaking fingers, I will them back inside my gloves, telling myself I can't hurt her.

I'd be no better than the monsters at this faerie revel.

She just makes it so goddamn difficult, snaking her arms around my neck like a boa constrictor, and that's when she gets her own claws out, raking them down the length of my spine. My body shudders, and I suppress another growl, heart pounding like a battering ram.

I want her. *Now.*

Against the wall. In the meadow.

Everywhere.

Our lips part as we press our foreheads together, sharing breath. My world spins, and I'm simply drunk on her scent. Honeysuckle floods my veins, pumping hotter and faster until I'm blind to everything but her.

"Let's go somewhere private," she whispers.

Her green-blue eyes are pure temptation, and my gaze darts towards a distant knoll where I spy several faeries doing the unspeakable.

It's the longest night of the year, and the Fae are celebrating in the best way they know how—dancing and fucking until they wear down the soles of their feet.

Ivy follows my gaze, and then she starts dragging me towards the knoll. I have dreamed of this from the moment I laid eyes on her, and it looks like my wishes are about to come true.

We crest the highest point of the knoll, tumbling down onto the wet grass when we find a shadowed spot. I make sure to lay us somewhere downwind. That way, the others won't pick up on the scent of blood when I take her for the first time.

Her hair pools across the grass like swathes of golden silk, and that's how we stay for a while, ignoring the groaning and gasping of the faeries around us.

Ivy throws my hood back, and my horns are exposed to the night. The others will finally see my shattered horn, my disgrace, but it's the furthest thing from my mind now.

A beautiful woman spreads herself below me on a silver platter, and it's all I can do to resist the urge to sink my teeth into her neck.

Ivy caresses the base of my injured horn, and a shiver courses right through me. She smiles mischievously. "Are you sensitive there?"

I meet her hooded eyes, giving her a surreptitious nod, and the wicked creature does the exact same thing again, running her fingers between the grooves this time.

A strangled sound wrestles free of my throat, and she finally moves her fingers away from my horn, biting her lower lip. "So hard..."

She needs to be careful talking like that. I'm already having a hard enough time as it is keeping my wits about me, yet she has to go and make a goddamn euphemism about my fucking horn.

Besides, it's my turn now. Time to torture her...

I brush my claw along her body, starting from her head as I make my way to her navel, and she leans into my touch. When my claw snags her top lip, she gasps, arching her back off the grass. I didn't mean to cut her there, and I need to be more careful with these claws of mine; it looks like I nicked the skin beneath her nose as a bead of blood gathers.

Yet my claws unfurl, desperate for more, and I suck in a breath, getting my shit together as I lean forward, licking the wound with my tongue as I taste her blood.

She groans, arching further. I can hear the rapid pulse of her heartbeat, and she's finally ready.

Nestling my hand behind her head, I gaze into her sea-green eyes, appreciating how those starbursts glow when she wears the glamour.

Her fingers splay across my pounding heart, and she trails them down my chest, stopping above my breeches.

I raise a brow. "You sure, Ivy?"

She grabs my cheek, massaging my skin with her thumb. "I've never been surer of anything."

My heart drums against my ribs, yet I still can't shake the feeling that I'm taking advantage. I cup her sweet, heart-shaped face with my hands, making sure my claws stay unsheathed this time. "It will hurt."

Fear shines in her big eyes, and I start pushing away, giving her back her space. But then she drags me back, whispering hotly against my lips, "I'm not afraid, Tegwyn. I will never be afraid of you..."

Honeyed pleasure trickles through my veins at the sound of her heartfelt declaration, and now my vision blurs as she becomes my sole focus.

Her mind is set.

I will be fucking her beneath the stars of the longest night of the year.

Ivy

Luminous eyes of molten gold are all I can see, and soon it's just me and Tegwyn, the festival and the revellers all forgotten.

Mama once told me that I shouldn't lie with a man unless I was absolutely certain that I loved him and that he loved me in return, but I feel Tegwyn's love with every beat of my heart.

Tegwyn will be my first, the furthest thing from a *man* that I have ever met, yet he's all mine, and I wouldn't have him any other way.

Once again, he rakes his devilish claw across my skin, and I sigh beneath his careful ministrations, wishing that his claws were all over me. I want them tearing off my clothes, exposing me to the elements.

Heat blossoms throughout my body, pooling between my legs, and I grind my hips, eager for his caress. A growl vibrates in his throat, but I push him further, yearning for his friction. His eyes burn like stars, stealing the very light from the night sky, and it's those gleaming eyes that scorch my soul, leaving me wanting, *waiting*...

My core thumps in time with my heartbeat, and I tug him closer, pressing my cheek against his. I mark him with my scent, savouring the coarse sensation of his skin on mine. I want that gritty texture inside me.

"A word of warning, Ivy...I'm far from gentle," he rasps, catching his breath.

I thread my fingers through his russet hair, meeting his lips with a soft kiss. "Is that a promise?"

His eyes erupt like flames, and I no longer see the slits of his pupils. "*Yes...*"

I smirk. "Then *ruin* me."

Suddenly, he's upon me, his teeth hovering mere inches from my throat, and for a few torturous seconds, he does nothing.

But when his pained gaze finds mine again, it comes to my attention that he's torn.

With a gentle coaxing of my fingers, I run them down his cheek, and he narrows his eyes, brushing his hand along my thigh.

My dress crumples with the movement, and soon I'm exposed to the air. He finds my opening, stroking his finger along my seam, and my body shudders, relishing his touch. When he brings his hand back up, gloved fingers glistening with my arousal, his dark expression says it all.

He's ready.

And so am I.

Suddenly, he's dragging me along the grass, aligning our bodies, and then he frees his length, brushing himself against my opening.

His heat brands my skin, and I wrap my arms around his neck, keeping him close so I can feel his heartbeat.

Tegwyn edges in slowly, and a sharp pain splinters right down my middle, taking me by surprise.

I grit my teeth, bracing against the pain. When he spies the discomfort on my face, he presses a kiss between my eyes, banishing my worry lines.

"The hard part is over. But I'll stop if you want me to."

"No," I pant, keeping my arms locked around his neck. "I...I want this..."

He swallows. "All right."

So, he pushes further, stretching me around him, and I squeeze my eyes shut as I wait to adjust. Soon, he's fully sheathed inside me, claws gripping at the sweet earth as he becomes delirious with lust.

When I reach for his horn, he seizes my wrist, laying it down on the grass beside me. "For...for the best. I'm already hanging on by a delicate thread," he pants.

A shame: I love how his horns feel beneath my fingers. They're enticing and hard as rocks.

His eyes flash, and then he cocks his head, resembling a predator. "You've really no idea how much I'm holding back, Ivy... How much I want to fuck you into the dirt..."

I know it's best not to provoke the beast, but I can't help it when I breathe, "Then bury me six feet deep."

An unnatural stillness befalls him, and his eyes lose all focus. And then before I know it, he's flipping us around, and now I'm the one on top, gazing down into his heated eyes.

His claws grip my ass, puncturing the skin deep, and I arch into his touch. When he flexes inside me, angling his hips at just the right position, I breathe faster, swallowing up his last few inches, and it's better this way...

Much better.

He smirks beneath me, his golden eyes branding my soul. "Fuck me, Ivy. Fuck me six feet deep."

His crude words echo inside my drunken mind like a bell, and finally, I thrust. He claws at my hips, prompting another deep moan of pleasure from my lungs.

I don't stop, rolling my hips over and over as I chase my release. My legs shake, so I plant my feet onto the grass, using them for momentum.

Lights dance in my peripheral vision, but I won't stop until I reach that glorious peak.

Tegwyn guides my thrusts, and if my eyes deceive me, he's *glowing*... His power thrums right through me, lighting up at the base of my spine, and with one final push, I explode like a newborn star.

Magic surges through me, and when I toss my head back, I spy the veins of each leaf high in the trees.

And as I rock faster, sweat dripping down the groove of my spine, his magic swells, and I hear the wind whistling between the blades of grass at my feet.

I'm drawing strength from his magic, and it lights up every nerve in my body. I spy new colours, ones naked to my eyes before, and they twist and spin like a kaleidoscope, sending my mind into a spiral.

Tegwyn has given me the gift of faerie sight, and it's more than I can take. I see and hear the world as he does now, and I can even hear the solid thump of his heart.

Soon, I clench around him, screaming once his magic reaches its final crescendo.

Tegwyn digs his claws in deep, yet he doesn't wound me this time. His magic heals me instantly, and that's the moment he finally lets go, spilling his seed as he finds his release. He sits up, pressing me flush to his chest as he slams hard into my hips, and then he crests for a second time. I teeter over the edge after him, meeting his thrusts with a cry of my own. I still see the world through his magic, and when I catch sight of my reflection inside his eyes, I do a double-take.

I'm glowing.

We don't move for some time, too lost in each other's embrace. We remain locked at the hip, even when he lays me down onto the wet grass, holding me close to his warm chest.

And as the night wears on, and his magic slowly ebbs from my system, I fall asleep to his soothing purr.

31

Tegwyn

Ivy slumbers like a goddess beside me as I lose myself in her honeysuckle scent, breathing in her golden waves.

I can't believe she's all mine. This beautiful human creature... Her skin is flushed, the glorious afterglow of sex yet to fade, and I brush a delicate claw down the curve of her spine, savouring every inch of her.

I'm still sheathed between her legs, her silken walls protecting me from the elements. If only we could stay this way forever.

The glamour worked like a charm in the end. No one suspected a thing, and I just hope our luck remains.

Ivy shudders, and I tug her closer, shrouding her beneath my woollen cloak to keep her warm.

It really is a cold morning. Soft flurries drift down around us, sticking to the grass, and my eyes widen in surprise. Snow? That can't be right.

I puff out a breath, watching as it fogs, and it's just as I feared. Winter has come to the village.

It looks as if Ivy brought some of the winter chill from the human realm when she snuck through the gate, and it's time we trek back to the mountain before anyone realises she's here.

I shake her gently, whispering in her ear, "Ivy."

She wakes with a soft sigh, smiling up at me lazily. Then she trembles, huddling beneath my cloak. "So cold."

"I know, and that's exactly why we need to leave. It's snowing."

The human merely yawns, and I get it. She's tired, and she may struggle to walk for a few days, but we need to make haste.

"And what of it?"

I meet the blue-green slits of her eyes. "It *never* snows in the village."

Her lids fly open. Then she rises, slipping free of my cock and allowing me to button up my pants.

She winces when I help her to her feet, and since I'm the reason why she's in so much pain in the first place, I tuck my hands beneath her legs and carry her the rest of the way down the hill.

Most of the Fae have gone home, and now only the most dedicated of revelers remain. Several have passed out drunk on the cobblestones, and we pass one group, in particular, that resembles a naked heap of tangled limbs. The air reeks of decadence. A lot happened while we were safely tucked away at the top of the hill. Once upon a time, Ivy would have blushed at all the debauchery, but now she barely gives the faerie orgy a second glance as we head to the gate. I feel like I'm tainting her innocent soul, but I can't help but feel a little proud of her; it must get tedious being the good girl all the time.

We find the alleyway, and the spriggan lets us through the gate without protest. A blast of white wind steals my breath the moment we re-enter the human realm, and it looks like we've walked right into the heart of a blizzard.

Snow swirls in thick sheets, and I've never felt a chill like it before. It sluices across my skin and soaks my hair, freezing me right down to the bone. It's not natural, whatever it is.

Ivy latches on to me tightly, chattering her teeth like a baby squirrel. I must get her back to the mountain quickly.

But I'm struggling to see ten feet. There is no way we will make it back tonight.

"What... what should we do?" she asks, trembling.

Dread leaches from my veins when I spy her bloodless lips. If I don't do something soon, she'll freeze to death.

All she wears is that flimsy gossamer, and even the vines and flowers are receding faced with this merciless storm. Hoarfrost seizes the dress's once lovely petals, and they wither and unfurl, succumbing to the elements.

Ivy will not meet the same fate.

We left her clothes back at Bannog's shop, but we can't return because the spriggan has resumed his ancient slumber.

The only way to go is forward.

I'm Fae. There's a strong possibility that I will survive this storm. Magic sustains the very blood of my veins, but Ivy will die.

I tug her closer to my body, bundling her up under my cloak, and she nestles her nose into the crook of my neck, shivering miserably.

"T-Tegwyn," she shudders, her breath warming my skin.

I hold her tighter, praying to Maghelena to show us a way through the storm. "I know. But I will get you out of this. I promise." She nods, putting her entire trust in me.

I can't let her down.

Through a gap in the storm, I spy the yawning mouth of a cave and send a silent thanks to the goddess. She heeded my prayers.

Ivy is barefoot, so it's no wonder she's slipping away. I scoop her up in my arms, keeping her buried beneath the cloak as I wade through thick carpets of snow.

Once we reach the cave, I settle her down onto the hard, uneven ground, unclipping my cloak so I can place it around her shoulders.

Then I step back outside, braving the tempest once again. "I'm going to collect some firewood. Stay here."

She doesn't reply, too numb from the cold. I need to act, and fast.

I find the sloping branches of a pine, deciding it will do for tinder, yet after a few failed attempts at a fire, I finally give up the fight and create a spark with my fingers.

A Rogue Fae must always remember to budget his magic, but desperate times call for desperate measures, and I'm not about to let Ivy freeze to death.

Ivy scoots closer to the flames, wrapping us both up in my cloak, but she needn't bother. My magic should be more than enough to sustain us until morning.

The fire illuminates the inside of the cave, and I cast my eyes around our temporary dwelling, taking stock of the snottites that drip from the ceiling like globs of saliva.

It's like being inside the mouth of a giant, but this smelly, rotten cave was our saving grace tonight.

Ivy huddles closer to absorb my warmth, closing her eyes as she tries to get some sleep. All the while, the wind continues to howl outside. We found a decent-enough spot downwind.

We may just survive.

It doesn't take Ivy long to fall asleep, and her complexion soon returns to its former rosy glory. I study her face, and not for the first time, I'm entranced by her beauty. If someone had told me when we first met that I would be buried deep between her legs on the longest night of the year, then I would have laughed myself senseless.

I may have been raised by humans, but that doesn't mean that I wish to consort with them. But I don't particularly care for the company of my fellow Fae either. In fact, I never really needed anyone.

Until I met *her*...

It seemed she was my undoing all this time. I did always have a weakness for blondes.

Ivy will be the death of me one day, but I wouldn't have it any other way. I would gladly lay down my life for this woman. Bannog's words repeat through my mind, and my heart grows as heavy as the blustering snow outside.

How am I going to tell her?

You don't. Simple. You know it would make no difference to you anyway, because you don't care about anyone but yourself.

I growl, grinding my teeth at the sound of her intrusive voice. She's still messing with my head.

"Leave me alone," I whisper to the gloom.

I'll never leave you alone, demon. Not after what you did to my son...

Red sprays my vision, and then I see his terrified face, a face I've tried so hard to forget.

Duke.

That was the day I finally took a stand against the boy who made my life a living hell. I can still taste his warm blood on my tongue as it drips from my lips, staining my fangs crimson, and I try to block him out.

Outside in the cold, she beckons me—a shadow silhouetted against the spiralling wind.

She's nothing but a wraith, tall and frail, and lacking any real flesh, and it's good to finally put a face to the voice.

Rosemary.

Another painful memory resurfaces, and then more shapes materialise behind her ghostly form. I recognise the glowing eyes of the villagers, and a gaping chasm opens up inside my chest, threatening to pull me under.

The whole village of Tillyfold has come to finish me off like they once promised. They weren't satisfied enough with my leaving, so now they're here to kill me for good.

For as long as I can remember, they've despised me. Vilified and treated me like a pariah. After all, I will never be one of them—the strange, green-skinned youth with the horns of a goat and the claws of a wolf.

"Don't ever step foot in this town again," Rosemary hisses, her voice close yet far.

Her gaze burns through the swirling snow, and I have never seen anything so vile, so inhuman.

"I'll butcher you like a pig *if you so much as breathe near my children."*

Why are they doing this? It was bad enough they chased me away from my home, but now they insist on torturing and killing me, too?

Mother, Grandpa...

They always treated me like family, but our short time together wasn't meant to last. Because in the end, I could never replace the son Mother lost—the one she gave up all those years ago. I wonder where he is now. Did the Fae merchant live up to his end of the bargain? Did the boy live like he promised?

Rosemary glides closer, floating atop the snow like a spectre, and her voice tolls like a death knell.

"Your mother never loved you. You were never enough to replace the loss of her *real* son."

My eyes glow, casting a sickly yellow sheen on the slimy cave walls. "Shut up and *leave*..."

"No. I will never leave, Tegwyn, because I'm a *part* of you. All your deepest fears come to life."

My body trembles, and then my claws peek from my gloves. When I look out of the cave, I find her hideous face staring back at me. She's barely human now, just an ugly imitation of the woman she's trying to emulate.

Rosemary is no more, and I finally see her for what she is. A boggart—a creature that feeds on the misery of those it deems less fortunate.

Well, it picked the wrong Fae. A snarl tears from my lips, and then I fly out of the cave, sending up a cloud of snow as I tackle the boggart to the ground. It continues to cackle with the face of Rosemary, its blackened teeth as sharp as blades.

The more gruesome cousin of the bugbear, the boggart not only manifests as their human victims' deepest insecurities, but that of their fellow faeries, too.

When they're desperate and hungry enough, that is.

I wrap my hand around the boggart's skinny neck, smirking when it melts back into its natural form.

The creature writhes within my grip, and when I lean closer, its rotten stench burns my nose.

I'm just grateful that Ivy's asleep. These cruel creatures have led many humans to suicide by merely convincing them that no one loves them and that their existence is meaningless. I must protect her.

"I said, *leave...*"

My eyes flash, reflecting off the boggart's dark, glassy teeth, and it finally dissolves with the wind, merging with a passing snow swirl. It will have to find its meal elsewhere.

I bury my knees in the snow, the spiralling wind howling all around me. Yet I don't move an inch. I may have defeated my foe, but its cruel words still linger.

Mother... *Did* she love me?

After all, she sacrificed her son just to raise me, but I guess I was nothing but a burden in the end.

Still, I think a part of her did love me. She was always so kind...And what she did for her son was truly commendable. Heroic even.

I never believed in true love, but her selfless act has almost converted me numerous times. Maybe one day, I can tell her in person that she is the bravest woman I've ever known.

But I will never get to tell her, because I am not welcome in the village anymore. If I go back, they'll kill me.

The cold finally consumes me, and soon I'm buried in a foot of snow. But then something appears in the storm, landing on my arm, and I turn to find a moth splaying its pink and green wings.

An Elephant Hawkmoth? In winter?

I gaze into its beaded eyes, watching as it waves its antenna, and a smile curves my lips. No wonder I didn't recognise him earlier. He's changed somewhat since I saw him last.

Back then, he was a green pile of mush beneath Duke's boot.

I may be delirious from the cold right now, slowly losing consciousness as my body falls into a magical torpor, but it looks as if my childhood caterpillar finally became a moth after all.

"Hello, Henry."

32

Ivy

It's stark cold as I pat the cave floor with a shiver, jerking upright when I don't feel him beside me. "Tegwyn?"

Fear feathers down my spine, and I scramble to my feet, jumping when a heavy cloak falls from my shoulders.

Tegwyn's cloak.

Picking up the garment with shaking fingers, I wrap it around my shoulders again and brave the cold. A bright, glittering forest takes my breath away the instant I step outside, every rock, tree, and brush covered in cotton-white snow. It reflects the light of the sun, and I shield my eyes against the glow, surprised to find a serene blue sky. There isn't a single cloud in sight, last night's blizzard apparently gone for good. I hardly notice the chill as I trek through the forest, following a neat set of tracks in the snow.

His boot prints lead me to a grove of trees, each branch dripping with melted icicles, and I stumble upon a scene that looks as if it were taken straight from a children's picture book.

A robin perches on a low-hanging bough to my right, its scarlet breast a perfect complement to its ripe red berries, and a squirrel darts up a pine tree, watching me with curious, glistening eyes.

The animals are acting rather oddly today, but before I can ponder the strange occurrence further, I freeze when his familiar figure finally appears. Tegwyn gazes forlornly alongside a frozen lake, several rabbits chewing at tufts of grass at his feet. A squirrel sits on his shoulder, gnawing at the hard shell of a hazelnut, and numerous songbirds perch on his horns. Heart pounding, I tread carefully, afraid of scaring away his little forest friends. "Tegwyn?"

The faerie turns my way, and I meet that frozen mask. Not a single muscle moves on his face, and his golden eyes are distant.

But as cold and detached as he is, the air around him ripples with warmth. There's a patch of lush green grass at his feet, and the rabbits chew at the fresh shoots eagerly, paying neither of us heed.

Wait... Could Tegwyn be warming up the forest with his magic? It would explain why my feet are so warm, despite the snow on the ground. It's like his magic lingers wherever he treads.

Shaking my head, I unwrap my cloak, clipping it around his shoulders. "Here. Before you catch a cold."

I take his chin in my fingers, and his cheeks are like ice. He's not just warming the forest; he's sacrificing the warmth of his veins. No wonder he's lethargic. His magic is waning. His skin, hair, and eyes are dull and lifeless. I must get him back to the mountain quickly. There's a spot by the hearth with his name on it.

"Tegwyn, you silly fool. You're freezing."

"Am I?" he replies without inflexion. He's becoming a husk. He really is an idiot.

"Yes, and you shouldn't just disappear like that. I was worried."

Despite the frozen muscles of his face, a small smirk still curves his lips, and there's the impish fiend I know. "Were you now?"

I roll my eyes, gazing at his gloved hands. They're cupped together, and I spy a furry tail tucked inside.

"What... what have you got in your hands?" The faerie merely blinks, opening his fingers up for my inspection.

The smallest of mice sleeps in the palm of his hand, and judging by the squeaks escaping its tiny snout, it's snoring. That's a dormouse, and I've never seen anything so precious.

I place my hand over my mouth, meeting his eyes. Tegwyn shrugs. "He was cold."

I'm not sure how to respond. Dormice hibernate in the winter, so the small rodent is currently experiencing torpor. He won't wake up for another few months.

Smiling, I cover Tegwyn's gloved hands with my own, hoping to add some extra warmth, and I can't help but notice how he keeps his claws sheathed out of respect for the mouse. Tegwyn really does have a heart of gold. All those cruel stories about him were wrong after all.

He's not a monster. In fact, he's the closest thing to an angel I have ever met.

"Poor thing must have fallen from his nest. Come on. Let's take him back."

As I guide the faerie through the forest, the animals are never too far, following close at our heels. Soon, we find the dormouse's nest at the base of a tree. I push aside a patch of dried leaves, finding a cosy nest lined with moss and empty hazelnut shells. I place the little mouse back inside so he can return to his winter sleep. Once I've finished tucking the mouse into bed, I rise to my feet, taking Tegwyn's hand. He blinks at our joined fingers, meeting my gaze.

He truly is more than meets the eye. Beneath those horns and the sharp teeth and claws is a heart that beats pure warmth, and I know it deep in my veins...

I am falling for him.

I just hope he feels the same way. He may have taken my virtue, but that means nothing in the grand scheme of things.

If not for Tegwyn, I would have perished in the storm, and he's my saving grace. I'd be dead ten times over if it wasn't for the Fae beside me, and sometimes I'm glad he found me that day drowning in the marsh. Because then, I never would have got to know him.

I squeeze his hand, leading him back to the mountain. "It's time to go home."

I make him a hot bath upon our return to the mountain. It took several trips to the waterfall with a cast-iron pot, and Tegwyn watched the whole time I ran up and down the tunnels like a headless chicken, an impish smirk slowly returning to his face.

On top of collecting the water, I also had to boil it over the hearth, and to say I was tired at the end of it all would be an understatement. I sense his prickling gaze on my back, wisps of pale blonde hair floating about my face as I'm still catching my breath.

"Do you need a hand?" he asks.

I blow a particularly bothersome strand from my eyes, trying to focus on my task. The water's not even close to boiling, and the tub is only half full.

"No. I've got this. You just let me take—"

I jump when the water bubbles behind me, and I glance over my shoulder, gasping when I spy swirls of steam curling from the brass tub.

"Tegwyn! I said I would fill the tub for you."

He sighs, stepping closer to inspect the water. "Well, you were taking too long, and if you must insist that I get inside this wretched tub, then I would like to do so quickly."

It looks as if the frost has finally thawed, metaphorically speaking, of course, and now he's returning to his old, chipper self.

Well, *almost.*

He's still jaded, still unimpressed by my fruitless attempts to make him a hot bath. Really, I think he's just looking for an excuse to show off his skills.

I startle when he bends over the tub, flicking water at me. "Hey!"

He chuckles, and I can't help but return the smile as I step towards the cupboard where we store the dried herbs. I'm sure we have lavender or rose petals. Anything that would infuse with the water and give it that sweet, aromatic smell.

Not that he needs it. He already smells amazing…

Ooh, rosemary!

He looks a little concerned when I return to the tub, sprinkling several sprigs of rosemary from a glass vial into the boiling water.

He picks up a leafy twig. "If I didn't know any better, I would say you were trying to cook me up, Ivy."

I glance at the small green twig in question. "Of course not. Mama used to put rosemary into my bath all the time when I was little. It always made the cottage smell so warm and welcoming."

He flinches when I mention my dear mother, and I cock my head. "Are you all right? You're not still cold, are you?" The faerie heaves a sigh, then starts removing his cloak. I take it from his hands, draping it across a chair. Then he peels off his long leather coat and unfastens his cravat and tunic until he's in nothing but his white blouse and breeches.

My eyes pop when I cast my gaze over his tapered waist, and I lick my lips, eager to see what he's hiding beneath.

I've given him my virtue, yet not once have I seen him naked. Nor has he seen me naked, for that matter.

We were still fully clothed on that high knoll in the village, and I'm still wearing Bannog's diaphanous dress of glistening gossamer, although the vines and flowers have long since wilted.

They didn't survive the storm.

Tegwyn pulls his sleeves up to his elbows, and I get a glimpse of the corded muscle beneath. My mouth waters.

He smirks, his golden eyes molten when they settle on me. "*Now* I see... This was all just a ruse to get me naked."

I stammer, shaking my head as I leave him to bathe in peace. "D-don't be silly..."

I don't make it two steps before he grabs me by the back of the neck, pulling me flush to his chest.

Only his blouse and my thin tablecloth of a dress separate us now. My nipples peak as they press against the hard muscle of his chest, and he shuts his eyes, breathing in the scent of my arousal. "*Fuuck*...you smell fantastic right now."

My own eyes are closed as I lose myself in his heady scent of pine and woodsmoke.

"I'll give you a deal, Ivy," he whispers, his voice a dark caress down my spine. "I will get in this tub on one condition."

My tongue darts out, wetting my bottom lip. "And...what condition is that?"

"You join me."

My eyes snap open. He can't be serious. We are not in the village anymore; I just got caught up in the moment. Now we're back in the real world. Still, our relationship will never be quite the same. We are paramours now, something a little more than friends.

A sigh loosens from my lips, and I meet those rounded eyes, the half-moon pupils now a thing of the past.

"All right. Except I have my own condition."

His brow jumps at that. "Yeah?"

A smirk creeps across my face. "You take off *all* your clothes, even the gloves. No more hiding."

Tegwyn falters, and then he angles his face away from me, muttering a curse.

I reach up, palming his face. My thumb caresses the golden flecks of his sculpted cheek. "I'm not afraid of you anymore, remember? I know your claws won't hurt me now."

His eyes scrunch shut, and I know he's thinking back to the day he accidentally cut me in the forest, when I failed to shoot the deer.

Placing both of my hands on his cheeks now, I lower his face until we're a breath apart. "Besides...I like it when you scrape me up a little..."

The faerie opens his eyes, and there's no missing the fire. Now I reach up to stroke a finger along the base of his horn, and he shudders when I rub those hardened ridges.

"I meant what I said...I really *was* holding back on that hill, Ivy...Don't tempt fate."

Moving closer, our lips brush when I whisper, "Then don't hold back. Unleash your beast."

His body trembles, and then he fists his hands, resisting his claws. His pupils swell, taking over his golden irises, and now I'm faced with the eyes of a predator.

But he manages to get a hold of his beast as he finally starts peeling off his gloves. My heart thumps in my chest as he prepares to bare it all.

When the first glove comes off, I stare in awe. His hands are no different from mine. His nails are a little sharper, but the tips are hooked and slightly tapered.

I spy a thick encasing on the beds of his nails, and when I press down on one gently, a shiny claw extends.

A nervous, giddy sound escapes me, and he grumbles, sheathing his claws once again. But before he can put his hand away, I grip his fingers, placing them over my cheek.

His breath stutters. "Ivy…"

I press down on his nails, pushing out his claws for him, and they prick the delicate skin around my eyes. Although it hurts, I don't remove his hand. I keep it on my left cheek as a show of trust. His eyes melt into liquid gold right before me, and he finally reaches up his other hand, combing his fingers through my hair. Then he slams his mouth onto mine, crushing me with a bruising kiss. A soft, mewling sound of pleasure escapes me, and he takes that as his verbal cue, opening my mouth with his tongue. I respond in kind, meeting each thrust of his tongue, and then I feel the sharp tips of his fangs.

He rips off my dress with his claws, and the thin material gives way easily, pooling at my feet with a sigh. Now I'm completely naked, but I don't care… I'm prepared to bare it all.

With feverish hands, I start taking off his own clothes. Tegwyn steps out of his pants in no time, and we feast our eyes on each other's bodies.

My gaze rakes up and down his torso, and a strange, strangled sound leaves my mouth.

He certainly isn't lacking in any department.

Sculpted chest of shimmering muscle, a chiselled eight-pack that looks as if it was carved from the finest bronze, and a narrowed waist. I almost become a woman possessed as I resist the urge to run my tongue between the grooves of his toned stomach.

And his long, thick shaft… It swings like a pendulum between his legs, all ten *inches*, and the underside bears the same ribbed texture of his horns. My lower lip wobbles, and then a deep pulsing grows between my legs as he extends towards me.

There's no missing the glistening bead at his tip, and I lick my lips, wanting my taste of him.

His heated gaze tells its own tale as he takes in every inch of me, and I spy that feral beast again. His eyes flash, and then his teeth bare as he prowls closer.

He backs me up to the wall, caging me in with his arms, and his claws dig deep into the ancient stone on either side of my head. The faerie's entire body trembles, and he's trying so hard to resist. He worries about hurting me, but I know he wouldn't. So, I display my neck as another show of trust, and I'm not sure why. I just have this strong urge for him to bite me there.

A strong desire to be closer to him...

Tegwyn aims for my throat. A squeal of shock escapes me when he bites my pulse, and soon I'm suspended in thick darkness.

But then a white flash appears in the murk, one that steals my breath and my entire vision, and when I come to, I swear I can taste blood. The moment vanishes, and the taste eventually leaves my mouth as I pant, opening my eyes. Tegwyn stares straight back, blood dripping from his fangs, his gaze unfocused. He's already fallen so far into the abyss, but I don't care. I don't want him to stop biting me, not for a second, so I push his face toward my neck, gasping when his teeth find their mark again.

The longer he prolongs the bite, the more I fall into eternal darkness, and soon that white flash returns, along with the sweet taste of blood.

Holy fuck... I just want to rake my claws up and down her spine, claiming her with my claws... But I'm afraid of hurting her...

I mean, *him*... I'm afraid of hurting Tegwyn with *my* claws... Not that I have claws.

Wait. Whose thoughts were those just now?

I don't have time to ponder the strange anomaly as his magic streams through me, burning hot through my veins just like it did at the top of the hill, and I soon come apart in his arms, wrapping my shaking legs around his waist.

Now I guide his mouth down my body, letting him take bites out of my flesh. He never bites too hard, just enough to puncture and nick the skin.

He has better control than he gives himself credit for.

When he stops between my legs, my heartbeat rises, and then stars explode in the corners of my eyes. Sweat rolls down my throat, dripping between the valley of my heaving breasts. When the faerie nicks my sensitive lips with his teeth, I arch my spine, pushing towards his mouth. "Oh, *fuck!*"

He growls once he hears my curse, and the sound vibrates, reaching a tender bundle of nerves deep inside, and the stars return.

I almost collapse above him, but I grip his horns like the reins of a horse as I ride his face. My hips buck toward his mouth as he explores me with his tongue and teeth, and when he finds the sensitive nub beneath the hood of my sex, biting down *hard*, I shatter into a million pieces. My eyes slam shut, and I scream, knowing that no one else will hear me all the way in the mountains. It's just me and Tegwyn... He could kill me, and no one would even know. I am completely and thoroughly at his mercy, but I wouldn't have it any other way.

This time, he uses his claws, and when he hooks them inside me, scraping at that sweet network of nerves yet again, I collapse. He captures me effortlessly, scooping me up, boneless, in his arms as he carries me to the tub. With a click of his fingers, he heats the water again, then steps over the lip of the tub, submerging us both. The rosemary has done its work, and now the cave is redolent with the herb as I breathe him in.

He lays me down on his chest, purring softly into my ear, and I listen to his thunderous heartbeat.

He's dripping with hot water, and I start peppering kisses down his chest, licking and nipping at his muscles with my tongue and teeth.

Tegwyn wraps his arms around the back of the tub as I create a path down his body, licking away the droplets that gather between the grooves of his eight-pack. It looks like this faerie works out, and it's only a show of his brute strength.

When I find his length, I run my tongue along the ridged shaft, and I hear his claws scraping against the sides of the tub.

"Holy shit, Ivy..."

I get my taste of him, kissing until I reach his swollen head, and then I lick away that bead of pre-cum. Then I rise to straddle his thighs and position him at my entrance. He flexes, and I finally impale myself on his cock.

I slide down his shaft, meeting him at the hilt, and he leans forward, claiming my back with his claws. We're face to face, nose to nose, as he fills me with his cock, and I have never felt so full, so complete.

He is all I ever want and need in this life, and I would die a happy woman if heaven struck me down at this very moment.

Tegwyn runs his palms down my spine, and I arch my back, pressing my nipples to his chest.

His upper lip ticks, and I can tell he's reining in that beast again.

His eyes flicker like a guttering candle, but he manages to hold back, letting me have my way with him.

The moment I thrust my hips, he freezes, and then he rolls his eyes back as I push along his dick. He shudders as I grind against him, chasing those lights as his ribbed shaft scrapes my walls.

I thank whatever goddess made this magnificent creature as I finally brace myself, slamming my hands down on his chest.

My vision brightens as pure, rapturous pleasure ripples up and down my body. Tegwyn follows at my heels, and then he sits us upright, pumping into me hard and fast as he wraps his hands around my neck and spine.

When he finishes off inside me, silence stretches through the cave, the only sounds our pounding hearts and heavy breaths. Finally, I curl up against him, listening to his thunderous heartbeat.

It beats only for me now, as mine does for him.

We soon fall asleep, the scent of rosemary and sex infusing the air.

The water never cools, heated continuously by his magic, and I drift off to his rumbling purr. There's nowhere else I would rather be than in his arms.

33

Tegwyn

I run my claw down the groove of Ivy's spine, making her body shudder all over. When she finally looks at me with those brilliant starburst eyes, I give a wicked smirk.

"So, you *are* awake..."

She scowls, and my chuckle reverberates through the cave when I spy that cute crease between her brows. This human is ridiculously expressive; it's amusing to watch.

"Yes, I am *now*. No thanks to you. Don't tickle me there."

"Where? *Here*?"

I scrape up the length of her spine again with the hook of my claw, and she gives a shrill gasp, slapping my chest. "Yes, stop!"

Yet the more she protests, the more I scratch, and she harrumphs, shoving my hand away. She finally settles, nestling down beside me again, using her hands as a pillow as she closes her eyes. The poor human is spent, and it'll be *days* until she regains her strength.

I have no remorse. What can I say? I'm a beast.

Ivy more than lived up to my expectations, and she tasted far better than I imagined. Like honey straight from the comb. It's going to take a lifetime to forget the sweet sensation of her arousal from my tongue.

If only we could lie this way forever, but alas, we must return to reality. I'm going to have to tell her what Bannog informed me of at the shop. Tonight. Before the light of a million stars...

Ivy deserves to see some beauty in this world before it's cruelly ripped away.

"You think too loud."

My heart thumps at her words, and now I steer my thoughts elsewhere. This moment with her, right here, right now. This is perfect. The way the heated water drips down her body, the candles turning her skin soft, buttery gold...

She lifts her face, hiking up a pale eyebrow. "I can hear your heart beating. You can't hide anything from me."

Fuck. She's on to me.

"What's on your mind?"

I swallow, and she watches the movement run down my throat.

Worry dances inside her eyes. "Tegwyn?"

She knows I can't tell a lie, so there's no way I can skirt around this. So, I focus on her gorgeous face, appreciating the way the candlelight casts a shadow on the dimple above her heart-shaped lips. The humans call it *Cupid's bow*... Quite fitting, given how besotted I was from the instant I spied her lush, red mouth. Rather than telling her the truth outright, I grasp the back of her head, threading my claws through her golden hair. "Later. I promise."

She regards me for a few moments. She's not an idiot; she knows it's something bad. Yet she lowers her gaze, giving me a nod, and I lean forward, bumping our heads together.

Ivy rises to her knees, water trickling down her alabaster skin, and it looks like she's getting out of the tub. But I want to indulge a little longer and drag her back to me. "Not just yet. I want to cherish this moment. It's amazing having your wet, naked body pressed up against mine, princess."

She smiles teasingly. "Oh, really?"

I return her smirk. "Really."

My heart pounds as she straddles my hips, pushing me back against the lip of the tub, and I'm rewarded with the sight of her pert breasts. When she moves her mouth close to my lips, I shut my eyes, savouring the sensation of her hot breath on my damp cheeks.

The water is still hot, fuelled by my magic and her insatiable lust.

It turns out that sex with Ivy is a good way to refuel my reserves. It all started from the moment I bit her neck.

She still bears my mark, the candlelight casting shadows on the indentations left by my teeth.

My next mark: her breasts. One of her dusky pink nipples has my name on it.

"My eyes are up here, Tegwyn."

Slowly, my gaze trails back to her face, and there's no missing her smirk. She reaches across, running her finger tortuously between my pecs. She gets in between my abs, brushing away the water there, then continues south.

The blood rushes hot through my head when she teases her finger down the V of my hips. I'm not going to last.

Any moment, I'll pounce on her.

Finally, her finger finds my cock, and a growl loosens from my throat.

"Easy now," she whispers.

My growling stops, replaced by a tick of my upper lip. This beast of mine is relentless, accompanied only by the thrashing of my heart. Without warning, she presses her palms to my pecs, grinding her cunt along the base of my cock, and that's when she rakes her sharp nails down my chest.

Fuck. That *hurts*...

She leans forward, pushing her hardened nipples against my tender pecs, then whispers into my ear. "Now, *I've* marked *you*..."

Suddenly, she rises, water dripping off her body like music as she steps out of the tub, collecting her shredded clothes off the ground. I remain in a state of shock as she pads out of the cave stark-naked, tossing me a final look over her shoulder.

My heart is still raging, my rapid breaths bouncing off the cave walls.

She... *marked* me...

Slowly, I gaze down at my chest, spying the gashes she left with her nails. I'm bleeding, and I look back in her direction.

She is full of surprises. With a heavy sigh, I slump back against the tub, slipping beneath the scorching water to relieve some of the tension. I guess I will finish myself off then.

Ivy

Tegwyn woke me in the middle of the night, telling me he had a surprise waiting at the end of the tunnel. Should I be worried? Hopefully, it's not revenge for marking his chest. If he thinks he's the only one with claws around here, then he can kiss my derriere.

Oh, wait. He already did.

"Skies should be clear tonight."

I raise my brow, gazing at the back of his horned head. "Clear for what, exactly?"

He glances over his left shoulder, oil lamp swinging in hand. "For stargazing, of course. There's going to be a meteor shower. One you don't want to miss."

My heart rate spikes. I did always have a love for the stars, and I bet they're even brighter in the cold, dark north.

We arrive at a fissure in the rock, and the moment I step out onto the cliff, a gust of icy wind takes my breath away. Yet the wind has nothing compared to the open sky. It's like an artist's canvas. I couldn't even begin to describe the colours she used: indigo, mauve, violet, sparkling silver... The way the paint swirls and bleeds with just a single brushstroke. Not even back at home did the stars ever look so spectacular, so vivid.

Bright, shimmering clusters blink across the span of the night sky, and I soon forget which way is up and which is down as I free-fall into oblivion.

"It's beautiful..." I whisper.

Tegwyn blows out his lamp, and we both gaze up at the sky now. A light streaks across the velvet expanse, and I jump. Then a series of others follow, and I can't stop laughing. "This is amazing. Look!"

I point north towards a hazy pillar of red light. Several other pillars materialise with the first, growing in brightness and intensity until they stretch skyward. Then they dance, rippling across the night sky like a curtain of red, green, and purple, and I can't believe it.

"The northern lights."

Tegwyn confirms my statement. "That's right. I was hoping they would appear tonight along with the stars."

They're breathtaking, the way they dance and light up the whole night.

The faerie chuckles. "If you think that's impressive, then you've seen nothing yet. Come here."

He grips my chin, drawing my eyes away from the pretty lights, and he plants a chaste kiss on my lips. I have no idea what he's doing. At first, I thought he was just being passionate, but when I look at the night sky again, that single brushstroke of star-kissed paint explodes into a river of sparkling dust.

And the lights... They burn magenta, lime green, and flaming violet now, overlapping as they dance more vividly than ever before, and I try to catch my breath.

Oh...so, this is how the night sky appears to the Fae?

It's phenomenal.

More stars streak across the now-living canvas, merging with the dancing aurorae high above, and there are no words. With my new gift of faerie sight, they're simply blinding, and tears gather in my eyes.

So many humans live their entire lives without getting to see a night sky like this, and I just wish everyone got the chance to experience it one day.

I glance at the faerie beside me, and the star-flecked river reflects inside his eyes. "Thank you for bringing me out here tonight. It was worth waking up for."

He returns my smile. "Don't mention it, princess."

The magic soon leaves me, returning to its original proprietor. Does he have to sacrifice a little of his own lifeforce just to share what he did with me tonight?

Now he appears crestfallen, and I step closer, taking his hand. "Tegwyn?"

He sighs, gazing up at the dancing aurorae. "It's time you finally knew."

My heart drops at his dire tone. "All right."

He shut his eyes. "You remember when Bannog and I were talking yesterday?"

A cold shiver rattles down my spine. "Yes."

"He...informed me of some grave news..."

The Fae sighs, reaching up to run his claws through his hair. He appears to be in pain. What has got into him?

I wet my lips, heart thumping. "It's okay. You...you can tell me..."

Finally, he looks my way, and I meet those dancing pillars inside his shining eyes.

"I'm sorry..."

I struggle for breath. "S-sorry for what?"

"Your parents. Bannog has contacts at the king's court. They're...they're gone, Ivy..."

The sky shatters like a mirror high above, and the sweet illusion of magic vanishes instantly as a grey cloud takes over. A life without colour.

Nothing.

Just...emptiness.

My head spins, the ground dissolving beneath my feet as I forget how to stand straight.

He captures me in his arms.

"N-no...they...they can't be..."

My lungs shrink, and I breathe through a narrow passage. The blood rushes through my head, and it's all too much. I had my suspicions. But I pushed them all aside, clinging to false hope.

"It's all right, Ivy. Deep breaths."

I can't even fathom breathing. My brain can't connect with my lungs. A strangled sound leaves my throat, and when my knees buckle beneath me, refusing to keep me upright, I finally collapse into his arms.

Nothing could have ever prepared me for this. It's like someone gouged my heart out of my chest, and it's bleeding on the cold, hard ground now, slowly losing life.

Once upon a time, the sky was a blaze of colour... But now, it's just black.

Suffocating.

"I'm... I'm yours, Ivy..."

His words pull me back from the depths of despair, and I meet those gilded eyes. A flaming ring of gold surrounds his pupils, and I find my stars again.

It seems I did the impossible; I won the heart of a once-selfish faerie...but how?

He presses his mouth to mine, and splashes of colour return to my eyes, as well as warmth and sunshine.

"You'll always have me. I'll be your family from now on. You won't ever be alone. That's a vow."

Alone?

Did I say that at one point?

Finally, I meet his kiss, drinking up his raw passion. "I'm... I'm yours, too."

A heartbeat passes between us. Then he whispers in a voice only I can hear, "*Tĕr nghalon...*"

My eyes open, meeting those rings of pure gold. "What did you say?"

He swallows audibly. "My true name is *Tĕr nghalon*. All faeries have one. Now, you command my every action. You can peer into my mind if you so much as wish, hear my most intimate thoughts. You can even make me *kill*... Best of all, you can tap into my magic, use it to heal yourself."

I... I have no idea what to say. He's giving me such a rare gift, and it's not one I could ever return. No bartering, no deals.

Just his trust.

His sheer faith in me stitches up the hole in my chest, helping me to breathe and think clearly again, and I finally say, "Thank you... *Tĕr nghalon...*"

He goes ramrod straight when I call him by his true name. Even its mere utterance allows me to peer into his mind, sensing myself in two places.

The two streams of consciousness are a little too much to handle, so I cleave free of his mind, gazing at him from my own perspective again.

We don't speak. Instead, I nudge into his headspace, letting him sense how much I love and appreciate him, and soon we embrace beneath the light of a thousand stars, two lost souls, forever entwined.

34

Tegwyn

THE DEER PEELS ANOTHER strip of bark off the tree, and I draw my arrow, aiming for a quick, clean shot. I've been tracking it all morning, and it seems my hard work is about to finally pay off. Just one shot and my hunt will be over, and then I can return home to the girl who never smiles anymore. But I would take even a sad smile over her faux happiness. Her sadness confirms she's real. That she's processing her grief.

Fae magic can only go so far. Nothing more than a shiny veneer that hides the true decay beneath, and the longer it continues, the more it festers. At first, she had begged me to mask her pain, and of course, I'd obliged, doing anything I could to help the woman I love.

I gave her my true name. Something that still baffles me, and yet she has not once abused my trust, even during the thickest fog of her grief. I don't harbour a single regret. With my true name, she can call to me from anywhere, and now it's impossible for us to ever be apart.

It's rare for Fae to share such secrets, even amongst themselves. A strong bond must be forged before such delicate information can be disclosed.

After all, it makes us vulnerable. In the wrong hands, a true name could be lethal. Anyone could bend me to their will, and my heart shudders at the very idea of someone squeezing the truth of my name from Ivy someday.

But I push the morose thoughts aside, focusing on my current task—the deer. Our reserves are running low, and we need the meat.

But the moment I look up, all the breath leaves my lungs. The stag—it's spotted me. The creature gazes straight into my soul, assessing me with its eyes of deep onyx, and I swallow hard. I draw my bow, heart pounding. Billowing clouds escape the stag's nostrils, and it backs into the forest, vigilant eyes remaining on me the whole time. If I don't shoot now, then I will miss my chance. This is the first deer I've seen in weeks. It's not a large male. Most likely a yearling, but meat is meat, and winters in the north are harsh.

It has small, forked antlers, barely big enough for a full lock with a rival male. So, it is its first set. The velvet is peeling, and it appears this deer truly is young. Precious even.

It loses its fear of me, finally sensing the wonderful magic that resides within me, and I hate it when that happens. The magic simply enthralls them, but I still make sure it's a fair fight. I never abuse this power.

The deer steps closer, and I keep my arrow drawn, never losing my focus. It sniffs the arrowhead with its wet nose, and when I gaze into its sweet eyes again, it's *hers* I find.

She wouldn't kill this creature. No, she would let it live, no matter how hungry she was. There's been enough death in this world lately. I could always make noise. Startle it, make it a fair fight.

But I lower my weapon, letting it lick my cheek. Its breath smells of tree bark, but I don't mind.

I guess we'll have to do without meat this winter.

It's fine; I can survive on a diet of porridge, fruit, and wild berries, too.

I hover outside her cave, carrying a steaming bowl of porridge. No longer do I wear gloves, deciding to be my authentic self. These claws of mine are ridiculously sharp, hurting friends and enemies alike, yet they're mine, and they're a part of me. So, I've finally learned to embrace them.

Though I don't do it for me... I do it for Ivy.

A lonely wind drifts down the tunnel, and for once, I feel the ominous chill of the north. I've felt it since the night of the blizzard, and it makes me wonder. Something is looming on the horizon, and whatever it is, we must brace ourselves. Ivy and I may be in for a harsher winter than I realised.

However, there is one good thing to come from the blizzard. Rosemary has finally gone. For now, at least.

Maybe the boggart took her away with it once I bested it in the snow, who knows, but there's one thing that does remain—Henry. I feel him flapping his wings with each beat of my heart, and he gives me strength. He gives me hope, which is something I've been in short supply of lately.

And now, that very same *hope* is going to be my driving force today. Ivy needs me, and I am going to help her get through this. So, when Henry beats his wings again, I step inside the cave, almost dropping the bowl the moment my eyes find her.

She's painting all manner of shapes along the grimy walls, and I blink to ensure I'm seeing correctly.

When I left her this morning, she was lying in bed. The only time she came to life was when I fed her my magic.

But magic only goes so far.

Yet this, however...this is new.

"Ivy?"

She barely hears me, hyper-focused on her task. Is this what happens to humans before they teeter over the edge? I must put a stop to this before it's too late.

"Ivy!"

"Hm?" she answers half-heartedly, hands flying over a series of whorls and spirals.

Shaking my head, I clear my throat, holding out the bowl. "I've brought you breakfast."

The human ignores me, fingers spinning around and around as she keeps painting a swirl. This is getting bizarre.

My stomach twists when I step closer, getting a good look at her face. Her eyes are shadowed, and her skin is dull and grey. And she's covered in paint. It stains her hands, cheeks, and even her hair.

I take a deep breath. "Ivy. Put the brush down and eat."

"I'm not hungry," she remarks coolly, never taking her eyes off her swirl.

Even her voice is devoid of life, and gone is the sweet, melodious song that once caused my heart to spasm. That's it. Time to get tough.

"Ivy, put the brush down and *eat*. Starving yourself won't help."

Her painting becomes frantic, and she draws yet another angry swirl. I yank the brush from her hand, getting paint on my own fingers. "Ivy!"

She glares at me, and her eyes shine a luminous green. They take my breath away.

She almost looks *Fae*. "*Fine*," she concedes, taking the bowl from my hands.

I stand and watch as she eats her porridge. I added a mixture of fruit to give it that extra sweetness, yet she still struggles.

She puts the bowl to one side, gazing at nothing. Her eyes are empty, and it's *happening*... The abyss has returned to remind her of what she's lost.

I bet she sees their faces. That's how it was for me.

"You...have to find them again..." she whispers absentmindedly.

I raise a brow. "What?"

She looks up, eyes vacant. "You must find your mother and grandpa again and tell them how much you love them. It doesn't matter that you ran away. None of that matters now... Don't live with regrets, Tegwyn..."

My throat bobs as her words claw their way into my memories, making old wounds bleed yet again. Fuck, she's right, and the guilt only tears me apart. But it's not that simple. I can never go back. That life is over.

She closes her eyes, face crumbling with grief. "I'm sorry. I spoke out of turn."

I inhale a shaking breath. "N-no, you didn't. You were right, but...it's not that simple, I'm afraid."

Ivy nods. "Because of Duke and Rosemary."

I told her everything, of course. I thought it was the least I could do while she was grieving. It seems we had pretty similar childhoods. People treated her like an outcast, too. Yet in her case, it was because she had been an extremely beautiful young woman who liked to dream.

I *hate* small-town mentality. You stick out like a sore thumb when you dare go against the grain.

I huff out a breath. "I did go back. Once..."

She looks up, eyes wide.

I continue. "About a year after I left the farm. I watched them from afar. Mother had a baby in her arms... It seemed like she'd moved on."

I've never told anyone this story. Not until now. But I want her to get a glimpse into my past. See what makes me tick.

"The way Mother looked at that baby...I couldn't take that away from her. If I'd knocked on that door, I would have brought all that old misery back. I had ruined her life. Made the whole town despise her."

The memories come rushing back, but I push through the pain, going on. "That baby could have been my sister in another life, but I wasn't going to ruin *her* future, either. I couldn't do that to either of them."

Finally, I glance her way, and my heart stops. She's crying. For me... The tears streak down her cheeks as warmth trickles through my veins when I see that life returning to her eyes.

I smile, transporting myself back in time again. "She always wanted a daughter... Hence why they were better off without me. She finally got her happily ever after in the end."

Ivy shuts her eyes, wiping away a tear. "Oh, Tegwyn..."

The smile leaves my face. "Such is life."

She stands, taking my hands. Then she presses a kiss onto my lips. "It's okay. You have *me* now."

I sigh, basking in her nearness. She's coming back to me.

"For what it's worth, I think your mother would have been happy to see you again, Tegwyn. People can surprise you."

Don't I know. Finally, we thread our fingers, and I spy the difference immediately. While her skin is soft, mine is coarse, yet in that moment, we are one. Two lost souls who found each other. She drags me to bed, and there we lie side by side. As she falls asleep, I watch her for some time, truly feeling like the luckiest creature in the world. Ivy is all the happiness and family I need in this life.

I wake that night to find the bed cold and empty and jerk upright. When I peer to my right, a deep chasm opens up inside my gut, sending me spiralling into the abyss.

Ivy. She's *gone*.

I search the cave, gasping when I find the face of a silver-eyed wolf sneering back at me from her painting. A shudder snakes down my spine.

That's what she had been painting all this time? And here I was, thinking she was painting at random.

My heart rings through my ears as I rush down the tunnel, and I stumble upon a handwritten note on the kitchen table. She's left her necklace, too.

Shaking my head, I snatch up the note, reading quickly.

I'm sorry. If I don't survive the hunt, then I want you to have it, Tegwyn. Find the happiness you deserve. Maybe you can finally find that island...

My hands tremble.

No. I already found my happiness, and I can't let her go through with this.

She's going after the wolf that chased her all the way to the north. When she'd described the beast to me, I knew it without a doubt in my mind.

That wolf was Fae. Most likely a member of the king's court.

If I have to kill that creature to save her, so be it. I will taint my soul once again, killing another member of my kind just to keep her safe. She's my family now, and I will protect her at all costs.

My eyes find my rack of knives. The hunting knife has gone.

Grabbing my bow and quiver, I don my cloak, making my descent into the early dawn.

I *will* catch up with her.

35

Ivy

THE MISERABLE GREY LIGHT of dawn filters through the trees, bringing with it a fine mist, but I keep on marching, determined to hunt down the one thing that has held me back all these months.

The wolf.

I know that vicious lupine is in league with the king. And I know that it was never a wolf in the first place, but a member of his court.

A Fae.

For Belle, I will kill it.

And for my parents, I will kill the king.

It's time to fight back. My mind is stuck. Somewhere inside, there is a smart girl banging on the glass, begging me to see reason and not to do anything rash.

But grief has taken over. The abyss sucked me right back into its cruel, black mouth, and now the creature has become me, its eyes searing deep into my soul.

My fingers grip the knife as I finally find the clearing where Belle and the wolf fought. It barely ended in bloodshed.

I don't even know what became of the horse; she just vanished with a blast of light, and I still don't fully understand what happened that day.

The clearing is overgrown with snowdrops, even though the winter frost has long since settled. But I don't question the peculiarity further as I focus on the surrounding trees, knowing that the wolf's out there.

I may not survive today, but at least I will die in a beautiful place. The snowdrops glisten with what can only be described as liquid diamonds. They drip from the petals, collecting inside the veins of each leaf, and the effect almost resembles magic.

Tegwyn would love this place.

Leaving him was one of the hardest decisions of my life, but I hope he understands that I do love him. He will just have to find his happiness without me. This will be the hill upon which I die. I've made my choice.

The hair pricks at the back of my neck, and I grasp the knife tighter. I'm not alone. Someone watches.

Finally, I spy a pair of floating eyes in the gloom—eyes that mock me. Every muscle in my body locks in fear, but I never take my gaze off the beast.

Slowly, it slinks from the shadows, a four-legged creature larger than life itself. My heart pounds faster. It hardly resembles a wolf now, just a devastating hell beast with pure bloodlust shining in its quicksilver eyes. Branches crack beneath its paws, paws bigger than my whole head, and its claws dig deep into the earth as it leaves its mark, letting the world know that it was here and that it killed the princess—the last living descendant of the Godwyn Dynasty.

My bloodline will end with me.

Its mouth widens, revealing a set of curved fangs that makes my knife look like a sewing needle, and it's hopeless.

I won't even make it to the king at this rate. This wolf will tear me limb from limb.

The hell beast pushes me towards a tree, and I press my back against solid bark, heart thumping so loudly that the creature stops a moment to savour the sound.

Its quicksilver eyes still taunt me, its hot breath burning my cheeks as it widens its jaws, and only death glares back at me now.

A low rattle rumbles in its chest, and it takes me a second to recognise the sound. It's *laughing...*

I find my voice, having had enough. "Just get it over with already and kill me."

It snaps its teeth, pinning me in place with its pinprick pupils, but I bare a snarl of my own. "What are you waiting for?"

"I'm not going to kill you."

My muscles seize at the guttural sound. It's like the creature is whispering to me deep from the abyss, a sound like cold, trickling water that ices my veins.

I swallow.

It never once moved its mouth. Instead, it used its tongue to form words, mainly because it was too busy peeling its lips back from its teeth.

There's no mistaking that the wolf is female. But it makes no difference to me.

Those fangs could still rend my flesh.

"I promised someone I would bring you back alive, and that is exactly what I plan to do, princess.*"*

There it is again, the *snark*, and someone really is mocking me... So, I guess that makes her a bitch. Well, this bitch is about to die.

Flipping my knife around, I plunge it deep into her eye, and her dark blood splatters my cheeks. She rears back with a howl, and I seize my chance.

I run.

Back to the only one who has ever had my back in this cold, grim place.

Tegwyn. I never should have left him.

Hopefully, I can make it back to him before the wolf regains her strength.

A shadow lumbers after me, and then I'm flat on my back, winded from the heavy impact.

I gaze up hazily into a burning silver eye. The left one is bleeding, and it looks like she managed to get the knife out.

My only regret is that I never got to see him again, but at least I got my revenge on one of my enemies.

That knife was for Belle. Wherever she is, I hope she's happy.

She opens her mouth, and her jaws encompass my whole head. The top half settles on my scalp and the lower beneath my chin, and I squeeze my eyes tight shut when her saliva drips onto my face.

"Fuck bringing you back alive. I'll just tell the king that you died on the road. Accidents happen."

She laughs again, and if only I had another knife to take out her other eye.

That's when I feel the hard press of steel at my back, making me widen my eyes.

Can it be?

It's hidden beneath the undergrowth, out of sight of the she-wolf, but can I grip the handle before she crushes my skull?

I bide my time, asking before I die, "Who are you?"

She only cackles harder, yet I go on. "Who sent you?"

"None of that matters now."

I don't remove my gaze from her tonsils as they squirm at the back of her throat. "No, I think it does. At least give me this courtesy."

She stops cackling. Then she growls, *"I don't know why my brother wants you so badly."*

Brother?

So, she's the king's sister.

Well, at least we have one thing in common; it's not as if I asked to be related to him either. He wants me dead because I'm a threat to his throne, so he sent his sister to do his dirty work for him.

"Now shut up and keep still while I kill you..."

This is my chance. I must strike, now. But then she pins my arms down with her paws, and I shed a silent tear.

I was too late. I'm going to die after all.

An arrow hisses through the air, puncturing the wolf's other eye, and I shuffle away, finally free from the rotten stench of death. I didn't have time to grip the handle, but none of that matters anymore. Because I'd know that arrow from anywhere...

Help has arrived.

The wolf whips her head around, flaring her nose, and I almost cry for joy when I spy him standing amongst the snowdrops, looking like a hero from a storybook as he draws another arrow.

His hood is up, and all I see of him are those glowing eyes. They're pissed.

"Ivy. Get behind me."

I don't move, peering back and forth between the wolf and Tegwyn.

"Now!"

At his command, I scramble to my feet, coming to his side.

The she-wolf snorts when she detects Tegwyn's scent. *"What have we here? The handsome prince coming to save the little princess from the big bad wolf? Cute."*

Tegwyn throws his hood back, and the wolf halts. Even though she's been blinded, she can still sense his horns, the claws, and his general *otherness*.

He chuckles. "No handsome prince, I'm afraid. Just another monster, like you."

The she-wolf bares her teeth, and it almost resembles a smirk.

Tegwyn speaks. "Change forms. I want to see the bitch beneath the wolf before I kill her."

She snarls. *"You're a disgrace to Fae kind. Falling in love with a dung?"*

"And you're a filthy cur," he chimes back. "Now reveal yourself."

Her eyes burn brighter than the moon upon the night sky of her face, and she finally lunges.

Tegwyn releases his arrow.

The projectile makes contact just as her teeth graze his shoulder, and I have no idea what comes over me.

One moment, I'm about to watch him die, and the next I'm leaping in front of him, taking the brunt of her sharp teeth in his place.

There's blood. It rents the air, a thick, coppery tang, yet I don't even feel the pain.

All I find are his eyes. Eyes so full of pain and regret.

"Ivy..." he whispers.

Before I can reach up and caress his cheek, my arm falls slack, and then my eyes close.

It's dark. But through the murk, I spy a bright light. A light so warm, I hardly feel despair. All I sense is love. It's Tegwyn's soul. And it's the most beautiful thing I have ever seen.

"Têr nghalon."

36

Tegwyn

Ivy bleeds out in my arms, and all I can do is hold on to her tightly, hoping she can hear me. "Ivy?"

She doesn't stir. Her eyes remain closed, her glow diminishing by the second, yet I try again, shaking her harder. "Ivy!"

No response. I squeeze my eyes shut. Just when I thought I couldn't hate myself further... I let the woman I love *die* for me.

She took the brunt of that monster's teeth, and all I can do now is watch, helplessly, as she dies in my arms. There's nothing I can do. Her wounds are too deep, and my magic simply isn't enough to heal her.

I've never felt so helpless.

"Ivy... *why?*" I choke, barely able to get the words out of my throat. It hurts. *All of it.*

Her breathing becomes laboured, and there's no mistaking the dreaded death rattle as her lungs give up the fight.

A wheezing sound catches my attention, and my eyes latch on to that naked female. She must have transformed back into her true form the moment my arrow pierced her flesh, and she's now dying as a result.

As she should be. Those arrows are tipped with iron. The bitch deserved it.

I'm not surprised she was beautiful beneath the dog suit. Most Fae are. Her limbs are long, slender, and her hips curved, but she's still a demon.

If only I had arrived earlier, I could have killed her before she had the chance to get to Ivy, but it's too late.

Pressing my forehead against Ivy's, I whisper her name, hoping she hears me somewhere.

Call it Fae intuition, but I can sense her calling my name... My *true* name.

After all, she can call to me from anywhere. Even from the place between life and death.

She's not dead, not yet.

There must be some magic I can muster from the dregs of my soul. I have to try at least.

"Ivy, it's going to be all right. I can fix this. Fix you."

Only silence greets me, but I feel her smile from beyond, and I close my eyes.

Last time, I healed her scratches with my tears. Maybe I can be lucky again.

Yet, my tears have zero impact this time when they drip onto her wounds. They truly are too deep for my magic.

Her blood blemishes her porcelain skin, and I finally lose hope. She really is going to die.

Grief like I've never known consumes me, and I let my cries carry across the forest. The sound seems to shake something deep in the earth, but all I can focus on is the human in my arms. She's slipping away, and fast.

What do I do? I think of the only thing I know.

I pray.

Someone, somewhere, has to hear me...

I can't be alone. Not truly.

Please, someone, anyone...Help.

But when help doesn't arrive, I shut my eyes, giving up at last.

I really am on my own. No one is coming to help us.

Slowly, I lean forward, kissing her pale lips, and then I whisper the three words I swore I would never utter to another soul again.

"I love you, Ivy..."

Suddenly, a blast of light bursts across the clearing, and I shield my eyes.

It's too bright, even for me.

When I re-open my eyes, I blink in surprise. My surroundings have changed.

No longer are we trapped inside the overgrown evergreen forests of the north, but in a small wooded glade, one blanketed in bluebells.

Songbirds trill from the deciduous trees, and I jerk my head left and right, trying to find a conifer.

These trees may shed their leaves, yet they're frozen in time. Because time doesn't move here, but the trees are still living and breathing. I can sense their roots through the verdant grass, roots that vibrate and hum like a heartbeat.

This land is beating with life.

It beats with *magic*...

Did I die after all? Because there's only one name that comes to mind when I cast my gaze around this serene place.

Heaven. Or something akin to it.

The sweet, pealing sound of children's laughter echoes through the trees, and while I should be afraid, I find that I'm not.

The laughter puts me at ease.

These spirits are not malicious. They're just as pure as the dewdrops that drip from the bluebells.

Finally, I spy them. They're nothing more than small orbs of light as they coalesce at the other end of the glade to form the tall, elegant shape of an ethereal woman.

Vibrant, sweet light radiates from her very form, and I stare, open-mouthed. My heart pounds, and I swallow.

"Maghelena."

She answers with a smile. A goddess in the flesh.

Or in *spirit*.

I'm not sure where we are or where she has transported us to, but when I look at a nearby cluster of humming bluebells, I finally realise… We're in her famous bluebell glade.

I *must* be dead.

Yet the knowledge doesn't upset me because Ivy is still grasping on to life.

How?

This place is for faeries. It's where our souls go when we pass.

So, why is she here?

Maghelena steps closer, or she floats, because the grass barely makes a sound as she glides across the glade, her long, silken robes flowing behind her as she heads our way.

When she stops before us, I lose all ability to speak.

I can't even begin to describe her. She has the long, tapered ears of a Fae, but her azure eyes are spheres of swirling light. Pure, divine light. Goosebumps rise up and down my arms.

She bears a large pair of translucent wings, and when I peer through a segment of her left wing, I spy the treeline beyond.

"Hello, my child."

My heart thumps when she speaks. Her voice vibrates through my bones, settling somewhere at the base of my spine.

It even sends a tremor through the green earth, yet I still can't form words. Our goddess simply leaves me spellbound.

Maghelena kneels, casting her blue gaze over Ivy. "So...this is what they look like? Endearing."

Endearing?

She meets my gaze. "I've felt them this past millennium, but I haven't had the fortune of meeting a human being just yet. Quite beautiful."

The goddess reaches her long, slender fingers across, brushing aside Ivy's blonde hair. The human's pained expression softens, and soon she breathes steadily at Maghelena's touch.

"It seems the time has come."

Finally, I find my voice. "What time? Your...your grace..."

Shit. How does one address a goddess?

Technically, she's supposed to be my mother. She's the mother of all my people.

Maghelena smiles. "The time for humans to prove they are worth saving. They've become corrupt over the last couple of centuries. A darkness plagues them, turning once great friends into foes, and it must be stopped before it's too late. But one human had to prove their worth first, acting as an ambassador for their people."

An ambassador?

The goddess takes my chin in her hand. "I saw what she did for you. She put your safety before hers, and a creature that inspires that much love in my eyes is worth saving."

The tears drip from my eyes at the memory. In Maghelena's presence, my tears come freely as she awakens my heart.

She wipes them from my cheeks like a good mother should, and I release a sob. "I... couldn't stop her, and now...now she's..."

I can't stop. The floodgates are wide open, yet she's here to soothe me through every wave.

"Fret not, child. She's not gone. She's still holding on. As your mate, your souls have become entwined."

Mate? How and when did *that* happen?

She brushes away another tear. "You bit her and gave her your true name, but both of you had a connection before you even realised."

Now that I think about it, I have always been attracted to Ivy's scent. Honeysuckle and buttery biscuits, it's indescribable.

"So, Ivy was my mate? This whole time?"

"That is correct."

"But... I thought only faeries found their fated mates?"

Maghelena runs her fingers through my hair. "They do. But there's a first for everything."

I guess there really is.

Now I ask the most pressing question on my mind. "So, will she live?"

She nods. "Yes. Through her act of selfless love. She may just be the one to bring back peace between faeries and humans. Someone needs to fight the darkness that has spread through the human lands like a disease, and she may just be our saviour."

The word sends shockwaves through my system. So, that's what she meant by ambassador?

"But she will need help, and that is where you come in, *Tĕr nghalon*."

Maghelena uses my true name, but I'm not surprised she knew it. She must know everything about her children.

In that case, has she seen all the stealing and cheating that I've done? Have I brought her shame?

Maghelena shakes her head. "No. You do not bring me shame. You're my child, and I will always love you. Just as I love all my children."

Her love wraps around me like a blanket, putting me at ease, and I am utterly speechless.

"But I've done bad things. I am not pure by any means. Ivy is good. I'm... I'm corrupt..."

She narrows her eyes. "Only because the humans in your life made you so. Humans are plagued by prejudice and fear. They seldom accept what is different from them."

Well, that's not entirely true. My mother was a good human, and my grandpa, too.

"Your human family are an exception to the rule, and maybe there are more humans out there like the one in your arms."

Silence falls over the glade as songbird continues around us.

"So, what now?" I ask.

Maghelena rises. "You return to the world of the living and help Ivy. From this moment on, you are both ambassadors of your people."

I don't care what I have to do. So long as I get Ivy back.

"I'll do it. We both will. We will bring back peace between our kind."

There's also the matter of the political strife amongst the Fae. The Seelie and Unseelie turned their backs on the Rogues a long time ago, around the time the human scourge spread through the lands, and that was when they finally closed the gates to the faerielands forever.

We can't go back.

But maybe I can make things right for the Rogue Fae and the humans. After all, we share a plane. It makes sense.

No longer do we have to live in hiding.

No longer will we be persecuted.

Shouldn't be too hard a feat.

Maghelena steps back, extending her hand. "When we meet again, child. Just remember, I am always close. When you need guidance, pray. I am always listening."

I grin. "I will."

I never believed she was gone. Other Fae have lost faith in her, but I always sensed her presence, and it seems I was right.

Always trust your gut.

Light bursts from the goddess's hand, and flowers and vines twine around me and Ivy. I hold her closer, pressing my head to hers as I kiss her lips. "It's okay, Ivy. We're returning home. Just hold on."

The light vanishes with another bright flash, and when I open my eyes again, I find myself back in the cold north.

A shudder rushes through me. Everything seems so dull in comparison, even with my heightened Fae eyes.

I'm just sad that Ivy never got to see Maghelena's glade, but it doesn't matter now. All that matters is that she's alive. Her wounds have finally healed, and she may as well be sleeping.

Carefully, I run my claw down her cheek, rousing her gently. "Ivy?"

She stirs, fluttering her lids, and time ceases to a standstill when I finally spy those luminous starburst eyes.

I don't remember them shining so brightly before.

As a matter of fact, she's dripping with magic. It shines from her skin, giving her hair a flawless glow, and she almost looks Fae.

I guess as an ambassador of the human race, it's only fair that she should be compensated in some way. Especially after she selflessly put my life before hers without a second thought.

A smile curves her sweet, rosebud lips, and my heart thumps back to life.

"I love you too, Tegwyn."

Tears gather in my eyes, and I send a silent prayer to Maghelena. *"Thank you."*

Ivy reaches up, stroking her finger along my cheek, and I'm too overcome with happiness, too overwhelmed by her gentle touch to take much notice of the new threat.

It hovers in my peripheral vision, a black, ominous shadow in the shape of death, and before I have a chance to react, Ivy springs into action.

She brings up the handle of a fine blade, one that was hidden amidst the undergrowth, then plunges it deep into the she-wolf's heart.

Wait. The she-wolf?

No, that can't be right. I saw the bitch die; I killed her with my own arrow.

But the shock soon wears off once I spy the way Ivy fights. The human dances circles around the lupine, and I've never seen her move so fast.

She has all the liquid grace of a Fae, but the constitution of a human. That steel would weaken any faerie, yet she wields it like a seasoned fighter.

The she-wolf drops to the ground as Ivy lops off its head, and it turns out that she wasn't fighting the she-wolf after all, but a bugbear.

The same one that came prowling around the mountain a few weeks prior, coincidentally.

The creature evaporates into dust, disappearing with a swirl on the wind, but I don't take my eyes off Ivy.

The starburst of her eyes glows like fire as she lowers the blade, and there are no words.

She really isn't the same girl anymore, and once again, I thank Maghelena for her gift.

Ivy is not only alive, but she moves and fights like a Fae, and I wonder what other gifts the goddess bestowed her with.

Perhaps she can wield magic.

The human wipes the bugbear's blood from her long, thin blade, noticing my curious gaze. A blush takes over her cheeks. "Erm…it was a gift from my father. I thought I'd lost it, but it turns out that it was just hidden in the undergrowth this whole time."

Well, that explains it.

"Well, it's a good thing you were so quick-witted. Should I be…worried?"

I eye the blade warily. The steel is making me a little sick, but it's nothing I can't handle.

She smirks. "Only if you piss me off."

I have nothing to say to that.

Ivy laughs, wrapping her blade up in her cloak to lessen the effects on my person, and I chuckle along with her.

"Come. Let's return to the mountain," I announce. "We've got work to do."

"Work?" she asks.

She really was out of it in the glade, but that's fine. I can catch her up.

I meet her gleaming, starburst eyes, a smirk arching my lips. I haven't lost my impish ways.

"Congratulations, princess. You are now the official ambassador of your people. Well done."

Her expression is almost comical, and now she's at a complete loss for words. But then her eyes land on the top of my head, a gasp drawing from her lips.

"Tegwyn…"

"What?"

She points at my head.

Heart pounding, I reach up, and my hand trembles when I finally brush my fingertips along a familiar curve.

Well, what do you know?

My horn grew back.

End

Want to read the free prequel novella, *Wicked Thief*? Then sign up **here!**

Afterword

Thank you for reading my debut romantasy!

If you would love to keep up with updates on **Book 2**, be sure to follow me on my socials below!

Mailing list
TikTok
Instagram
Facebook Page
Kayleigh Rymer's Reader Group
Bookbub
Pinterest

About the author

Kayleigh Rymer is a UK-based romance author.

When she's not flying and taming wild dragons, or out frolicking through the woods befriending faeries, then she's writing her latest book.

Kayleigh likes to write about deep, complex, and often highly flawed characters who dictate when she sleeps and when she eats, and even what music she listens to.

Printed in Dunstable, United Kingdom